THE KING'S QUESTIONER

THE KING'S QUESTIONER

NIKKI KATZ

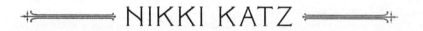

Swoon READS

New York

A Swoon Reads Book
An imprint of Feiwel and Friends and Macmillan Publishing Group, LLC
120 Broadway, New York, NY 10271

Our books may be purchased in bulk for promotional, educational, or
business use. Please contact your local bookseller or the Macmillan Corporate
and Premium Sales Department at (800) 221-7945 ext. 5442 or by email at
MacmillanSpecialMarkets@macmillan.com.

Library of Congress Control Number: 2018945045

ISBN 978-1-250-19544-9 (hardcover) / ISBN 978-1-250-19545-6 (ebook)

Book design by Liz Dresner

First edition, 2020

10 9 8 7 6 5 4 3 2 1

swoonreads.com

To Katelyn, my firstborn,
who has the uncanny ability to read my mind.

CHAPTER

1

Taking a breath to steel his nerves, Kalen turned the key. The door opened on silent hinges to reveal the hazy scene. A woman stood in the middle of the room. She seemed larger than life, towering like a giant scylee bird over the little girl in front of her. Her features were exaggerated, her mouth open wide as obscenities poured forth. The words hung jagged in the air, ugly and crimson. The girl cowered and tucked into herself. Dirty, blond strands of hair curtained her face. The woman stretched taller; her hands curled into fists, and her knuckles enlarged to twice their size. Sobs shook the girl's tiny frame. The woman's arm drew back. The fist swung forward, striking the girl on her cheek. Her head swung to the side, and her hair parted to reveal massive eyes. They were round and fringed in spider lashes like the dolls sold in the market shops.

The girl screamed. A cobalt ribbon slipped from between her lips to twist and weave through her hair. Tears settled dewlike on her lashes. The woman froze. Her arm dropped to her side. Her knuckles shrank to normal. Her stature collapsed. She turned away, head falling and arms crossing across her stomach as she bent over.

A fog curled in from the edges of the room, dense and cold, to shroud the two figures. Kalen shoved the door closed, turned the key, and removed it.

He opened his eyes. A wave of nausea swept over him, and he fought to stay upright. His forehead felt hammered with a thousand nails.

"She's innocent," he said. *Of the accused crime anyway.*

He yanked his fingers from the woman's wrist and stepped away. She wouldn't know what he had seen in her mind, but she knew he'd seen something. She swallowed hard, unable to look him in the eye. Most people couldn't, and, honestly, Kalen was okay with that.

"What do you mean 'she's innocent'? This woman is our best lead." Ryndel, the King's Law, was entrusted with matters of crime and punishment in the kingdom of Mureau. He paced forward from a dark recess of the small interrogation room, not happy that Kalen had failed to find what he'd been looking for. The flickerfly lamps set in the wall cast a light that cut his features in half, and his wiry, black hair stuck out in all directions. His emerald brocade jacket was open to reveal the unspotted white shirt underneath. He never got close enough to the prisoners to get dirty.

Kalen cracked his neck side to side and withdrew his

gloves from the interior pocket of his vest. "Do we need to repeat this conversation every time?"

Ryndel only wanted to hear the word *guilty*. Innocent meant more work, and the King's Law frowned upon anything that kept him from being drinking buddies with the king. That did, however, mean steady pay for Kalen—with all the false accusations Ryndel brought him as soon as he had even the hint of a new lead—so Kalen wasn't one to complain.

"I'm never quite sure you're telling the truth," Ryndel said.

"No, you can't be." Kalen met the man's watery green eyes and pulled on one glove. "But you know my abilities." He leaned in, bare fingers of his other hand a hairbreadth away from Ryndel's arm.

Ryndel scooted away.

It hadn't been easy for Kalen to prove his talent. Even he hadn't understood it at first, when, as a child, he'd caught glimpses of thought the second he touched someone's skin. He thought he was going a bit mad. But once he understood his ability, it wasn't the memories that drew his attention—it was the secrets. Secrets locked and hidden away so people wouldn't suffer from constant reminders.

When he entered a mind, he found pathways. Sometimes trails in a forest. Perhaps hallways in a home or distributaries from a river. Memories were structured in a variety of ways, but there were always arteries and branches, and at the end, hidden down dark hallways, in twisted mazes, or behind false walls, lay the secrets. The darker a secret, the harder to find. And the harder to unlock. He tugged at the key that hung on a leather cord around his neck, a mirror to the one he used when exploring someone's memories. His fingers stroked its length once before tucking it beneath his shirt. The cool metal soothed his hot skin.

Ryndel knew firsthand about Kalen's powers. The King's Law had been a test subject when Kalen was a youth and had to prove the ability to the king, who was himself unwilling to expose his mind to someone who could unlock its secrets. In fact, the king always kept Kalen at a distance of several yards and mandated that the young man never remove his gloves in his presence.

The Law was not the only person at court to distrust Kalen for his magick, but Ryndel had little to worry about. His secrets were mundane. A love of mulled wine and an unhealthy obsession with a young duchess. Not exactly appropriate but hardly anything treasonous.

A steward rushed forward with a mug of tea. Kalen accepted it with a nod and gulped it. The headaches had worsened over the past year, and on days when Ryndel kept him busy, sometimes the only relief came when he was actually inside a prisoner's mind. The tea also helped to ease the pressure in his forehead enough for him to unclench his jaw.

"I told you I didn't do nothin'." Marcella spat the words from behind him.

"I wouldn't say *nothing*," Kalen said.

"I didn't do no stealin'." Her voice softened.

"That is correct." Kalen finished the tea and set the mug down on a narrow shelf against the wall. "You did not steal a letter from the king's courier." Of course she hadn't. Ryndel was intelligent, but not when it came to matters that should be handled by the guardsmen. This woman was of a stocky build, a heavy breather. There was no chance she could have snuck up on the courier, who was most likely on horseback the entire time, to steal correspondence as it was brought into town.

"Who did?" Ryndel asked.

"Damned if I know. And she doesn't, either." Kalen hooked his thumb in Marcella's direction.

"Can I get goin' now?" the woman whined. "I have a daughter who needs me—"

Kalen's head whipped around, and her words stopped. He glared at her as Ryndel waved a hand in dismissal. The steward led her to the door, and she scurried through without a backward glance.

Kalen's gloved fingers rubbed at his temples.

"What's so important about this letter?"

"It's none of your business."

Kalen sighed. "Perhaps not. But you do know that if you find the culprit and use me to prove it, I will learn the contents of the letter in the process."

Ryndel frowned and rubbed at his chin, as if the thought hadn't quite occurred to him. Kalen knew most of the kingdom's secrets. Whether he wanted to or not. His talent made him equally as much of a target as an asset. His family could attest to that.

"Have a good day, gentlemen." Kalen handed the steward the empty cup and raced into the hall to catch up with

Marcella. She was slowly making her way up the stairs when he moved next to her and leaned in. "Was that your daughter you tormented?"

"I don't know what yer speakin' of," she said.

"It won't happen again." Silence fell. A sticky, stifling sort of silence, like she didn't know if she was supposed to respond. "Repeat the words."

A pained whisper. "It won't happen again."

"I will find out if you harm her again." He paused to let his words sink in. "Consider this your one and only warning before I have you thrown in prison for a much more punishable offense."

"You couldn't."

"Try me. Or ask around. It's not that difficult to blame someone for a crime when there's nobody to refute my allegation other than the accused." He let the truth weigh her down. "If you were a juror, who would you believe? Me or you?"

Her shoulders sank.

"You shouldn't find it that hard." Kalen stood. "Only keep your hands to yourself and your voice to a motherlike volume. You may come to find the girl loves you."

Although most likely not.

TWENTY MINUTES LATER, Kalen stood in the middle of the courtyard, a sword gripped between his gloved hands as he worked his way through the meditative steps of Hakunan. The concentration on movement always settled his nerves and relieved the residual aches in his head after a questioning.

Eyes closed, Kalen crouched, keeping his weight centered over his feet. With a slow and steady movement, he brought the sword above his head to point at the sky and then lowered it to the ground in front of him, acknowledging both the gods and his ancestors. From there the sword swung up to the right and behind his head, down to the left and up again. He spun and danced, the sword a mere extension of his arms and a tool to center his focus. His breaths settled into a deep rhythm of inhale and exhale. His mind cleared of thoughts of revenge and anger. He was simply present.

Time passed in a void. Kalen had begun the final sequence when he felt the barest shift in the air at his side. He jumped back. His eyes opened, the glare of the sun a slice of pain through his forehead.

He caught a glint of metal and a blur of sapphire in his peripheral vision.

Cirrus.

And then the young man stood before him, still and stoic and just out of reach of Kalen's sword. They were of the exact same height, and Cirrus's brown eyes glared into his.

"Good reflexes." Cirrus winced as he spoke, as if the words pained him. They probably did. The compliment was the first Cirrus had thrown in his direction in years.

Kalen nodded in thanks.

"I didn't mean to interrupt your playtime." Cirrus's gaze fell to Kalen's sword, now clutched awkwardly at his side. "You can continue. I'm sure you could use the extra practice."

Kalen's jaw tightened. "I think I'm done for the day."

The false sense of calm blanketing Kalen mere moments before was now gone. He lowered the sword and dug the weapon's tip into the dirt before leaning against it. His entire body felt heavy and sore. He ran his gloved hand through his hair and fought the urge to yawn. He refused to show Cirrus even the smallest weakness.

"Haven't seen you around much." Cirrus spun his own sword like it was weightless.

"You, either." Not that Kalen made much of an effort to see Cirrus, or anyone really. He pretty much relegated himself to his room between questionings.

"I've been busy touring the countryside. Fresh air does wonders."

"Yes, if only my work here wasn't so very important."

Cirrus glared at him.

Kalen knew Cirrus hated his ability, even if the king seemed to appreciate its usefulness. "Well, I best be going."

Cirrus's eyebrow rose. "Off to town for a little female distraction?"

"That sounds like a great plan." Kalen turned around to walk toward the weapon rack. Nobody ever turned their back on Cirrus without permission. Nobody but an ex-childhood friend anyway.

Kalen knew it would irk Cirrus, and he hated that they always seemed to return to immature behavior and juvenile slights, ruining one's meditation and making insinuations. Although he guessed it could have been worse. Cirrus could have still hated him. Kalen thought most of the time he did.

When his magick had first manifested, the king had

brought Kalen's family into the fold of the royal court. It was meant to look like an honor, but Kalen soon realized it was actually to keep him close and at the king's mercy. Two young boys in the castle, he and Cirrus had bonded over their mutual love of climbing trees and skirmishes with wooden swords. They'd schooled together and shared secrets, including Kalen's concerns about how to control his ability. He feared losing himself in someone's mind.

Cirrus had invited Kalen to practice on him, in the hopes Kalen could learn how best to use his magick, so one afternoon the boys sat in a clearing, Kalen's hand resting on Cirrus's arm. A storm hovered, and the air felt heavy with humidity. They were both tired and had taken a break from play. Kalen raced through Cirrus's mind, knowing most of the memories as his own—they had shared so many of them. But this time he pushed farther, faster, and he spotted something he'd never seen before. Not necessarily new, but hidden, on the fringe of Cirrus's thoughts.

Clouded in darkness.

A door.

And locks.

Kalen stepped closer, his fingers brushing over the metal of the lock faces. One was a shiny silver color with a large plate. Swirls and floral designs were etched into the surface, tightening around the center. The second was diamond shaped and of a matte finish. The final lock was round and plain in design but fabricated of a black onyx stone. He didn't understand how it was attached to the door. The design was seamless.

And he didn't know how to access it.

He retreated from Cirrus's mind and told him what he'd seen. Cirrus shoved Kalen away and jumped to his feet. "You're lying. You didn't see anything."

His tone and words were angry, but Kalen recognized the look that flashed through his eyes. He was afraid.

After that, Cirrus distanced himself from his friend. He took to insulting Kalen and calling him a freak. Kalen never mentioned to anyone what he had seen, but he began to find locks in other people's minds. His own powers manifested in a mental key, exact in shape and size to the one he wore around his neck, the key to his chambers, the only place he felt safe. He learned how to unlock the doors and find the secrets hidden deep behind them.

And he always wondered what memory Cirrus kept locked away, what secret had cost them their friendship.

———◦•◦———

THE SUN HUNG just above the upper lip of the courtyard walls on its descent toward the horizon as Kalen placed the sword into its slot on the rack and made his way over to the wall and the trough of fresh water. He dipped in a tin cup and lifted the cool liquid to his mouth. After several gulps, Kalen tilted his head forward and poured the remainder onto his hair, letting the cool water soothe his scalp. He shook his head once, droplets flying, and tossed the cup in the bucket on the side.

He allowed himself one glance back at Cirrus as he paced across the courtyard toward the large door leading into the main wing of the castle. Cirrus had moved to the sparring ring, where he now stood facing Terrack, the head guardsman. Terrack towered over him, his massive frame making Cirrus look like a woodling. Kalen shook his head at the sight, wondering if the king had chosen Terrack for this task because of his skill or because he was the only one who would agree to spar with Cirrus, who was the prince, after all.

CHAPTER

2

Kalen rifled through the obscene amount of clothing that filled his wardrobe to find something a little less sweaty and cleaner scented to wear. And that's what he chose. The wardrobe held a vast array of brightly colored shirts and vests in rich fabrics and patterns, all gifts from the king and meant to be worn for the many royal events that Kalen tried to avoid, but even so, the space was mostly filled with black garments. Another pair of black breeches with a black undershirt and tight-fitting vest.

He removed a pair of older boots off a shelf that held many of the same style in various states of wear. A low dresser held his gloves, and from it he removed a clean pair made of supple leather. He snagged an overcoat and returned to his bedchamber. The massive bed took up much of the room, the covers pulled neatly to the pile of pillows, not because any attendant or servants made his bed each morning, but rather because Kalen didn't sleep there. The makeshift pallet near the door worked well enough. It kept him grounded, and he never wanted to let his guard down again. His parents had taught him a difficult lesson, and although he'd come to understand their decision to flee in the years that had passed since they'd abandoned him, the lesson was one he would never allow to be repeated.

Never get too comfortable.

A glance out the window showed the sun had slid farther over the horizon, shading the sky's canvas a darker spill of blue, and Kalen caught a star winking at him. He had just enough time to stop at the kitchen to grab a bite to eat before heading into town.

Kalen exited his room and shut the door behind him. He used the key around his neck to turn the lock, squared his shoulders, and headed down the stairs. Minutes later he walked through the great hall, outside, and across a small courtyard into the kitchens. They were offset from the main buildings in case a fire started in one of the dozens of ovens.

The building was frantic with people hurrying this way and that, arms laden with bags of flour or pots filled with soup or trays piled with pastries. Kalen stayed close to the outer wall and worked his way along the edge. He rarely ate with the royal family or their honored guests, whatever lords happened to be vying for attention that week.

He stopped near the hearth and slopped a large ladle of stew from an oversize pot into a bowl. Cradling it close to his chest, he stepped into the pantry and grabbed a hardened roll. Away from the kitchen chaos, he leaned against the wall and dug into the food. The roll served as a spoon, and he scooped vegetables and buttery chunks of meat into his mouth. He hadn't realized how hungry he was until he'd licked the bowl clean and his stomach ceased clenching.

He dropped the dishes with all the other dirty ones in an overflowing barrel and slipped out. Within minutes he was outside the castle walls altogether. He followed the main path away from the gates and immediately wove through the side streets to dodge the marketplace at the center of town. It would be mostly cleared out at this hour, with only a few remaining vendors packing up their goods and townspeople haggling for a last-minute deal, but Kalen avoided it anyway.

He walked along the avenues, twisting back and around at seemingly random intervals. A spy himself, Kalen knew the king employed many others, and this time he preferred to keep his whereabouts unknown. While always on the lookout for information, he would rather have an hour or two to relax, and this time not have to use his magick.

Kalen kept to the shadows, even though it would have been cleaner to avoid the refuse collecting in the alleyways. A sharp left and he stood in front of his favorite place of solace.

The Milked Goat.

He still thought it was a ridiculous name for an establishment, but, like every other night, when he pushed through the doors, he was greeted with the noise and sour scent of a crowd. The low ceiling didn't help either of those, nor did the fire roaring in the hearth against the back stone wall. A fiddler held court in the corner, and a few girls lifted their skirts to twirl on a makeshift dance floor in front of him. A table had been set up for cards in the back of the room, and a group crowded the counter where Reap—the tavern keeper nicknamed for the tattoo rippling up his forearm—was making his signature drink.

He cracked several eggs into a pitcher and whisked them together, showing off his massive biceps to the girls who seemed intent on staring. Pouring in rum and molasses, Reap continued to beat at the mixture. He added in a seemingly random amount of beer and then paced to the hearth. A fire poker rested in the flames. Reap grabbed the handle and lifted it up over his head so as not to maim anyone with it. He plunged it into the pitcher and stirred quickly, creating a frothy drink that steamed and sizzled. He tossed the cooling poker to the side and poured the concoction into the already waiting mugs lining the counter. Patrons scooped them up, clinking them together in cheers before chugging the drink.

Kalen stepped to the end of the counter and tipped his head in acknowledgment.

"Usual?" Reap asked as he used a stained, damp towel to mop up the alcohol that had spilled as he poured. Kalen glanced around, looking for a clean one to throw him, but there were none to be found.

He waited as Reap reached for a mug under the bar and poured boiling water over tea leaves. Kalen never drowned his sorrows in anything stronger than caffeine. Alcohol left him too susceptible to letting his guard—and his gloves— down. Cirrus, on the other hand, would have joined in with the rest of the patrons to gulp a mug of Reap's mixture.

Kalen took a gulp of the tea, threw Reap a coin, and made his way to the card table. He collapsed into the lone vacant chair and traced his gloved finger along the familiar crack running down the curved wooden arm.

He hated gambling but loved anything that served to sharpen his mind. Kalen could focus on both the game and the conversations going on around him, tucking away details, like love letters to dissect later. It was a great way to gather information. Not exactly sanctioned by the king, but if Kalen used his knowledge of the kingdom's happenings while in someone's memories, he could complete the questioning much quicker and get out of their minds.

"Keepin' busy?" Damien, the young fisherman sitting to his right, asked.

"Same as always." After pushing a pile of coins to the dealer, Kalen was dealt a hand. "How's it going at the docks?"

"Good. Brought in at least three barrels o' crawfish this afternoon."

Kalen glanced quickly at his own hand. A pair of knaves and a run of three clovers. He continued chatting with Damien while he watched the other players discard and receive new ones. One of the regular players rubbed at his chin, a tell that Kalen knew meant he had a good hand. Play reached Kalen, and he immediately tossed the clovers on the table and requested three new cards.

"I swear, ya don't even pay attention to what yer doin'," Damien said with a shake of his head. He folded his cards and stretched his arms so his hands laced behind his head. "There was some interestin' activity today."

Kalen nodded encouragement. This information was what kept him returning to the Milked Goat.

"A new ship came in. I woulda guessed it was a pirate ship, what with the black hull and black sails, but the constable came down ta greet 'em and take 'em somewhere private."

Black sails. *Antioegen.* Antioege was the port city of the kingdom of Ehren, situated just north of their own. He wondered why the ship was in port. It wasn't part of the normal trading cycle, as the moon was nearing full and the winds were not cooperative.

As Kalen pondered this bit of information, he picked up his new cards and added them to his hand. He slid them apart just enough to see he'd been dealt another knave and two minstrels. He tossed a coin into the middle of the table to increase the bet. Two players folded, but the fifth, an older gentleman sitting on Kalen's left, called Kalen's bet and raised him. Kalen bit back a sigh, knowing the man was about to lose. He matched the bet, and the dealer signaled for the gentleman to show his cards. Two pair. Kalen flipped over his own cards to reveal the full ship.

The gentleman pursed his lips in defeat. "You win some and lose some. Good game." He pushed away from the table, and a waif of a girl slid into the vacant seat. Her hooded cloak mostly covered her shock of silver hair, and her equally silver eyes turned to Kalen.

Luna.

She blinked lazily at him, and her lips tugged into a half smile.

Kalen couldn't help but smile in return, but then clamped his lips shut. He was supposed to be angry with her. A week ago he'd asked her to be his lookout, and she had disappeared.

This was the first time he'd seen her since, and he had questions to ask. Why she'd left. Where she'd gone.

The dealer passed out another round of cards, and Kalen drew his close. Not a good hand, but he didn't care. He slid four of the cards away, keeping only the wizard of clover.

Luna asked for only one new card, and play moved around the table until it reached Damien. He appeared intent on staying in the hand, his tongue caught between his front teeth as he debated which cards to surrender.

"How many ships were there in all?" Kalen asked him.

"Damien finally dropped two cards to the table. "Just the one. Came in kind of late."

Kalen mulled this as he was dealt two more wizards for three of a kind.

But wait.

He glared at Luna and cleared his throat. She raised her silver eyebrows as she rearranged the cards in her hand. The long sleeves of her cloak billowed out at the wrists, offering a glimpse of the tattoos that he knew traced up her arms and down her torso. Twisting loops of chains and rose stems, covered in thorns. They circled her neck and waist, too.

"Give it back," he said out of the side of his mouth.

"Give what back?"

"My wizard."

Luna was a thief, and a good one at that. He hadn't even realized she'd swapped out his card with a squire.

"I have no idea what you mean." She fluttered long eyelashes in his direction and pushed several coins toward the center as she raised the bet.

A yawn stretched the mouth of the player at her side.

Monet was an aristocrat in his midthirties, known to spend his inheritance on gambling, women, and ridiculously expensive clothing . . . not necessarily in that order. He shoved a stack of coins to the center, raising Luna's bet.

When play returned to Damien, he folded his hand. Kalen was quick to follow suit, tossing his cards on the table. Luna was about to run the table, and he didn't need to add his coins to her winnings, not that it much mattered. Her gaze flitted from her cards to the coins and back again until Monet slapped his palm to the table in annoyance. Finally, she pushed all her money to the center. "All in."

"Oh come on," Monet said. "I'm not falling for that." He pushed another stack in to match her.

Luna grinned and flipped her cards. A flush of clovers, wizard high.

Monet growled as he turned over a straight. "You're cheating again."

"Who, me?" Luna feigned innocence while the coins disappeared into her sleeves. She rose from the table. "I'd say I'm sorry to have to limit your time with Jezebel this evening." She tossed the last coin to the dealer. "But I'd be lying."

She strode toward the exit but stopped midway and turned to look over her shoulder. "By the way, that hat is ridiculous."

Monet stroked the scylee bird feather stretching away from the brim and glared at her. Kalen gathered his coins and followed her out. It wasn't difficult to catch her, considering her stride was probably half of his, but the second he was within reach, his gloved hand gripped her shoulder. Luna had a way of disappearing into the shadows, and he didn't want to lose her.

"You could have been a little more subtle," he said, when she stopped and turned to him.

"He's weak. Besides, he wouldn't do anything that puts him in poor favor with my mother . . ." Her eyes widened at something behind him, and Kalen spun around. Monet had stormed out of the Milked Goat and now walked in their direction.

"Return it to me." He nearly spat the words as he held out a hand, palm facing up, toward Luna.

"Return what, exactly?" She widened her deceptively innocent silver eyes and stared at Monet.

"My. Pocket. Watch. Return. It. Now." His hand shook with fury. He lunged forward, but before he reached Luna, Kalen had whipped off a glove.

"Be careful." Kalen wiggled his fingers. "I'm sure you have some secrets you don't want spread around town."

Monet's eyes narrowed to slits, but he stepped quickly away. "Keep your hands to yourself, freak."

"I suggest you do the same."

"She took something from me." Monet glanced quickly to Luna and then back to Kalen, not risking taking his eyes off the questioner. "It's a family heirloom. Give it back."

"Fine." Luna reached into her cloak and pulled out a golden watch strung on a thin chain. She tossed it to him. "I figured it was no use to you since you always run over on time at the brothel."

He cradled the watch and tucked it into the interior

pocket of his coat before readjusting his hat and walking toward the tavern.

As soon as the door shut behind him, Kalen turned to face Luna. "I wish you wouldn't do that." He shoved his fingers into the glove.

"Kalen, you don't always have to come to my defense."

She was right, but still. She was his friend. "Why did you let yourself get caught?"

She snorted. "I'm pretty sure I would have been home already if you hadn't stopped me to give me a warning."

"I stopped you because we need to talk."

The clock tower began its toll, ending with a single chime.

"It's late, and I need to get back." What was late for the rest of the city was early for her mother's business.

"We still need to talk," Kalen said.

"You know where to find me." Luna tossed a grin over her shoulder as she walked away. A second later she was gone.

CHAPTER

3

A loud knock woke Kalen the next morning.

"You dressed?" Terrack's voice rang through the door.

"Does it matter? The door is locked."

Kalen stretched and rose from the pallet before walking over to open the door. Terrack blocked the hallway with his bulk, and his mouth moved like a horse's as he chewed on a piece of bark. "Actually, I just wondered if you had a girl in there."

"Have I ever had a girl in here?"

"There's a first time for everything," Terrack smirked.

"To what do I owe the pleasure of your company so early in the day?"

"I'll give you one guess."

Kalen steeled himself for yet another headache. "Give me a minute."

He shut the door and splashed water on his face from the basin. He quickly changed and grabbed a pair of gloves before returning to the hallway. Terrack hadn't moved. Kalen shut the door, turned the key in the lock, and followed the large man down the hall.

"Who is it?" Kalen asked.

"Ship captain," said Terrack. "Arrived yesterday."

The Antioegen ships Damien mentioned.

Kalen's worry over his impending headaches disappeared. This would be interesting. Much more interesting than a woman falsely accused of stealing correspondence.

They wound down the curved staircase into the darkness of the cellar. Rough stone walls caught at the sleeves of his coat, as if clawing him into the depths. The cool air was thick with moisture that gathered at the back of his neck. They reached the cellar floor, and Terrack turned in a different direction than the one leading to Kalen's normal interrogation room. Kalen's chest heaved with a silent sigh. This way were the holding cells.

Kalen despised having to go into the mind of someone shackled by chains.

They approached the two cells, heavy doors facing each other from across the narrow hallway. The slits in one door allowed flickers of dusty light to dance into the hall. Terrack pushed that one open, and Kalen got his first glimpse of the prisoner.

The captain was tall, in his midthirties perhaps, with

sun-weathered skin. Limp, long hair fell into his eyes, one of which was nearly swollen shut. He stood upright, his arms hanging at his sides. His wrists were wrapped in metal cuffs threaded with a heavy chain linked to the wall behind him through a ring just above his head. His breaths came fast and shallow, like he couldn't fully inhale. Kalen imagined that underneath the captain's jacket and all those gold buttons were whip marks or bruising . . . or both.

"Why is he in chains?"

"The Law's orders. He put up a good fight when he arrived."

The prisoner attempted a laugh but winced as soon as his chest expanded. The sound was more of a wounded cough.

Footsteps echoed in from the hall behind them, and the King's Law swept into the room. His black cloak swirled and settled around him, flashes of the green silk interior visible as he threw back his shoulders.

"Good. You're here." Ryndel nodded at Kalen. "I think we're ready to get started."

Ryndel grabbed one of two stools tucked into the corner and placed it behind the prisoner. He kicked forward, knocking the captain's legs from behind so they buckled and he fell back against the hard seat. His arms lifted awkwardly as the chairs held firm, making him look like a wounded marionette. Ryndel leaned in. "I would suggest you behave yourself."

Kalen waited until Ryndel had returned to his side. "What am I looking for?" he asked.

"The ship was carrying valuable cargo. It's no longer on board, but Captain Belrose here denies ever seeing it. I want to know what happened."

Silence filled the room.

"Well?" Ryndel raised his hands in impatience. "What are you waiting for? Get started."

"What exactly is the cargo?" Kalen hated the vagueness of these requests.

"I'd rather not disclose further information. You'll know it if you see it. Let's leave it at that."

Kalen sighed and removed his gloves. He stuffed them into the interior pocket of his vest and turned to Terrack. "I'm going to need tea. Double brewed." Terrack called into the hall for a steward.

Kalen stepped forward until he was toe-to-toe with the captain. "I'm going to touch your hand. It won't hurt, but please remain still. Otherwise they'll make this a lot less comfortable."

Belrose stared at the wall behind Kalen's head.

Kalen grabbed the other stool and sat on its edge. He leaned forward, stretching his bare fingers and thumb to encircle the captain's wrist, above the manacle. Before he could dive into the man's mind, Belrose thrashed and broke the connection. Kalen stood abruptly, the stool rocking once before it fell on its side.

"He warned you." Terrack grabbed the chain and hauled the captain to his feet. He kicked the stool to the side and then yanked on one end of the chain so the slack tightened and the links slid through the manacles. Belrose was forced to shuffle backward until he stood flat against the wall. Terrack continued to pull, wrapping the chain around his hand and elbow in a looping motion. Belrose's wrists were now pulled together and his arms stretched above his head. Terrack didn't stop until the captain was nearly on tiptoe, his back arched.

Belrose didn't bother to flinch.

Terrack pushed one of the links onto a hook in the wall to lock the chain in position before pulling the coiled links from his arm. He squatted and grabbed two additional manacles lying open on the floor. He attached them to Belrose's ankles with a second set of chains and stood.

"He's all yours."

Kalen righted his stool and dragged it over to the captain. He sat and eyed the strip of skin exposed between Belrose's shirt and the waist of his trousers. It was much more intimate than the wrists, but Kalen couldn't remain standing the entire time. This would have to do.

With a deep breath, Kalen touched Belrose's waist and spiraled into the captain's thoughts.

He walked along a cliff that butted up against the edge of a stormy sea. Lightning-fast flashes of memories glimmered. A few locked chests rested along the path, presumably holding some of the captain's recent secrets. If there were missing cargo, Belrose would have most likely locked the thought away.

Kalen removed the key from around his neck. He squatted on the rocky ground and inserted it into one of the chests. His mind shifted the shape of the key's metal blade and bits to fit the grooves and nuances of the lock. He sensed the ward spacing, the heights and angles, and made adjustments accordingly.

With a click, he threw open the chest, and the secret swelled around him.

He stood on a deck so clean it nearly shone. As in all the memories Kalen unlocked, the colors were heightened, every detail exaggerated. Belrose stood at the helm, concern drawing lines in his forehead as he noticed his normally jolly crew now slinging indigo ribbons of anger at one another. The master gunner and one of the sailors began to shove each other across the deck. Suddenly a knife appeared in the master gunner's hand. He lashed forward, the movement slowing in the memory. Moonlight glanced off the knife, the weapon a comet of white light as it inched forward and sliced through the other sailor's shirt and across his abdomen. Blood sprayed in a thin line. The attacker dropped his knife and, with the blade spinning on the deck, grabbed his bleeding comrade and tossed him over the rail. A scream of orange terror and a splash.

Time sped up again. Belrose shouted to drop anchor and lower a boat overboard. While his crew searched for the fallen sailor, Belrose and his first mate were able to secure the master gunner and bring him belowdecks. The only locked door on the ship opened into a claustrophobic room, barren save for a small wooden chest sitting on the floor.

The master gunner thrashed against the rope now binding his wrists. Orange and black traced his screams. "Get me away from it! Get me away!"

His feet dug into the floorboards, and he threw his head backward, trying to hit Belrose in the face. The captain and his first mate shoved the master gunner in farther, raced out of the room, and locked the door behind them.

They were unable to find the sailor thrown overboard, and the night grew progressively worse. More scuffles and arguments, completely out of character for a crew that had sailed together for years.

"It's whatever is in that chest." The first mate approached

Belrose, his words a gray strand of apprehension. "We'll never make it to Mureau at this rate."

Belrose paced his small quarters, a knuckle caught between his teeth as he mumbled to himself. "We need to get it overboard. Do I dare drop it in the sea? No, I need to find somewhere to bury it." The ribbon of words, green and crimson, wrapped around him like chains, tightening until he could hardly speak. He directed the first mate off course, to a deserted island. As soon as they were close enough to land, Belrose and his first mate retrieved the chest and dropped it into the tender. Belrose himself rowed the cargo ashore. He carried it up past the high-water mark and found an outcrop. He moved some of the rocks aside and dug a large enough hole in the sand to hide the chest.

He couldn't flee the area fast enough.

As soon as Belrose reboarded his ship, everyone returned into their rhythms. Belrose visited the windowless room. The master gunner had calmed. Now horror-struck by his actions, he asked for a trial and the worst possible punishment: death. Belrose said he would address the crime when they returned to Antioege, but he knew a part of the fault lay with the cargo. In the meantime, they needed to restock their ship in Mureau.

The edges of the secret dimmed, and the scene ended.

———————

EACH BEAM FROM the flickerfly lantern pierced the skin of Kalen's forehead with long needles.

"Where is it?" Ryndel's breath was hot against the back of his neck.

"Give the boy a minute." Terrack urged Ryndel away until the steward had given Kalen the tea.

Kalen gulped at the hot drink, wanting nothing more than to sleep and forget the pain. He donned his gloves and stood.

"There was a chest on board."

The captain sucked in a breath. "How could you see—"

"Where is it?" Ryndel interrupted. He looked from Belrose to Kalen, waiting for one of them to answer.

The captain pursed his lips together, and his glare turned sharper than the knife blade Kalen had just glimpsed in his memory.

"On an island," Kalen said. He held up his hand to silence Ryndel. "But he did what was necessary. The captain had no choice but to remove the cargo in order to save his crew."

Ryndel tugged at the sleeves of his shirt and frowned.

"I recommend clemency." Kalen passed the empty mug of tea to the steward. "I also recommend a thank-you to the captain. We don't want the contents anywhere near our kingdom."

Ryndel paced a tight square around the room, his boots clipping a steady tune that rattled Kalen's head. He stopped abruptly. "You're right. I'll have Terrack clean up the prisoner and return him to his ship. You're free to go."

Kalen had expected Ryndel to ask for more information, but he seemed distracted with other things.

It wasn't the first time Kalen was left to deal with the remnants of someone else's memories.

CHAPTER

4

I t was late afternoon, the sun casting long shadows across the landscape, when Kalen left the castle and headed along the back roads to a property on the edge of town. He stood, leaning against the wooden fence and staring at the columns lining the front of the residence. The paint had faded, but it still presented a formidable expression, awnings like heavy eyelids over aged eyes and a gaping mouth of massive double doors. Kalen felt the weight of them against his shoulder as if he had walked through them only yesterday.

But it had been six years.

Suddenly he heard his name being shouted. Terrack rode up on horseback. "The king needs you."

Kalen took a deep breath. Questioning requests usually came from Ryndel, but on occasion the king required

Kalen's services for nonroyal matters. He didn't look forward to whatever the king had in store.

The next words, however, were a surprise.

"The prince collapsed and has yet to awaken."

He extended a hand to help Kalen up onto the horse behind him.

They galloped away, and Kalen gave one more sweeping glance at the yard before it faded into the distance.

He wondered if Mathew remembered Kalen chasing him up the winding staircases or exploring the backyard maze where they tried to catch flickerflies.

He wondered if his younger brother remembered him at all, or if his parents had wiped the family free of the stain of his magick.

Terrack muttered to himself. "I didn't mean to hit him that hard. He attacked me out of nowhere. We were no longer sparring, I tell you. I had to protect my life."

"What does the king want with me? Did he ask Jenna for help?" Kalen glanced at Terrack. As the king had done with Kalen, he had a way of snagging the few *sorciers* in the kingdom and bringing them into his fold. That way, he kept a pulse on their abilities while keeping them under control. There were currently eight *sorciers* in Mureau, and their abilities covered a wide range of magick: the ability to find water sources, read emotions, manipulate dreams, manipulate others' movements, communicate with the dead, attract things—and Kalen's own talent.

Jenna was several years older than Kalen, and her ability was diagnosing ailments via touch. She could trace her way through the body and recommend a course of action, although she couldn't do much to heal.

"She found nothing, nor did the other *sorciers* or the physician. The prince hasn't so much as blinked. I think the king is hoping you can access his mind and see what's going on."

Of course Kalen was the last resort . . . the king kept Kalen's abilities at arm's length, so it made sense to keep them away from his son as well.

They continued on in silence until they reached the black iron gates leading to the castle grounds. The click of hooves echoed off the stone courtyard before they stopped near a waiting stable boy. As soon as they dismounted, Terrack handed the reins over and motioned for Kalen to follow close behind him.

Terrack and Kalen paced through the massive main entrance, past the myriad columns, up the ornate staircase, and down a long hallway lined with portraits of the royal family and their ancestors. Plush carpets flattened under Kalen's boots, and strings of bulbs, each filled with a dozen flickerflies, pulsed overhead.

Finally, Terrack pushed open an engraved door and urged Kalen in. "I'm not invited," he said.

"Why?"

"I'm still at fault here. We'll see if the king forgives me."

Kalen stepped forward and found himself in the king's own quarters. The king jumped up from a chair near the hearth. His eyes were bloodshot, and his hair was bunched at his scalp where he appeared to have gripped and yanked at it. The king was relatively young, and Cirrus was his only child. The queen had died when Cirrus was a toddler, so it was only the two of them. Distress wafted off him like a sour cologne.

Or perhaps that was mulled wine.

"Please, Kalen, you must help."

Kalen nodded, although his stomach clenched. He wasn't a healer. "I'll do my best."

The king pointed Kalen toward the bedchamber. Cirrus lay sprawled on top of a rich maroon coverlet stretching across a raised four-poster bed. He was still dressed in his breeches and boots. His shirt had been unbuttoned, leaving his chest bare, and the physician bent over him, tapping on his ribs with some sort of hammered instrument.

"Make room," the king said, the words polite yet firm.

The physician stepped away, and Kalen neared the bed. He slid out of his cloak and draped it over the footboard before he sat on the edge of the mattress at the prince's side. He quickly removed his gloves and tucked them in his pocket.

"I can't promise anything." Kalen looked at the king. His palm hovered over Cirrus's chest near his collarbone as he debated the sanity of delving into the prince's mind. If Cirrus died—whether it happened now or in the next weeks—Kalen could be blamed. While he wouldn't mind not having to serve as the King's Questioner, he didn't know that he'd like to spend the rest of his life in a tower cell. Or eternity without a head.

"I won't hold you liable." The king seemed to read his mind.

A promise easily dismissed. Still, Kalen closed his eyes, lowered his hand to the prince's skin, and was swept under.

His world spun, disconcerting as ever. After doing this

gods knew how many times, Kalen thought he'd be used to it by now.

He took a moment to orient himself, but he was already familiar with the open structure of Cirrus's mind. Not much had changed in the arrangement of the prince's memories since he'd been a child. There were certainly more doors and locks, secrets Cirrus had formed over the years, but on the extreme edge of the horizon, clouded beneath a shroud of darkness, Kalen could still make out the heavily locked door.

Kalen settled in the open space and looked around, determined to see if there had been any injury to Cirrus's mind. He spent a minute observing, not exactly sure what to look for. Perhaps a disturbance or fading thoughts, but nothing appeared out of the ordinary or faulty. He'd once been in the mind of someone suffering from mental illness, and it had looked like a spiderweb. Memories sticky and stretched, woven into other memories and thoughts. It had made him dizzy, and he'd removed himself from that mind immediately.

Kalen knew he should do the same now—pull away and reassure the king, but he was drawn to the dark, clouded door like a moth to flame. He walked closer, the key searing against his chest. He pulled the cord up and over his head, and his fingers worried at the metal.

The locks were still familiar in their arrangement and shapes, as they'd been a constant subject of Kalen's dreams— nightmares for a while—ever since Cirrus had abruptly severed their friendship.

His fingers traced the top lock, and he inserted the key.

The locks in someone's mind weren't like locks in the

outside world. Kalen's key had to trace the wards, often reshaping midturn. Wards of the mind were uneven and inconstant, requiring focus and concentration.

The key finally made it through to Cirrus's memory. A satisfying click and the bolt slid clear from the wall. Kalen took a breath and removed the key, turning his focus to the second lock. The cloud thickened around him, the temperature cooling and the tendrils thickening to a soupy texture.

It took longer to open the second than the first, but soon enough Kalen had unbolted that one as well. The third took the longest, time seeming both to stop and stretch endlessly as the atmosphere turned even gloomier and darker. The wards were infinitesimal in width and shifted constantly, forming a bending wave in nearly all directions. The key kept catching, and he was ready to exit Cirrus's mind when the lock finally gave way.

Kalen stretched the cord and dropped the key back over his neck. He gripped the knob and shoved open the door, tripping into a world of chaos.

A darkened room, sconces flickering along the wall. Long shadows thrown everywhere. A wailing newborn. A young boy crouched in the corner. A woman laid out on the bed, her eyes cold and her skin the pasty color of death. Another woman standing in the middle of the room. And a much younger version of the king, distraught beside her.

"I want her out of my sight." The king's voice was strangled, the words a dark sash of plum wrapping his throat. He pointed at the newborn. "I want her gone from my kingdom."

The boy wrapped his arms around his knees, his reddish

hair and freckles more prominent against the white of his skin as he fought against a sob.

"That goes against every vision I've seen, my lord," the woman said. Her words were the stark white of truth, as white as the long gown draped over her thin frame. She tugged at the fabric and wound it between her fingers.

"I don't care about your visions. She killed my wife." The king's voice cracked. "She killed the queen. She's lucky I don't have her decapitated today."

The prophet rested a soft hand on his shoulder. "She's a baby. She's your daughter."

He wrenched away. "She is nothing to me."

Her hand fell to her side. "She couldn't control herself."

The king glared at the prophet, his words biting and full of venom. "You came here *today* to tell me not to send her away. You could have come to me *yesterday* and told me of the vision, so I could have prevented the entire thing. I should have *you* killed."

The prophet stared at the king until he turned away. "My sight doesn't work in that manner, and you know that. I only had the vision as the queen gasped her last breath. It was clear. If you send the princess away, she will be the death of us all."

"I don't believe you. I don't believe it. I'll send her far enough away that nobody can find her. She'll never know her true heritage, so what does it matter?" The king spun around and began to pace the length of the room.

The boy inched upward, his back wedged into the corner. Slowly, with bated breath, he snuck closer to the bed. His hand brushed the queen's hand.

"That's not the way it works," the prophet said again.

"The vision shows destruction of the kingdom, an occurrence directly related to her banishment."

The boy slipped from the queen over to the bassinet. He peered inside at the baby girl, at her startling blue eyes. Enormous tears built in the corner of them and trailed down her face to splash on the blanket beneath her head. Her arms extended, as if reaching for him, and she started to wail, an indigo noose that wrapped around the prince's throat. He gasped, hands fluttering to his neck.

The king raced over and spun the boy around. "Cirrus, are you okay?"

The boy's eyes bugged wide, and he fought to breathe against the sobs racking his chest. He crossed his arms tight as he fought to take a breath.

"Look. She's doing it to him, too. She'll kill us all if she stays here." The king's voice rose, and he spun to the prophet. "Leave us alone so I can make plans."

Resigned, the prophet walked toward the door. "What of the boy?"

"What of him?"

"He's heard the truth. He may speak of it."

The king dismissed the thought with a wave of his hand. "I'll have the memory removed. It will be better for him never to have known he had a—"

⋅—•—⋅

KALEN'S MIND WRENCHED from the memory as his body was flung off the bed. Cirrus bolted upright, his eyes wide and nostrils flaring.

"What are you doing?" In his voice was a mixture of

hatred, awe, and uncertainty. Jaw clenched, he choked out the words. "What *were* you doing."

Kalen sank to the carpet, and his head fell forward, nearly to his knees. His hands gripped his hair, trying to pull the pain out through his scalp. Nails pounded into every pore. The room spun around him in a lazy circle, and it took him a moment to realize that he had failed to relock Cirrus's memory.

He groaned and reached out his hand for the mug he knew Terrack would have requested for him. The herbs began to take effect, and then the reality of the memory slammed into his mind with even more force than the pain.

He stood, the tea still grasped in his hands, and moved away from the bed until his back was against the wall, much like the young prince had been in the memory. The king had stepped forward to sit next to Cirrus and bombard him with questions, drilling him on what had happened out in the courtyard with Terrack, was it the guard's fault and should he be punished, was Cirrus in pain anywhere, did he need something to eat or drink.

Cirrus said not a word, only stared straight ahead into the middle of the room.

The king motioned for the physician to return to Cirrus's side. The older man reached over to rest his fingers on Cirrus's wrist to check his pulse and leaned in, face-to-face, to examine his pupils.

Panic tightened Kalen's chest. Had leaving the memory unlocked done something permanent to Cirrus's mind? He feared he had damaged the prince and wondered if there was a way to repair it. He pushed away from the wall, ready to touch Cirrus again and delve back into his thoughts.

But Cirrus squeezed past the physician and stood. "I'm fine. I'm tired and hungry. I'd like to eat and go to my chambers." He nodded at the king and the physician in turn. "Thank you for your concern."

And he walked away, leaving everyone staring after him.

CHAPTER

5

K alen fought the desire to follow Cirrus, knowing the prince had to be shocked over the unlocked memory. He himself had lost a sibling.

A sibling. A princess. A prophecy. There were so many things at stake. Kalen swallowed hard. The king couldn't discover that Kalen had unlocked the memory, or that Cirrus now knew. Especially since he'd never heard of a prophet *sorcier*. What had ever happened to the woman in white? The king must have banished her as well.

"Your Grace."

The king turned toward him. "Yes, Kalen?"

"I saw nothing of note inside the prince's mind. Other than the usual hostility toward me, of course." He gave a self-deprecating smile. "He seems to have all of his wits and thoughts intact."

"Thank you for helping." The king turned toward the doorway. "I wish I knew why you two fell out of favor with one another."

"I can answer that." The king's attention swung to Kalen as if he wondered about the memory. "I'm the better sword-fighter." Kalen's lips pulled into an even broader grin, and the king's shoulders relaxed.

"You two were such great friends. And then you weren't. Hopefully someday you can sort it out. It would be nice for Cirrus to have someone he can trust on his side."

Kalen took the last gulp of tea and nodded. "I agree." He tipped his head in acknowledgment. "I'd best be going."

"Of course." The king waved him toward the door. "I will see you around, I'm certain."

And I'm certain you'll make sure of it.

Kalen stepped out of the chambers and walked steadily down the hall, though his pulse leaped and his legs itched to run. He couldn't put enough distance between himself and the king. The king had to wonder what Kalen had seen and why Cirrus had reacted the way he had.

Kalen followed the hallways through the servants' quarters and out the side door to the supply path and gate. With a nod at the sentry, he passed through and into the forest beyond.

He avoided the trail, and as soon as he was within the dense cover of trees, he wove a meandering course through the brush that he could have followed with his eyes closed. And he had as a child, when the forest was a daily exploration. *Step over the fallen log here, push away the jutting branch there, sidestep the never-ending puddle here, and leap over the stream right there.* Now he only walked this path when he needed to be alone in the fresh air to gather his thoughts.

The sun had started to set, and the western sky pulsed with pinks and yellows, visible when he stepped into a small clearing that opened in front of him. A soft bed of grass covered the ground, and a circle of flat, gray boulders lay scattered at the center of the open space. He sprawled on his back across one of them, one boot on the rock's surface and the other planted on the ground.

His arm draped across his forehead, and his eyelids sank closed. The thunder of his pulse slowed to an easy rhythm as the sounds of the forest settled around him.

A snap of a branch.

Kalen quickly sat upright. Cirrus stood at the edge of the clearing. His hair was slicked to his scalp like he had dunked it in the water tub. He probably had.

"I figured I'd find you here."

"I figured you'd come." This was the spot it had all happened, when Kalen had first found the door in Cirrus's memory. It was only fitting they have this discussion here.

Cirrus shifted his weight side to side and then walked closer. He lowered himself to sit on one of the rocks and glanced up at the moon. His long legs stretched in front of him. He opened his mouth and closed it again. Finally, he spoke.

"So," said the prince.

"So." Kalen felt sorry for Cirrus, but he still felt a significant amount of tortuous history between the two of them. He wasn't about to orchestrate the conversation.

"Do you think it was true?"

"Yes." Kalen answered before Cirrus had even closed his mouth.

"Why?"

Kalen contemplated the best way to explain. "Some people have a way of remembering thoughts or events in a manner that may not be true, but I can always tell. There's a hue or haze over the entire memory, and the words coming from their mouths don't match what they are saying." He paused. "I don't see thoughts the way the world is around us. There are magnified colors and shapes and senses." Cirrus's forehead wrinkled in confusion, so Kalen returned to the original question. "Your memory held nothing that would cause suspicion. Plus, it was hidden away when you were too young to manipulate it. I have no doubt that what we saw is the truth."

Cirrus took a deep breath. He pulled his legs back toward him and leaned over to curl into himself. "Bloody crow . . . I have a sister."

Kalen stayed silent and allowed Cirrus to continue to process this development.

"I have a sister, *and* she has magick. But what is her ability?"

Kalen stared at him until Cirrus lifted his head to look him in the eyes. "You tell me. It looked like she was strangling you."

Cirrus shook his head. "She wasn't strangling me." He said it as if it were an impossibility, the mere idea of someone with their hands around his neck. "I remember feeling sad about my mother, seeing the baby, and suddenly being a hundred times more distraught. I couldn't breathe through the anguish, felt like I was choking on it."

"Something to do with controlling emotions." Kalen drummed his fingers against his lips. "You were sad, and those feelings heightened. The ability might have had to do with enhancing emotions."

"But my mother. She was happy to have the baby in her arms; then suddenly she was panicked and fell."

"Perhaps the princess projected her own emotions." For some reason, Kalen's thoughts turned to the captain's chest, which seemed to have cast an emotion of anger on the crew. He wondered briefly if the two were connected.

"Is that possible?" Cirrus arched an eyebrow. Kalen imagined the prince hated the idea, hated all of it as much as he hated Kalen's own magick. "Her ability could be that strong, that young?"

"I don't know," Kalen said.

"Do you think she's still alive?" Cirrus feigned nonchalance, but Kalen heard the shift in his voice, a wishful undertone beneath the words.

Kalen swung his legs to the side so he faced Cirrus. "The prophet said she would bring destruction to the kingdom, which hasn't happened yet, so I'm guessing she's still alive."

"That's not necessarily true." Cirrus grabbed a stick and began drawing overlapping circles in the dirt. "Prophecies aren't always what they seem." He glanced up. "You know I was forced to study all this."

Kalen shrugged a nonanswer. He didn't know. How would he have known? They both knew he hadn't been the prince's confidant for a while now.

"Anyway," Cirrus continued, "if I'm understanding the prophet's words correctly, sending the princess away would mean destruction of the kingdom. But that could mean decades from now. Hundreds of years from now. Perhaps she meets someone and has a child who ends up waging war against Mureau." He made an x in one of the circles. "Or maybe she was banished to another kingdom, where she accidentally killed someone. They beheaded her at the age of five but eventually will discover she was the princess, and they then band together to seek revenge on Mureau." He added an x to another circle. "She might be alive or dead. There are dozens of possible scenarios. Hundreds even. The prophecy was merely based on the act of banishing her from the kingdom."

Kalen nodded. "Valid points. I'm impressed."

Cirrus raised an eyebrow and combed back the dried hair now falling into his eyes. "Do you change your answer now?"

"No. I don't." Kalen paused. "I don't think she's dead, because somehow I think *you* would know. I can't imagine how you must feel having only now learned you have a sister somewhere out there. But I feel you would've known something was amiss if she had died." He had no idea if what he said was true, but he knew it was what the prince wanted to hear.

"I wish . . ." Cirrus stood.

"Yes?"

"Nothing. Never mind."

Kalen chewed at his lip as he pondered his next steps. Did he want to get involved with this? He risked much. "Do you want to find your sister?"

"Of course I do." Cirrus paced across the clearing and spun around. "The prophecy says her banishment would end in the kingdom's destruction. Maybe if we bring her back, that will all be negated."

"You just said we couldn't change things, that there was no way to decipher the meaning."

"But what if we can?"

Kalen did feel an urge to learn the truth in this matter, as he had in all matters in his life. But he could not deny that self-preservation was the stronger motivation. In the secreted memory, the king appeared willing to do anything to conceal knowledge of the princess . . . anything. Including disposing of the prophet. Kalen had an increasingly unsettling suspicion that, despite his value as the questioner, he would be an easy casualty if the king found out he knew what had transpired on the night of the queen's death. But if Kalen could use the girl as collateral against his own life, or at least proof against the judgment of the royal council, he might walk away with his head.

And most importantly, Kalen knew he was the best man for the job. He was used to uncovering secrets.

"I'll help you find her." Kalen stood.

"I don't need your help." Cirrus crossed his arms in front of his chest. "You'll just get in the way."

Kalen ignored him. "I know a place to start seeking answers here." He would find Captain Belrose before his ship sailed back to Antioege, whether Cirrus wanted his help or not. "In the meantime, you need to placate your father," Kalen said. "I don't know what anger you might have toward him and the lie he's kept all this time—however, he can't have even the slightest idea that you now know the truth. It impacts me as well, because if you know, then I know."

Kalen was sure the prince didn't care much about what happened to his former friend, but Kalen valued his own life too much to linger in Mureau.

Kalen turned away from Cirrus and pushed through the foliage at the edge of the clearing. He glanced over his shoulder. "Return to the castle, and I'll see what I can dig up. Meet me here at midnight."

And he let the branches close behind him.

"I HAVE A proposition for you. But first I need to know what happened last week." Kalen stared at Luna, hoping she had an explanation.

He liked to check in, from time to time, on some of the subjects he'd questioned. Those who acted out in untoward manners—but hadn't quite committed crimes against the throne that warranted being thrown in the dungeon. This last visit had been to a reformed wife beater. Kalen had found the memories while questioning him for Ryndel and now dropped by on occasion to make sure the man stayed on the right side of morality. He would need to start doing the same with Marcella, or have Terrack follow up if he went off in search of the missing princess.

The only problem with this last visit had been Luna disappearing from her lookout position while Kalen dove into the man's memories. He wanted to know why.

He and Luna sat opposite each other in an opium-hazed corner of the lounge situated at the front of the brothel run by Luna's mother. It was still early enough in the evening that they had the room mostly to themselves. Kalen sipped a hot tea while Luna gulped a frothy, pale pink concoction. Her cloaked sleeve slipped down her arm as she lowered the glass.

"I wondered when you'd ask."

"I wondered when you'd offer." Kalen set his cup on a table and stared at her.

She sighed. "My sister."

"What about her?"

"I was at the lookout point, and she appeared. Mother was in trouble again, a patron that wouldn't leave at the appropriate time." She took another sip. "I figured you were okay. I *knew* you were okay. Everything was going as planned, and I honestly didn't think you'd ever find out."

She was right. They rarely reconvened immediately after a job. Except this time, he had almost gotten caught. And he'd gone to look for her.

"Why didn't you give the signal? I would have left with you."

Her skin flushed, as much as it could with its strange tones. "I handled it myself."

"Luna, I can't have that happen again. I put you on lookout for a reason. His wife got home early."

She bit her lip. "I'm sorry."

"I don't know if I can forgive you so easily if it happens again."

"But I'm forgiven now." She winked and loudly slurped the rest of the drink. "That's all that matters."

Suddenly a small ball of twisted dark hair and tiny limbs raced into the space and attacked Kalen in a hug.

"How are you?" Kalen ran a gloved hand through Amya's tangles. She had none of Luna's silvered features, which wasn't surprising, as they had different fathers, and Luna most certainly took after her dad.

"She's tryin' to make me read again." Amya hooked a thumb at her sister and stuck out her tongue. "I don't wanna. Books are for ninnies."

"Ignorance is for ninnies." Luna shook her head. "Will you talk some sense into her, please?"

"Your sister is right, Amya. How about I find you some more interesting books to read. Say, ones that have fighting and magick?"

"Yes!" Amya thrust a small fist into the air. "She be making me read poetry. It's all a bunch of gibberish."

Luna ignored her. "What's the proposition?"

Kalen glanced to the girl and then to Luna. "Are you able to leave for a bit of time if needed?"

"Depends on the *why.*"

"No, you can't go." Amya's lips trembled, and her large eyes welled with tears as she stared at her sister.

Kalen knew Luna would feel guilty about leaving Amya behind.

"Terrack will come hang out with you," Kalen said to Amya. He knew the girl had a fondness for the giant. "And I'll bring you the books I promised. Deal?"

She managed a valiant smile. "Deal."

"Shouldn't you be getting ready for bed?" Luna urged her sister away.

"Where's Baba?" Kalen asked. He had given her a stuffed sheep years ago, and she slept with it most nights.

"In bed."

"I think I hear him. He needs some company." Kalen lowered her to the ground and rose to his feet. Luna stood beside him and watched as Amya ran off down the hall, past two girls lounging in doorways who ruffled her hair.

"Why does she always listen to you?" Luna shook her head.

"Because I'm not family."

Jezebel, with her short skirt and legs that stretched for yards, walked past and kissed Kalen on the cheek. She knew he wouldn't touch her. He wouldn't touch any of the girls, and they all knew it.

"Are you kidding me?" Luna choked. "Not family?"

Madam had taken him in after his parents disappeared, when he had wanted nothing to do with the king's offer of a room at the castle. While he'd loved the attention and friendship that had surrounded him at Madam's, he hadn't gotten much sleep, what with the doors opening and shutting, and the rehearsed laughter of the girls. A year later and he had moved into the castle room where he still resided.

Luna reached out and rubbed something off his cheek, most likely a smudge of lip stain. "So you've convinced my sister that I can leave her. But you haven't convinced me. That *why* again?"

Kalen rubbed at his key. "Honestly, Luna, I don't want to tell you too much yet. I'm worried for my own safety—"

Her forehead furrowed. "That doesn't sound good, but you know I don't ever divulge secrets."

"There are ways to torture someone, you know."

"Why not go to the king with this?" she asked.

"That's the problem . . ." His voice trailed off.

Her eyes widened. "So it's finally happened, as I always said it would. He turned against you?"

"Not yet, but I do fear him discovering what I've learned."

"So where are we headed?"

"I'm not exactly sure yet." He motioned for her to walk ahead of them to the door. The air was cool and crisp, a delicious contrast against the smokiness inside. "First thing I want to do is to meet up with a certain captain I was forced to investigate yesterday."

"We're not going sailing, are we?" Her skin turned a shade of green in the cast of the flickerfly lamps as they walked down the street. Luna was not a fan of boats.

"There's a pretty good chance the answer is yes. Second thoughts?"

She shook her head. "I'll figure out something. There's always ginger root and passion flower." She patted her cloak, where Kalen knew a myriad of items sat tucked away in hidden pockets.

Kalen began a meandering path toward the docks as he filled her in on the captain and his strange chest. He wanted to further question Belrose about the chest and where he'd obtained it. The projection of emotion seemed distinctly similar to that of the princess, especially in the indigo color of the tension. He wondered if the two were related and would give them a good place to start looking.

A spray of mist dotted his cheeks, and the scent of fish and salt filled his nose and throat. The shops and bars gave way to warehouses, until finally the sea spread wide before them. Kalen immediately spotted the single black Antioegen ship, anchored well offshore. They walked farther down the dock, and Kalen stopped short, his arm thrown out in warning to Luna.

"What?" She nudged his arm away.

It was the sailor who had killed his shipmate aboard Belrose's ship. He paced back and forth, pausing every few seconds to look out toward the ship and then the city. He spotted Kalen and froze.

"Where's your captain?" Kalen called out as he slowly made his way forward. The man had appeared repentant in Belrose's memories, but one never knew.

He scowled in their direction. "Who is asking?"

"Someone who might be interested in hiring him for transport."

His voice lowered. "We aren't a ferry service."

"I think he might consider it." Kalen paused. "Now, where is Belrose?"

The sailor straightened. He eyed Kalen up and down, his eyes catching on the gloves. He stepped away. "Not here."

"Is he on the ship?"

"No, he's still in the prison."

"That's not possible—he was released this morning." Kalen's forehead furrowed.

A snort. "Released? Says who?"

"Says me." The words slipped out before Kalen could contain them.

The sailor's eyes went to his gloves again. "I've heard of you. What are you doing here? Is this a trap?"

"No." Kalen hated interactions like this, when his reputation preceded him and the immediate response was one of fear and distrust. "It's not a trap. Honestly, I only want a few minutes with the captain."

"He's not here. I told you that. Perhaps you might want to revisit your cells."

Kalen spoke through gritted teeth. "And I told you, he was released."

"No, he wasn't." The sailor looked out at the ship again with a sigh. "He was released for all of five minutes before they dragged him back behind the walls. Captain Belrose has been found guilty of privateering."

CHAPTER

6

Luna leaned over to whisper in Kalen's ear. "This doesn't seem to be going well."

"Thanks for pointing out the obvious," he muttered.

"Who's she?" the man asked. "She's not getting on our ship, not for any amount of gold."

"We'll see about that. But first I guess we need to see about the captain." Kalen sighed. "Get your crew ready. We will be sailing out tonight."

He spun on his boot and caught Luna's elbow gently in his grip to lead her away.

"What's the plan?" she asked as they walked up the street.

"Head to the brothel. Pack. Make any final arrangements for your sister. Meet me in two hours at the postern closest to the dungeon."

They worked their way through the southern border of the town, keeping to the alleyways and side streets, weaving in and around the vacant storefronts and collapsing homes of this poorest part of Mureau.

Kalen held his cloaked arm up to his nose in an attempt to keep out the stench. They turned a corner and raced down an alleyway, dodging puddles of sludge and rotting trash. Luna's boots slid, and she cursed under her breath. They turned onto a street just as a tavern door was thrown open and two men tumbled out. Kalen and Luna slipped into the shadowed doorframe of the tannery right beside it.

"You're wrong." A tall man with an even taller hat stood with clenched fists at his sides as he turned and faced his adversary.

Shorter but with massive biceps, the other man jabbed his finger in the tall man's chest. "You're naive. The king has done nothing to move us forward. We're sitting at the edge of the world, waiting for things to happen, when we could be out exploring."

Another man joined in. "We could conquer the seas!"

Suddenly all the patrons filled the street and yelled over one another.

"Our army is getting weaker!"

"They don't care about us; they only care about growing what's in their vault!"

"Isn't that the truth?" Luna mumbled. She looked ready to join them, but Kalen reached out and gripped her shoulder.

The crowd's agitation grew, even though they were all on the same side. Two of the men began to scuffle, though they'd in essence been shouting the same facts at each other. One swung at the other's jaw. He ducked and turned around, accidentally knocking into a woman. She growled deep and charged him, the top of her head connecting with his gut.

Kalen felt drawn to the melee as well. It was as if someone were pushing on his lower back, nudging him forward, and his thoughts felt clouded, in a haze of black discord. He tripped toward the action, but his attention snagged on someone at the fringes of the crowd. A figure, short with wiry hair and wearing a cloak edged in green embroidery, whispered to a man at his side. He pointed toward the opposite side of the group.

Kalen knew that stance. He knew that hair. And he certainly knew the green embroidery of the King's Law. What in the world was Ryndel doing here?

Shouts came from the opposite end of the street. A trio of guards ran toward the brawl. "Break it up!" one of them shouted as he withdrew a short sword from the scabbard at his hip.

Ryndel slipped into the shadows, his hands sliding into the pockets of his cloak, but not before Kalen spotted something in his grasp. Ice blue, it glinted in the light of the lamps lining the street.

The crowd turned on the guards, weapons pulled and shouts filling the air. Before Kalen could blink, Ryndel had disappeared. Kalen wondered what the King's Law had been up to, because he certainly hadn't been trying to talk the crowd out of their anger, and he obviously hadn't wanted to be caught.

At the thought of being caught, Kalen grabbed Luna's sleeve and tugged her around the door into the now-empty tavern. The barkeep eyed them warily from where he wiped spilled ale from the countertop.

A roar erupted from the crowd outside. "Down with the king!"

Kalen again felt drawn to join the crowd, but Luna stepped in front of him, pushing at his chest so he walked backward through the double doors leading to the kitchen. They were suddenly blanketed in the steaming heat and peppered scents of the back room. Nearly rotting vegetables and raw meat sat chopped on a counter slab, soon to be added to whatever meal sat bubbling on the hearth. Flour and dough decorated the floor in random intervals. Luna kept pushing Kalen through the narrow path between the counters and ovens toward the exit. She eased open the door and peered outside. She stepped through, and Kalen followed as Luna maneuvered along the alley and several streets.

"What was that?" she finally asked.

"I'm not sure, but Ryndel was involved."

"The King's Law definitely had something up his sleeve."

"Literally," Kalen said, thinking of the ice blue object.

They arrived at the brothel, and she stopped in front of the door. "Is the plan still the same?"

He nodded. "I'll see you shortly."

Kalen raced inside the castle walls and to his room. He grabbed a change of outfit and thrust the clothing into a travel bag. Crouching on the closet floor, he opened a chest tucked in the corner and scooped out coins. A bag of loose tea rested on his dresser, and he threw that in for good measure. A razor and comb, as he hated using other people's toiletries. He figured that was enough for the trip.

He had another hour until Luna would meet him, so he went out in search of Terrack. He found him in the nearly empty dining hall, eating a late supper. Kalen's stomach growled, and he realized he hadn't had any food since noon. He slipped onto the edge of the bench, and a kitchen boy appeared with a bowl of stew and a small loaf of bread.

"Thank you," Kalen called after the disappearing head of blond hair. He tore off a chunk of bread and drowned it in the gravy.

Terrack stabbed a piece of meat and looked out of the corner of his eyes in Kalen's direction. An invitation to speak.

"I have a favor to ask."

Terrack chewed slowly.

"Actually two. I need you to spend some time with Amya for me. Read to her. She gets bored over there. I also need you to check on Marcella and make sure her daughter appears healthy."

Terrack's eyes narrowed.

"Just a precaution."

"For how long?"

"Maybe a week? Until I get back, whenever that is." He speared a piece of softened root vegetable and jammed it in his mouth.

A nod. "Of course. I don't really need an excuse to pop in to visit Madam, but this gives me more than one reason. Where are you headed?"

"A lead on my family." Kalen knew that would shut Terrack up faster than claiming royal business and the excuse would prove more effective because the head guardsman could bring it up to the king the next time they met.

Terrack nodded again. "Best of luck to you."

"Thanks," Kalen said. "It shouldn't take too long. Hopefully, I won't come back to an overflowing dungeon." Every time he left for more than a few days, he would return to find a queue of prisoners waiting for him to unearth their secrets. Sometimes they were released to their own homes to await his arrival and assessment. Other times they were locked in cells. It made his return something to look forward to even less.

He truly didn't know how much longer he could keep this up. Kalen had a fear of dying from his gift. His curse. Whatever anyone wanted to call it. The headaches only continued to grow worse, yet the king would never allow him to slow. Another reason to leave the kingdom for a bit of time.

"And one more thing." Kalen shoved the bowl away. "Can you keep an eye on Ryndel?"

Terrack's gaze cut to him. Kalen didn't know how much to divulge, but he didn't want Ryndel running wild while they were gone. "Is there anything I should be aware of?"

"I'm just a little leery as of late." He stood and clasped Terrack on the shoulder with his gloved hand. "I'll be in touch as soon as I return."

———

THE GROUNDS WERE cast in moonlight as Kalen approached the postern at the back of the royal property where it jutted up against the tree line.

Luna waited for him, her own bag hanging from two fingers at her side.

"Let's leave them here," he said. They nudged their sacks against the base of the wall.

"What's the plan?" she asked. "You're the one that's good with locks. I don't exactly need to *steal* the prisoner away."

"I need you to distract the guards."

"Oh great." She rolled her silvered eyes. "I'm here to charm them with my feminine wiles?"

"If that's your preferred method. Or I'm sure you have a vial of night lily in one of your pockets."

Luna was a veritable apothecary. At times she'd pull out the most random of tinctures and dried powders. The night lily would be a vial of crushed pale purple flower petals.

"Is it necessary? It's my last one." Luna tucked her hand in her cloak as if to protect it.

One inhale of the poisonous flower and the guards would be out for thirty minutes each. Unfortunately, the petals were rare, and any exposure to air lessened the effectiveness of the powder. There were perhaps a dozen potent doses per vial, and then it would be rendered useless.

"I'll replenish it when we return, but for now it's necessary. I don't want anyone to suspect me, or you, until we are long gone." Kalen had debated walking in and demanding the guards release the captain, or finding Cirrus to do it for him, but then the King's Law would know exactly where they'd gone. He would certainly suspect it when he realized Belrose had escaped, but this would hopefully buy them *some* time. Time he could work with.

Luna nodded, and they snuck through the gate and inside the walls. They darted across the lawn to the dungeon tower entrance, where they crouched in the shadows and caught their breath.

"Try not to make it too obvious, or they are bound to sound the alarm." Kalen peeked around the corner to make sure they were still alone. "There should only be three guards on watch. A guard or two will be stationed just inside, along with one at each level of the keep. Incapacitate them all, and then we'll free the captain."

"What's the signal for all clear?"

"A whistle is fine."

Kalen stepped around the side of the tower and waited for Luna to open the door.

He heard a muffled "How can I help you?" and then Luna's low, smooth voice. A mere minute later and a soft whistle escaped the narrow opening left when the door hadn't quite closed behind her.

Kalen stepped through and shut the door behind him. He threw the bolt in place and stepped over the guard's prone body. The guard lay at an odd angle, one arm caught under his side as he had collapsed.

The room was edged in stone bricks, rough and cold gray in color. It was a small space, with three solid doors leading off to holding cells. The solid doors hid the worst of the prisoners. Two rooms were currently empty. The other held a well-spoken aristocrat who had murdered his entire family while they slept. Kalen still struggled with the nightmare of that memory.

Two thin windows cut down the length of the right-hand wall, letting the moonlight slice blades across the floor. A darkened set of stairs led up to the left, and Kalen stepped closer. He listened for Luna's voice.

"I only need to see him for a moment," she said.

"I recognize you from somewhere." A pause. "Wait. What's that?"

A thump.

"Hey. You. Boy." The words came from the cell closest to him. Kalen recognized the voice immediately. The aristocrat. "Exhale before you pass out. I know you're the Questioner, but you've never come with a girl before. I wonder what the two of you are up to."

Kalen heard a whistle and started toward the stairs. He took them two at a time, turned at the landing, and soon reached the second floor. The layout was much the same as the floor below, although this one only held two cells, and the doors themselves contained barred cutouts in the wood, allowing visibility into the rooms lit by dirty windows placed high on the exterior walls.

"How did you get up here?" A third guardsman spoke from the floor above, the words loud as they echoed down the staircase to Kalen.

A face popped up at the bars of one of the doors. "What's going—Oh. It's you." The prisoner glared at Kalen's gloves and started to turn away before his pale blue eyes caught on the guard lying on the floor. "Say, what do we have here?"

"You'll keep your mouth shut." Kalen pulled at the fingers of the glove. "Or you'll face the consequences."

The prisoner, a thief who had stolen from the king's treasury, threw his hands up in surrender and stepped back.

Kalen knew they didn't have much time left. He bounded

up the stairs, his elbow brushing against the rough bricks as he turned onto the upper story. The guard on this landing gripped Luna's wrist as he tried to peel open her fingers. She twisted her arm to the outside to free herself from his grasp and jammed her knee into his groin. He doubled over with a grunt. Her other hand twisted at the cap of her night lily vial. She waved it quickly in front of his nose, and the guard dropped to the floor, heavy as a stone.

Luna slipped the vial into her cloak pocket and faced Kalen.

"You're welcome." She turned to the two cells. "Now which one are you freeing?"

Against one of the barred windows, yet another face wedged itself between the metal rods. "Get me outta here!" The mercenary's stringy blond hair fell into his face, and his facial hair had grown in fuller since Kalen had seen him last . . . gone into his mind last.

"Not that one," Kalen muttered.

The prisoner's eyebrows knit together, and he spat through the bars. "You think you know everythin', but you're nothin' but a spineless little ferret. I see how much you hate it. Hidin' behind your gloves and all."

Kalen ignored him and moved closer to the opposite cell. He peered through the slits. Belrose squatted in a corner, one wrist locked onto a cuff and chain connecting to a metal ring on the wall. He lifted his head and stared at Kalen.

"Hey." The other prisoner spat again. "I'm talkin' to you."

Kalen crouched to look at the door. It was simple enough. Kalen knew his picks would open it quickly. But so would the guard's keys. Kalen stepped over to the guard and crouched at his side. He dug into his jacket pockets and finally found a key ring attached to a chain clipped to his vest.

"What, no lock picking today? I'm disappointed," Luna said.

"While I like to keep up my skills, I think the most efficient use of our time is freeing the captain."

"Suit yourself. I'll go keep an eye on our friends downstairs." Her boots whispered across the floor, and she disappeared into the stairwell.

Kalen's fingers danced through the keys. He finally gripped one and slipped it into the lock. The key turned easily, and he threw open the door.

"What are you doing here?" Belrose scowled at him and shifted upright as much as possible with his wrist caught in the cuff and holding him close to the floor. Unlike the other prisoners, he didn't seem afraid of Kalen, and his eyes didn't go straight to Kalen's hands.

"Isn't it obvious?" Kalen twirled the keys.

"No." He stared at him. "You could be here to inflict further pain. Seems to be a common theme around here."

"I recommended clemency, if you remember." He knelt at the captain's side, fighting the urge to turn away from the angry red welts on the captain's forearm. Instead he stared at the lock and felt his way through the keys again. He knew, even by touch, that none of them would work. He cursed under his breath.

"Your King's Law has it," Belrose said.

"Ryndel?" Kalen couldn't imagine why he would keep the key to the prisoner's bindings. Terrack perhaps, but not the King's Law.

Belrose nodded, and Kalen let the keys fall to the ground. He removed his lock-pick tools from his vest pocket.

"You might want to speed it up." Luna's voice drifted from below.

"I'm trying," Kalen shouted down.

The thief on the second floor began to realize this wasn't a normal interrogation. He rattled the bars and yelled, "Let me out!"

"If you're freeing people, you could let me go too," the mercenary chimed in. "I'll give you part of my treasure."

Kalen ignored them both and worked the tools into the lock, deftly twisting them until the cuff clinked open and the chain fell to the ground.

"This one's coming to." He barely heard Luna over the shout of the other prisoners.

Kalen cupped his hands and yelled, "Give him another dose." He reached out and helped Belrose to his feet. The captain rubbed at his lower back. His jacket pulled tight against his chest, and he winced.

"Can you walk?" Kalen held his hand toward the door, urging the captain in front of him.

"Yes. I can probably even run."

"Good, that may be a possibility." Kalen walked to the guard and clipped the keys to his vest. He looked at Belrose. "Let's go."

"What about me?" the mercenary called out.

"Consider yourself safe and well-fed," Kalen said as he crossed the small antechamber.

Belrose walked toward the stairs, seeming to accidentally

trip over the guard, although his steel-tipped boot caught the prone man's cheek with a sickening crunch. "Oops."

Kalen led the way to the floor below. The thief's blue eyes peered at them from between the slats of the left cell door. As soon as he saw Belrose, he began to beat against them. "Let me out!" He screamed the phrase again, over and over. Kalen worried he'd wake the guard, but Luna's second dose appeared to continue to work.

Through the prisoner's shouting he heard Luna grunt from the first floor. "Let. Me. Go."

Kalen's step quickened as he raced down. The guard had his back to him, but his burly arm wrapped around Luna's neck, and he'd lifted her high enough that her toes barely touched the floor. "Not fast enough this time, were you?"

She lifted one foot to kick out to her side but couldn't get enough leverage.

Kalen went to rush forward, but Belrose was even faster. His hand came down at an edged angle into the guard's neck. The guard's arm fell and he crumbled into a heap.

Luna barely leaped out of the way to avoid being crushed. She rubbed at her own neck as her eyes flitted from Belrose to the guard. "That move may be more effective than the night lily. You need to teach it to us."

Belrose nodded. "Sometimes your hands are the only weapon you need."

Luna unbolted the door, and the trio slipped outside, leaving the shouting prisoners behind them.

CHAPTER

7

The moon was practically overhead as they raced from the dungeon tower to the back gate. The woods had darkened to shadows, the tall trees stretching up until they blended into inky sky. Off in the distance flicker-flies darted through branches, daring one to follow their tiny paths of light.

Kalen and Luna stopped to grab their packs. Luna threw hers over her shoulder and pulled up her hood, which had fallen during their sprint. Her silver hair glowed in the dark, and she hid it all beneath the black fabric.

They readied to begin a path along the wall when Belrose grabbed Kalen by the shoulder. He slowly turned around.

"I need to know I'm not walking into a trap," the captain said.

"I just freed you. Why would I go to those lengths only to lead you into a trap?"

"One would wonder why you freed me in the first place. What do I owe you?"

"Passage to Antioege?"

"Shouldn't be too difficult as I'm headed that way anyway. But why?"

Kalen paused. "There's not enough time to explain right now, but that chest in your memory may lead us to something we're looking for. We need more information, and since you obtained it in Antioege, that seems the best place to start." He began to walk backward away from them. "Please know I speak the truth. Nobody knows of my intention to free you or to leave the country."

Belrose stayed silent for a few seconds. "It will take a while to prepare to sail."

"I already warned your crew." Kalen started forward again, traversing a completely different route than the one he'd taken earlier that day.

Silence built, heavy and humid as the air around them, until they finally neared the harbor.

Kalen turned a corner past one of the buildings and did a double take.

Cirrus lounged against the side of the building, his boot against the wall and a bag casually sprawling on the ground at his other foot. "Planning to leave without me?" he drawled.

Kalen had forgotten about his meeting with the prince. "Actually, I was hoping you'd change your mind," he said. Kalen moved to edge past. Cirrus would make the trip hell. The prince was spoiled, and the two of them in close quarters would not fare well.

Cirrus shifted his head and looked past Kalen. "You're the captain, I presume?"

Kalen frowned. "What have you heard?"

"An argument between Terrack and Ryndel. Right before the unconsciousness . . ." He rubbed the back of his head as if the memory had triggered a pain. "Terrack said you'd recommended clemency, but Ryndel refused. He wanted to know exactly where the cargo had been abandoned and told Terrack to torture the prisoner until he revealed the location of the island. Next thing I knew, a sudden rage flooded my senses and took over. I was charging Terrack, and he knocked me on my back."

The thought pricked at Kalen and he remembered feeling that same pull when he was near the crowd earlier. He'd been drawn against his will to the anger of the crowd. Kalen's mind churned these details. Ryndel had been in both locations. He was also after the chest and was willing to imprison and torture to get it. Kalen wondered if the king knew Ryndel was arresting citizens of neighboring kingdoms without his command. He glanced at Belrose. "Did they get the island's location out of you?"

Belrose glared at him as if offended that he questioned his ability to withstand torture.

Luna interrupted and pointed at Cirrus. "He is *not* coming with us."

While Cirrus had tolerated Kalen's lack of royal bloodline as a child and counted him as a friend, he tended to look down on Luna and her family. It had been years since he'd last slighted her, but Luna was known to carry a grudge.

"Au contraire. It would be *you* who is not going," Cirrus said.

"Stop it, you two." Kalen squeezed his temples. "I'll leave you both here if you don't promise to stop."

"Time is wasting." Belrose's words were clipped.

"Let's go." Kalen reached for Luna's arm and leaned in. "There's something I haven't yet told you," Kalen said.

Cirrus grabbed his bag, caught up, and loudly whispered, "And it involves me." Then he stepped away, like that would be the end of the discussion. In essence, it was. They both were along for the ride, whether anyone liked it or not.

The foursome passed boats moored along the length of the dock on either side. At the end, a lone person sat in a shallow tender. The same sailor they had spoken to before waited for them.

Kalen eyed the sailor warily. The chest was gone, and Belrose obviously trusted his crew, but Kalen only wished he hadn't seen what the man was capable of.

The captain motioned for Luna to board first. She took a deep breath, closed her eyes, and mumbled something toward the moon above. The boat rocked as she stepped in, and a light moan escaped her lips before she settled on the back bench, her pack at her side. Kalen and Cirrus followed after.

Belrose slipped the rope off the piling. "Ready to push off, Jasper?" he asked the sailor, who nodded. The captain dropped the rope and stepped into the boat just as Jasper began rowing away from the dock. They made their way quickly toward the ship, which waited in the bay beyond the other boats, black sails extended.

Luna rested with her forehead against the tender's edge. "This is going to be horrible." And with that said, she vomited over the side.

Jasper flinched and looked away. "This is just one of the reasons we don't sail with girls," he said.

———•———

IT WAS WELL after midnight when they boarded the ship. Belrose immediately began directing his skeleton crew to pull up anchor and take advantage of the outgoing tide and westerly winds. The sailors quietly focused on their work. No celebratory atmosphere accompanied their escape from Mureau with their freed prisoner of a captain.

Kalen asked the captain if he could do anything.

"Perhaps see about finding something to eat belowdecks. I don't know what provisions are left, and we obviously didn't have time to restock." He paused and rolled a shoulder. "I could also use some fresh water if you can find any. I'd like to clean up a little."

"Water." Luna collapsed at the bow of the ship, her head propped against the side and her body swaying to and fro along with the waves. "Can you bring me some?" She weakly patted at her cloak, and Kalen gathered she wanted to mix herself some tea with the herbs in her pocket. He nodded and climbed down into the ship's galley.

Once inside, Kalen made quick work setting a pot of water in the fire hearth to get it boiling. He rummaged through some of the cupboards and found salted cod, biscuits, and butter. On the counter sat a dented pail, which he used to carry the food and a jug of ale.

The water boiled and cooled and Kalen grabbed the pot in one hand, the pail in the other, and made his way above deck. The moon was near full and cast the entire ship in a pale silver sheen. For once Luna didn't look at odds with everyone.

Kalen lowered everything to the floorboards and reached around her shoulders to help her sit up. A tin cup rested on top of the food, and he filled it with the water. She took a deep breath and pulled out two packets of dried herbs. A pinch of each went into the cup, and then she raised it to her lips. A few forced swallows and she seemed a little steadier. Kalen reached into the pail and tossed her a biscuit. With deft fingers she broke a piece off and bit into it.

Kalen gathered the water and food and shuffled across the deck as the ship dipped into a swell. He moved to distribute the food and drink among the crew on deck.

"Need help?" Cirrus suddenly appeared at his side.

"Not really, I've got it—"

"Perfect." Cirrus grabbed the pail of food and followed.

They made their way to the quarterdeck, where Belrose stood talking to his first mate. The captain suggested a change in course and then motioned for the two of them to follow him to his quarters. Kalen took in the room, all the small clues to the captain's personality. Everything had its own place. Books stacked along a shelf, in order from biggest to smallest. The bed neatly made with corners tucked in. Not a speck of dust on any of the furniture or the nautical paintings framed in wood. Belrose was meticulous, detail oriented, and cautious. He had nothing to indicate a family back home.

Belrose accepted the water from Kalen and poured it into the basin.

"So we are heading to Antioege?" Belrose asked.

"Yes." Kalen knew the captain wouldn't like the next part. "But first I want to stop and see the chest."

Belrose shook his head vehemently. "Absolutely not."

"I'm paying you." He removed his pack and pulled forth coins until Belrose seemed content. "We will head to the island first. You don't even have to disembark from the ship, since I know from your memories where the chest is hidden. We will leave it there, so there's no need to worry I might bring it aboard the ship."

Belrose exhaled slowly. "Well, thank you for that, I guess."

"What chest?" Cirrus leaned against the wall, one foot propped up behind him. "Now seems as good a time as any to fill me in on exactly what's going on, considering I was left from any sort of plan making. Good thing I showed up on the docks when I did." He raised an eyebrow at Kalen.

"Good thing," he muttered.

"So, why did you free him?" Cirrus pointed at the captain, who had taken off his jacket and was now hanging it neatly on a hook on the wall. "And what are we doing here?"

As Kalen filled Cirrus in on the interrogation and what he'd seen in the captain's memory, Belrose began to unbutton his shirt. He winced as he eased it off his back. Welts lined the skin there, some raw and weeping.

Kalen flinched. They certainly had tried to torture the island's location from him. He wondered why the King's Law was so interested in the chest.

"The chest reminded me of another power we saw somewhere recently." Kalen cocked his head to the side, willing Cirrus to understand. He didn't want to reveal the knowledge of an abandoned princess to this captain from another kingdom. "I went to ask Belrose for further details, only to discover that instead of granting him clemency as I'd suggested, Ryndel had thrown him back in the cell. That's when I decided to free him myself. With Luna's help, of course."

"Thank you." Belrose cupped his hands into the basin and scooped water to splash on his face. It dripped into the bowl, and he grabbed a towel to wipe at his forehead and cheeks.

"Why did you come to Mureau?" Cirrus asked him. "You knew you'd be questioned about the chest. Why not return to Antioege as soon as you left it on the island?"

Kalen wondered the same. He didn't understand why the captain had sailed into port only to be tortured.

"It's my job to transport goods between the two cities— sometimes during the trading cycle, and sometimes just for hire. This one was given to me by a stranger right before we set sail, a personal request—and a good amount of money— instead of a merchant. I underestimated its importance upon arrival, figuring I could just land, load for my return, and return to Antioege." The captain dipped the towel into the water and reached behind himself to wipe at the wounds on his back. His breathing hitched, and he exhaled slowly as he pressed the cloth against his skin. He rinsed the towel and wrung it out. "Instead I was thrown in prison."

"There's more." Kalen started to tell Cirrus about the

skirmish outside the bar, but the prince looked even further confused.

He held up a hand. "Wait. They were complaining about the king? And our army? They have no idea what I've seen out in the countryside—"

"You don't have to convince me," Kalen said. "I'm on your side." Kalen loved his kingdom, and, as a member of the royal court, he would always defend the king. Perhaps when Cirrus eventually took his place as monarch, Kalen would have an easier time. Whatever Cirrus was, he couldn't imagine him demanding questionings with the same zeal. "And that's not even the shocking part."

Cirrus reached into the pail, grabbed a stale biscuit. He took a bite and talked around it. "What else could there be?"

"Ryndel was there."

"Perfect. So he stopped it? That's not surprising." Cirrus swallowed.

Kalen shook his head.

"That's impossible. They were talking treason. Ryndel would have had them all thrown in the dungeon before you could blink."

"And yet he didn't. He also had some sort of object in his hand. It flashed in the light."

"Was it magicked?" Cirrus asked.

"I don't know. But I can't help but wonder if this is all tied together."

Cirrus ran his hands through his hair. "The King's Law is more afraid of magick than anyone I know."

"Even yourself?" Kalen mumbled.

Cirrus rolled his eyes. "He wouldn't be a part of this.

You must be mistaken." He turned to the captain and asked if Ryndel had had any involvement with the shipment.

"Not to my knowledge. He was nowhere on the manifest."

"There you have it," Cirrus said to Kalen. "These are all just coincidences."

"I don't believe in coincidences." Belrose hung the towel on a hook and faced them. "You say he was there with an item and that the crowd seemed distorted in their emotions. Aggressive even?"

Kalen nodded. "They agreed with one another, and yet they fought all the same. I even felt this strange pull to join in, and I don't believe in what they were saying."

"What did it feel like?" Belrose asked.

"Almost like I was being pushed from behind to join. My mind sort of went into a fog."

Belrose took a drink from a cup on his desk. "That does sound similar. We never saw the contents of the chest; it may hold a similar item. Has it happened before?"

Cirrus nodded. "There has been some general unrest lately. Pockets of rallies and protests, and the council hasn't been able to pinpoint an exact source or way to address it."

"Has the King's Law been a part of those conversations?" Belrose asked.

Cirrus paused a moment to think. "He has been pushing for more patrols, more guardsmen out at night."

"And did they intervene?" Belrose asked Kalen.

"Yes. They arrived and Ryndel disappeared."

"It's possible he's intentionally creating this cycle." Belrose rested the cup on his desk. "A mob mentality and then he encourages the guardsmen to break it up. The tension will continue to escalate as both sides feel justified and fueled to continue. The subjects start to believe it's them versus the king and council."

"And then what?" Kalen asked. "What's the purpose behind it?"

"It makes no sense," Cirrus said. "What does Ryndel gain if the subjects are against the council?"

"Perhaps he wants to overthrow the king."

Cirrus crossed his arms over his chest. "He's the biggest coward I've ever met."

"I don't know," Belrose said. "He wasn't a coward when he had a whip in his hand."

"The council would never approve it. They would crown me as king."

"Perhaps he plans to dispose of the council. And you as well."

Cirrus's lips pulled into a frown. "Good luck with that."

Kalen shoved his hands through his hair. "We need to learn more about these objects, find the source, and destroy any others being sent to the kingdom."

"And return to see if Ryndel is up to anything," Cirrus added.

Kalen glanced at the captain. "I'm glad you kept at least one of these objects out of the King's Law's hands."

An eyebrow rose in their direction. "And yet I'm taking you right back to the island to place it in yours."

CHAPTER

8

A loud bang startled Kalen awake, and he jumped out of the hammock. Pale light flooded the room through the two portholes set high on the outer wall. Another knock sounded.

"Coming." He pushed his arms through the sleeves on his shirt and buttoned it up the front. His gloves were tucked in the pocket of his coat, which hung on a hook on the wall. He grabbed them but left the garment itself.

He opened the door just as the boat swayed, and he nearly fell into Cirrus. The prince looked casually effortless and well-rested, as always. His auburn hair was darkened with water and raked back from his brown eyes and freckled face. "We've anchored."

"Where did you sleep?" Kalen asked as he climbed the steps behind Cirrus.

"Up here. No way am I sleeping below."

The sky was an angry gray, and the sea frothed beneath it. The wind tugged at Kalen's hair as he made his way over to the small silver ball that was Luna. They had attempted to get her to come belowdecks to sleep, but she had refused. The tea had helped, but she needed the cool breeze above deck and the ability to see the horizon. Kalen had grabbed a couple of blankets and brought them to her. One was currently tucked beneath her head, the other wrapped around her chest and pulled to her armpits as she sat with her back to the rail and her knees to her chest. The ship rolled, and her face blanched.

The captain approached. His hand lifted to point at a visible bump of land in the distance. "The island is there. I'll give you two and a half hours, and then we are leaving. I can't risk my crew turning on one another again."

"Do you want to stay?" Kalen asked Luna.

"I'm going," she mumbled.

He bent at the waist to talk to her. "Maybe it's best to remain on the ship than spend an hour in the tender." There would be more waves and movement on the small boat, especially with what seemed like a storm brewing.

"I am going." She pushed herself up on unsteady feet. "I need land, even if it's for a brief moment."

Kalen knew better than to argue, as there was no way he would win. She'd swim to shore before she'd allow him to say no.

The prince joined them as they climbed into the tender, and Kalen began to row them in the direction the captain had pointed, directly opposite the sun. The captain refused to allow any of his crew to assist them, which meant Kalen would spend much of the allotted time getting them to and from the island.

Luna lay across the bench, her eyes closed as she took shaky breaths.

"I'm going to teach you some fundamental steps of Hakunan," Cirrus told her. "It will help with the nausea. You'll gain a better sense of balance and breathing."

One eye opened to glance at him, as if she doubted the sincerity of his words. After a few seconds, she nodded and closed her eye again. "Not yet, though."

"Obviously," the prince said. "We need much more space. When we return to the ship, we will get started."

"And you"—she didn't open her eyes, but Kalen knew she spoke to him—"seem to have forgotten to fill me in. Since we have some time to kill, why not get started? Why are we here, and where did this all start?"

"I'll tell you where it started." Cirrus surprised them both by offering. Kalen sat silent while the prince told Luna about the memory of his sister. By the time he was done, she sat upright, slack jawed, her eyes open and her nausea forgotten.

"You have got to be kidding me."

Kalen shook his head. "He's not. I saw the memory."

Luna leaned in toward Cirrus. "You must be reeling."

"You have no idea." Cirrus chewed on his lip.

Luna lay down only to bolt upright again. "I think it's better to sit." She stared at the island. A small, brown bump when they'd first viewed it from the ship, it now sported trees and a cliffside. "I'm still confused how this all ties together. Why the trip to Antioege and free the captain?"

"What I saw in Belrose's memory was similar to the princess's abilities, so it seemed the best starting point."

"And now the Law is involved." Cirrus stared at the island.

"Last night and the crowd?" Luna asked, and Kalen nodded. "Did you feel anything?"

He nodded again. "A slight tug."

It wasn't a surprise she had asked as Luna had an ability as well. She was a shield. Magick didn't work on her. Kalen couldn't enter her mind, which was probably another reason they were great friends.

Cirrus heaved a dramatic sigh. "It looks like we might have a series of problems on our hands." Leave it to him to point out the obvious.

Kalen had been keeping a lookout for the small cove the captain had used when he'd landed on the island a few days prior. He finally recognized it from Belrose's memory: the narrow strip of coastline and unexpected cluster of jicou trees signaling the trailhead beyond. He rowed them into the inlet.

Luna launched herself over the side of the boat and rushed onshore. She bent over at the waist, gulping air. Her body swayed slightly, the residual effects of the ebb and flow of the water. "I'm not getting back on that boat. You can leave me here."

"With no food or shelter? I think you'd change your mind pretty quickly." Kalen followed her overboard and pulled the bow of the boat forward. His boots dripped water to mix with the fine sand at his feet as he strained to keep the boat from being sucked out with the tide. Cirrus finally decided to help, and they wedged it farther onto the beach.

Kalen knew their time was limited and began to walk through the hardened sand toward the group of trees. The wind had picked up and continued to pull on Kalen's hair like some invisible sprite. Strands twisted free from Luna's braids to fly around her face. The terrain turned rocky beneath their feet, first loose pebbles and then hardened stone. Bits of greenery pushed through the cracks in the rock, spines and tiny unfurled leaves stretching toward the cloud-filled sky.

The path wound around the jicou trees and then sharply inclined. With the wind blowing straight down the hillside, Kalen had to bend over and strain for any forward movement.

Cirrus suddenly spoke from behind them, words hard as if spoken through gritted teeth. "What did you say?"

Kalen looked over his shoulder. "I didn't say anything."

"Really? Because I'm pretty sure I heard you say my name."

The wind howled around them, and Cirrus rubbed at his eyes.

Ignoring the prince, Kalen pressed forward, his course driven entirely by Belrose's memory. The path flattened somewhat but began winding, first left and then right.

"This is going to take too long." Kalen dragged a hand through his hair, catching it between his fingers to stop the wind from tugging it. "Why isn't the trail a bloody straight line?"

"Because the slope would be too steep," Luna said at his heels. "The switchbacks allow—"

"I know!" Kalen shouted, interrupting her. He knew the purpose of the switchbacks—they just annoyed him was all.

Silence fell as Kalen approached a fork in the path. He immediately veered off to the left, where the trail spread out onto a flat ridge that followed along a narrow canyon carved into the boulder beneath them. The clouds pressed on them like the gods wanted to bury their bodies in early graves. Kalen's entire body felt weighted with dampness, with exhaustion, and with a sudden burden of anger.

"Where is it?" he shouted again.

"You're a horrible guide." Cirrus moved to pass him. "I'll find it."

Kalen shoved at the prince's shoulders with his gloved palms. "Stay back. You have no idea where you're going."

"I'm positive I have a better idea than you." Cirrus shoved harder, and Kalen found himself precariously close to the edge of the cliff.

"Boys." Luna suddenly stood between them, her small frame preventing them from touching each other without hurting her first. "What's going on?"

"Step back, Luna," Kalen said.

"Hey." Luna grabbed the collar of his shirt and yanked it tight so the material dug into the back of his neck. She maintained her grip until he looked at her. "You're under the influence of the chest. Stop bickering and focus on finding it."

Kalen shook his head to clear the fog from his thoughts and then pulled away and looked around. Before Cirrus could start something again, Kalen walked quickly along the ledge, but now a few steps from its drop-off edge. No sense in encouraging the prince to shove him over.

Several yards away, he spotted it. A pile of rocks, each one as big as his fist, colored light gray with darker spots. He grabbed one of the stones, but it slipped from his glove. He yanked the gloves off and tucked them into his pocket. With bare hands, he moved several rocks aside. He glanced behind him at Cirrus, who stood with his arms crossed, glowering at him.

"Care to help?" Kalen asked.

Cirrus lunged forward, grabbing at a rock. He held it over his head as if to use the force of it to shatter Kalen's skull. Kalen skittered away, his palms digging into the pebbled pathway as he tried to get distance from the prince.

"Enough." Luna grabbed at Cirrus's waist from behind and yanked. She unbalanced him enough that his grip loosened and he dropped the rock.

"Luna, don't!" Kalen feared Cirrus would attack her, but he just stared at her with teeth bared.

"You're being a nuisance," she said to Cirrus. She lifted her arm and pointed back the way they'd just come. "Go wait for us at the trailhead."

Cirrus mumbled some obscenity and stormed away.

Kalen took a deep breath to settle his thoughts and turned his focus to the rocks. He continued to shove them to the side, now with Luna's help. Finally his fingers dug into the dirt. It was loose and gritty, easily moved as he scooped up handfuls and let it fall through his fingers to the side. Minutes later he had cleared away the top of the chest. He dug along the sides of the box until he could lift out the small container and place it on the ground. Swirled etchings traced their way over each side, marred only on one face, where a deep crack cut through the design, revealing some sort of metal lining severed along with the wood.

A gust of wind swirled past. His teeth ground together and his jaw clenched as he ran his hands through his hair again.

An intricate lock jutted from the side of the chest. He removed his tools and began to pick it. His lungs felt increasingly tight, and his breath grew shallowed. Lightning flashed farther north, over the sea, white against the somber clouds. Thunder erupted through the air seconds later, followed by a low rumbling sound.

The lid popped open, and inside, nestled into a pillow filling the bottom half of the chest, sat a pendant, very similar to the one Ryndel had been holding back in Mureau. A clouded blue crystal was embedded into a bronze circle strung onto a simple chain. Kalen fought the wave of anger overtaking him. He wanted to throw something, hit something, but his brain knew that these emotions didn't come from him. He closed his eyes and fought to focus on his surroundings. The feel of the damp air on his forehead, the sound of the wind howling through the canyon below.

A scream built in his throat, but suddenly Luna wrenched the chest away.

"We have to destroy it." She grabbed the amulet out of the chest and laid it on the ground. Her hands reached out for a large rock, which she raised above the gem. "Step away. We have no idea what this will do when the magick is released." Her mood had remained even, calm, unreactive to the jewel's powers. She was the voice of reason in the chaos on the cliffside.

Kalen shuffled a few steps back and wondered for a brief moment if the escaped magick could shift into something new when freed. He assumed Luna would still be immune, but perhaps the magick would absorb elsewhere. There was only one way to find out. Luna brought the rock down hard on the jewel. A large crack split open the face, and a tendril of black drifted forth. It dispersed into the clouds, pulled up and away with the next gust of wind.

The pressure lifted from Kalen's sternum. He could breathe. Anger no longer flooded his mind.

Luna lifted the cracked jewel and moved as if to put it into her pocket, but Kalen stopped her. "Belrose won't want it on the ship. It's best to bury it again." He held out his palm, faceup, and she dropped the jewel in his hand. The stone felt cool against his bare palm and fingers as he curled them around it. He paced over to the box and laid it inside before closing the small chest and returning it to the hole. His fingers scooped the damp dirt over the chest, and he moved the rocks to cover it again. He finally rose to a stand and brushed the dirt off his hands onto his pants. The wind swept over the cliff's edge, and he reached for his gloves and pulled the supple leather over his fingers.

With one last glance over his shoulder, Kalen made his way to the trail. Luna fell into step beside him. They reached the trailhead, but there was no sign of Cirrus. They proceeded down the hillside and onto the beach. Cirrus stood motionless at the bottom, his feet pointed toward the sea, his eyes bloodshot.

He glanced at Kalen. "I'm sorry."

Kalen shrugged. "It wasn't all you."

"I hate how susceptible I am to the magick." His hand rubbed at his throat, as if remembering what his infant sister had been able to do.

Luna sighed as she stared out at the frothing waves. "You teach me Hakunan, and I'll see if I can teach you how to lessen the impact of magick."

Kalen glanced at her. "You can do that?"

"I doubt it. But who knows. Nothing seems impossible anymore."

Kalen urged her toward the tender, but she didn't budge. "I don't want to go back on the water," she said.

"I know, but we have to return." He threw an arm around her shoulders and nudged her forward through the sand. They edged up to the boat, and Luna pulled a biscuit from her pocket. She picked at the stale crust as she settled on the bench, and Cirrus climbed in behind her. The tide swelled beneath the boat. Kalen propelled the tender toward the sea before lifting himself in and grabbing the oars. Cirrus reached out a hand and took one.

"Let's get away from here," he said.

Kalen's teeth started to chatter while a cold sweat erupted down his spine from the exertion of rowing. He clenched his jaw and dug into the water harder and faster. The ship was in their sights, but the sea was determined to keep them off track. Wave after wave pushed them back, and they had to shift their direction to row at an angle almost parallel to the vessel. Kalen hoped the captain was keeping an eye on them and could see they were making an effort to return. It took nearly twice the time to return to the ship as it had to row to the island. Kalen's shoulders burned, and the skin on his hands would have rubbed raw save for the gloves protecting them.

After they climbed on board and Belrose directed his crew to weigh anchor, Kalen and Cirrus collapsed against the rail and breathed heavily, while Luna turned into a puddle on the deck. Belrose looked both troubled and relieved to see them.

"Did you locate it?" He looked at their hands like he expected one of them to be clutching it.

"We destroyed the contents," Kalen said. "Actually, Luna did. We left everything there, figuring it wouldn't serve to even chance negatively impacting the crew."

His tone must have been emphatic enough, as the captain only nodded and said, "Where to next?"

"Antioege." Kalen peered off into the distance. He hoped the princess would be there, or that at the very least they would find a clue to her whereabouts.

"Antioege it is." Belrose turned to his first mate. Within minutes the sails had unfurled, and they were on the move.

Cirrus joined Kalen as they faced into the wind. Luna stood and swayed next to them.

"Do you think we'll find her?" Cirrus asked.

"I don't know."

More than that, Kalen wasn't sure exactly *what* they would find if they did.

CHAPTER

 9

Luna finally perfected a mixture of herbs that eased her nausea and returned a bit of color to her face. Once she had kept down a few stale crackers, Cirrus grabbed a mop handle and used it as a staff as he began walking her through the foundations of Hakunan: breath, balance, and focus.

She stood with both feet planted on the deck, the staff held horizontally in her hands.

"Initially we will use the staff as a way to keep your balance. Sort of like a tightrope walker." The boat swelled, and Luna hardly moved other than to angle the staff to the left. "See, you can use it as a tool instead of exhausting your body with movements. The staff doesn't always have to be a weapon."

Cirrus had her close her eyes and focus on her senses

before they moved into breath work, deep inhales to fill the stomach.

As the sun started to set, the mist turned into a drizzle, moisture working its way along Kalen's collar and down his back. He wandered into the captain's quarters under the pretense of asking how much longer the trip might take, but also in the hopes of staying dry.

The captain waved Kalen over to join him at his desk. Maps papered the surface. Belrose pointed just offshore of Mureau, which was situated on the coast of the country of Sandrasia, halfway between its northern and southern borders. The kingdom of Ehren was to the north. It was a small kingdom with only a few named cities. Antioege was the farthest south, a peninsula jutting out from the mainland.

Belrose traced a line from their current location at sea to the city of Antioege. "Two days more."

North of Antioege was another city, Leon, on the edge of the border with the kingdom of Artenglia, and to the east, deep in the mountains, sat the city of Servaille. Two other kingdoms, one to the south of Sandrasia, and a narrow one to the east that ran the entire length of the shore, made up the whole of the continent of Topia. The kingdoms shared a universal language and currency, as well as a united goal of peace. There were rare skirmishes and battles along the borders, but it had been over one hundred years since war had been declared, between or within kingdoms.

Kalen hoped it stayed that way. Imprisoning an innocent captain didn't seem to be a good way to keep the peace. He glanced at Belrose. "Thank you for all your help," Kalen said. "I appreciate you getting us to Antioege safely and quickly. Please let me know how we can help."

The captain straightened. "Perhaps you could round up supper for the crew?"

Kalen slipped out the door, his boots scuffing the deck as he walked its length. His mind lingered on all the unknowns. The crystals' exact powers. How they seemed to project magick into crowds. Where they originated. Their possible connection to the princess. Ryndel's part in all of it.

He made his way past Luna and Cirrus, who was walking her through the four directions and touch points of Hakunan. "Across your body is on an inhale." He stood behind her and gripped her wrists in his fingers, slowing the movement as she brought the staff around to her left.

Kalen searched the galley, opening barrels and cupboards and digging through boxes. He gathered salted fish and biscuits, dried apricots and plums. A cask of rum lay unopened, and he filled several bottles. When he brought the meal above deck, Jasper and the rest of the crew went straight for the alcohol, and much of the crew settled against the rails to eat.

Luna sank beside Kalen and chewed a dried apricot. She sipped at more of her homemade tea, not even turning her head as she said, "I heard that."

Across the deck, Jasper looked over from where he had been whispering to another sailor.

If there was one thing Kalen could say about Luna, it was that she had exceptional hearing. And deft fingers. And ridiculous night vision. Actually there were a lot of things Kalen could say about Luna.

Jasper's pale eyes narrowed and fixed on Luna.

"Do I bother you even more now?" she asked as she pinched another piece of the sticky fruit between her fingers.

Belrose took a sip from his mug and leaned closer to Luna. "Women are unlucky on ships. You set them on edge."

"As does my silver hair and pale skin." Luna gave a slight shrug. She was used to the ogling and comments.

"Where are you from?" the sailor to the right of Jasper called across the deck.

Luna let the cloak fall from her head, and her hair settled in a heavy sheet around her shoulders. She looked up at the stars dotting the sky and then over to the sailors. "Where is anyone from?" She swept a hand up and over, from the heavens to the horizon. "I don't know who my father is. But my mother used to tell me a story when I was young."

Jasper rolled his eyes, but the others leaned in as Luna opened her mouth to speak again. Sailors loved stories, and Luna loved to distract people. Usually while she pocketed their trinkets and coins, but in this case she could perhaps gain their trust.

"There once was a girl who was afraid of the dark. Every night her mother would light twelve candles and place them around her bedroom so that the girl could fall asleep. She would watch the flickering lights from each candle until her eyelids felt heavy enough and she would sink onto her pillow. The girl grew into a teenager, and her fear of the dark grew right along with her. She couldn't stand the pure blackness of it all, the seamlessness of the sky above and the ground below. The day held the sun and an array of colors, but the night . . . the night held nothing—"

"What about the moon and stars?" Jasper interrupted. Another sailor shushed him.

"One day the girl's mother left to visit an ailing relative. The girl stayed home to take care of her younger siblings and the farm. Her brothers and sisters took forever to fall asleep, and night arrived swiftly, so fast that the girl didn't have a chance to light any candles. She sat in the dark, paralyzed. She couldn't even see her hand in front of her face.

"Terror was a living thing inside of her, itching, crawling its way up her arms and legs, across her torso, inching up her throat until she thought it would strangle her.

"And then suddenly the darkness lifted. Black turned to a dark gray, and she could faintly see the shape of the table across the room. The change came from outside her window, a pale light that poured indoors. A small glint moved slowly, drifting in and out of the trees in the forest beyond the house. The girl stayed rooted to her spot in the middle of the room. Her eyes followed every movement, her fear dissolving slowly as the light grew closer and larger. A part of her mind told her to be afraid of the unknown, to question the source of the light. She chose to focus elsewhere.

"A soft knock on the door broke her reverie, and she tiptoed across the room. Outside stood a boy, about her age. His entire being glowed a strange white light that emanated from within. He was beautiful. Stunning in the way a living statue might be, porcelain come to life. She wanted to touch him.

"So she did.

"She reached out and brushed her palm against his forearm. His skin was soft, smooth, and, most curious of all, warm. Her fingers trailed down to thread through the boy's fingers, and he pulled her gently from the doorway into the yard.

"His light filled the space around them, illuminating the path that cut through the wildflowers and grass. They walked a few more steps, and he spun her, his arms wrapping around her lower back. She stared at his face, trying to memorize the sharp lines of his cheekbones, the slight arch of his lips, the long eyelashes framing his dark eyes. Her hands reached to clasp behind his neck, and suddenly the solidness of the ground beneath her feet disappeared. They spun slowly into the air, weightless. A breathless laugh escaped her lips; her only fear at this point was that he would leave.

"They spun higher, until the ground below was no longer visible and it seemed they were the only two beings in the universe. They hung for what felt like forever, speaking with their eyes and minds and hearts. He tipped his head, and his lips brushed hers. Light and love burst forth, tiny pricks of light that spread and settled across the expanse of sky. Their hearts swelled, and an orb burst forth, lifting higher until it hung bright above them.

"The girl knew their time together had ended and he had to go. He returned her to her home, and, after one last kiss, she went inside. The door shut slowly between them, but the light outside remained. She leaned with her back against the door, heart pounding with fear as she waited for the darkness to close in again. It didn't. Every night the glowing ball hung in the sky, and the pricks of light stayed, spread all around it. She never saw the boy again, but she was also never again afraid of the dark."

The sailors all glanced at the sky above, at the moon cresting the apex of the heavens. The sea reflected its bright white light. For a moment they might have believed that they sailed through pure starlight instead of dark waters.

The men appeared mesmerized by Luna's story. Everyone but Jasper. His head tilted to the side, and he stared right through her. "That didn't tell us anything."

"Sure it did." His mate jostled him with an elbow. "She's born from the girl who was afraid of the dark and the boy who loved her. Just like the moon and stars."

Jasper shook his head as if the idea were ridiculous. "It's a metaphor."

"Back to work, boys." Belrose commanded them to their stations. He turned to Kalen. "You might want to get her belowdecks for the rest of the night."

Kalen glanced at Luna, and she raised an eyebrow. Together they gathered the empty pails and remaining bits of food to take down to the galley. Cirrus followed close behind, tossing the staff from hand to hand as he went.

"Where did you guys sleep?" Luna asked when they were done putting everything away.

"I'll be sleeping above deck." Cirrus pointed at the ceiling with the staff.

"There's a room over here with hammocks." Kalen nodded at the cabin two doors away.

"Mind if I join you?" Luna looked at Kalen. "If you can keep your hands to yourself, that is."

Cirrus snorted. "Kalen doesn't like girls."

"He does. Just not me," Luna said, her hand over her chest like the thought wounded her. Kalen knew she was joking, though. They'd always had platonic feelings for one another. Sure, Luna was stunning and certainly unique, but they were more like siblings than anything else. He opened the door to the room and allowed her to enter first.

Within minutes they'd kicked off their boots and fallen asleep to the rocking of the ship.

———•·•———

THE SAILOR WALKED into the captain's room and said, "They are gaining on us."

"I'm not surprised." Belrose bent over to rest both hands on his desk. He stared at the sailor standing in the doorway to his room.

"Wait. I'm confused." Cirrus lounged against the wall, his arms crossed in front of him. They had stopped in for an update and to get out of the crew's way.

"Did they stop at the island?" Belrose asked.

Kalen watched for the sailor's response. A shake of his head.

"Can we back up a minute? I'd like a proper introduction." Cirrus waited as the sailor introduced himself as Milo.

Belrose waved for Milo to join him at his table, where maps still covered the surface. "Where are they now?"

Milo tapped the map with his index finger. "There. It's not a significant gain. They won't reach us before we make landfall if we keep up this pace." He glanced out the porthole at the darkening sky. "Unless the weather hits us first."

Cirrus opened his mouth as if to speak, but Belrose held up his hand. "And their course?" he asked. "I'm not sure how they've closed any gap whatsoever since yesterday."

"They are hugging the coast," Milo said.

Belrose nodded. "A treacherous route with the outcroppings and sandbars, but better winds." He eased into his chair, wincing at the movement. He glanced from Kalen to Cirrus and back again. "Milo is a tracker."

"I track objects," Milo clarified. "It's a type of magick. Not one easily determined, but I realized when I was young I could sense lost objects. It took a while to hone in to the skill set I have today."

"How does it work?" Kalen rubbed at the key around his neck.

"I have to identify the object ahead of time, see it in person, and touch it. Then I can sense its location."

"How many things can you track?" Cirrus asked.

"At this distance, only one at a time." Milo scratched at the scruff growing on his chin. "It's all I can focus on. I've lost the location of all other objects until I release this mark."

Kalen released his key. "And what exactly are you tracking?"

Milo looked to Belrose, who nodded his approval.

"I figured when the captain was arrested that we might be having trouble later, so I just happened to 'lose' something on the ship most likely to follow us. I've been following the *Impérial* since it left port yesterday morning."

Cirrus and Kalen glanced at each other. The *Impérial* was a ship in the Mureaun navy.

"Can you tell who is on board?" Kalen asked.

Milo shook his head. "I can only track the object, not anything else about it."

Kalen's mind spun. He glanced at Cirrus. "Do you think Ryndel would have sent someone after us this fast?"

"I think you know him better than I do at this point. I'm questioning all I knew. Father made it a habit of sending me away to the further villages to provide a royal presence, but it seems the real action was in Mureau."

That must have been the reason Kalen had seen so little of him lately. He'd selfishly thought Cirrus was either avoiding him or off playing. He felt a twinge of guilt that they had become so distant over the years. Then his heart hardened at the thought. It wasn't his fault. The prince was the one who had shut him out all those years ago. He was the adoration of the subjects of Mureau, while Kalen was ostracized for his abilities.

"How do people view magick in Antioege?" The question was out of Kalen's mouth before he realized he had spoken the words.

"It's tolerated well for the most part, although I think people are still nervous about those with abilities, because they are rare and inconsistent." He paused. "And in Mureau?"

"The same," Kalen said with a sigh. "I think people's reactions depend mostly on the ability in question and who wields it." He wiggled his fingers. "Suffice it to say nearly everyone seems opposed to the idea of a *sorcier* entering their mind and discovering their secrets."

Cirrus pushed away from the wall. "I should work with Luna on the next lesson of Hakunan. Care to join me?"

The pair found Luna at the bow, talking to Jasper of all people. As soon as he saw the boys approaching, he ducked away.

"What was that about?" Kalen asked.

"He decided to show me some self-defense moves." She shrugged. "Apparently I'm a weak girl in need of saving."

Kalen held back a snort as Luna leaned against the rail, closed her eyes, and took a deep breath.

"How close are we to land?" she asked.

"Still another day, if we aren't attacked first." Kalen filled her in on the tracker and what he'd seen.

"So Ryndel knows we fled?" She opened one eye to look at them.

"There's no way to know what exactly he knows," Kalen said. "But it's best that we assume a low profile in Antioege. The prince should stay out of sight as much as possible, and we need to seek out information about the princess immediately."

"Don't worry about me," Cirrus said, stretching his arms overhead. "It's not like my orders don't outrank Ryndel's."

Kalen glanced at the horizon. "I fear we are all wanted criminals at this point."

"True. You did liberate an incarcerated captain," Cirrus said with a half smile.

"I don't know that you're free of suspect. Again, I think we all need to keep a low profile."

"Easy enough for me. I can stay hidden." Luna sipped from a mug of tea.

"I still don't understand how. You stick out like a scylee bird whenever you're actually spotted." Cirrus shook his head at her. "Ready for your next lesson?" He didn't wait for a response before leaving to fetch the mop handle again.

"How are you holding up?" Luna asked.

Kalen stared off at the horizon. "Honestly?"

"Have I ever asked you to speak untruths?"

Kalen rolled his eyes.

"Honestly, I feel a lot of things," he said. "My headaches have eased now that I'm not having to use my ability. It's a relief, but leaves me feeling bitter toward the king." He paused. "And bitter toward this quest as well. I know I'll have to use it again."

Luna stood at his side. "Maybe you won't. Maybe we can get answers through regular means of questioning."

Kalen steadied himself as a swell rocked the boat. "Here's hoping that's the case." But he knew better. He knew the quickest way to obtain answers would be to scour the minds of Antioegens as soon as they landed.

And Luna knew it, too.

CHAPTER

10

A day later and they stood at the helm of the ship, Luna's mouth gaping.

Kalen didn't blame her. Antioege held no resemblance to their home. It was glasswork and color where Mureau was dour and imposing.

Much of the city was built over the sea. Across the entire bay, posts extended into the water to support massive buildings topped with spindles reaching high into the heavens. The setting sun reflected off the metal and glass that made up most of the buildings, blinding Kalen and Luna with brightness. Farther up the shore, the city extended into the foothills. Homes dotted the landscape, their windows also reflecting the light.

Milo informed them that the *Impérial* was half a day behind, so they needed to find a place to stay, off the beaten path, by nightfall. Before they exited, Belrose commanded

Jasper to go onshore quickly and purchase clothing for the trio to change into.

"When the *Impérial* arrives, they will question who exited the ship. If you leave in those outfits, you will definitely be flagged as foreigners."

"He's right," Cirrus said with a frown. "But I really would rather not wear Antioegen fashion."

"Is it that bad?" Luna asked.

It was that bad.

As they prepared to disembark, Luna gripped the skirt of her too-short dress, all thin and lacy and covered with poppies. It was long-sleeved so as to cover her tattoos, and her hair was tied back and covered in a scarf.

Kalen felt equally ridiculous in royal blue silk trousers, a buttoned white shirt, and a vest. He felt exposed, like the bright colors would call attention to them, even though it was the normal attire for this city. Meanwhile, Cirrus strutted around like a peacock in his turquoise attire.

"It's not as bad as I remember," he said. "Or perhaps my tastes have changed."

"I had hoped this was just a prank on Jasper's part," Luna muttered.

They all thanked the captain for his service and boarded the tender. Jasper rowed them toward the shoreline, pulling against the solid quay, where he threw his rope around a post.

Luna again leaped out of the boat first. Even though the Hakunan and tea had kept the sickness at bay all day, she seemed thrilled to be on land, even if land was actually a dock shifting with each swell of the waves.

Kalen led Luna and Cirrus toward the first intersecting piers. A light breeze swept in from the sea, ruffling the colored silks and scarves worn by the townspeople. The citizens walked light on their feet down the piers as they greeted one another and stopped to browse the stalls filled with shell wind chimes, woven hammocks, and the spicy aroma of baked sweets. A graceful and pale nationality, they looked delicate, even though they thrived on the sun and the sea.

"I know a place we can stay," Cirrus said. "We boarded there the last time I was here."

"On an ambassadorial mission?" Kalen asked. "We both know we shouldn't stay anywhere you boarded with your guardsmen. You can't be recognized . . . Your Highness. Let's head through town, see if we can learn anything, and then find a place on the outskirts."

Kalen inhaled the salty air and removed one of his gloves. He hated this more than anything, but he needed to get a pulse on the city and hunt for news from Mureau.

Luna leaned in. "You don't have to do that."

"We need answers sooner rather than later." Especially with the *Impérial* right on their tail.

He slowed his steps as they approached the crowded city center in the middle of the bay. He pretended to be interested in the wares and let his fingers brush against the residents' bare skin. A hand here, a forearm there.

Bits of recent memories spilled into his mind.

A girl trying on gowns in a shop, exclaiming she'd found the perfect red dress for the festival.

A man getting more and more angry as he attempted to negotiate a sales contract with a supplier.

A mother staring at her son as he left home that morning, fearing he was up to no good and would end up a criminal or a lockpick.

Hey, it's not so bad, Kalen thought.

His forehead began to sting with pinpricks of pain, and Kalen shoved his hand into his pocket. There wasn't anything newsworthy in their thoughts.

The trio moved further into the city center, where pathways widened and stalls lined either edge. Keepers shouted the worth of their wares. Bands for seasickness, silk pillows, and flickerfly jewelry and lamps. Cirrus seemed especially interested in that stall. Kalen sidled up next to a shop owner selling throwing stars and asked the proprietor about the metalworking of the weapons.

"These are forged in high-temperature ovens in the mountain of Ornatio." He held out a small set of gilded stars. Kalen feigned interest, leaned closer, and brushed his hand against the owner's palm as he cupped the stars. He figured a weapons dealer would be on the lookout for any fugitives if word had been sent ahead. Instead Kalen saw that he had been lying to the local ironsmith about costs.

Kalen thanked him for his time and walked toward Luna and Cirrus.

Luna tugged on her skirt. "Well I didn't learn much except that this city is full of pretentious idiots. You?" Luna asked.

"Nothing of note." Kalen pulled on his glove, and they made their way through the piers leading toward shore. Here the colors muted, as if the artist had run out of paint on the edges of Antioegen's canvas. Even the citizens dressed in more subtle clothing. At the base of the foothills they found an inn that looked promising, in that it was set back and run-down and looked like a place where nobody would ask questions.

"You two stay outside. I'll see if there's availability," Kalen said.

He walked into a large dining hall and an array of smells. The spicy scent of roasting meats and potatoes enticed him after the repetitive meals on the ship—but first, lodging.

A woman behind the bar waved him over. Her low-cut blouse and apron failed to support her ample bosom.

"Good evenin'." She flashed a bright smile. "What can I be doin' for ya?"

"I'd like to rent a room."

"For how long?"

"A week. At minimum." He hoped they'd be long gone, either returned to Mureau or searching elsewhere, but wanted to appear reliable. It wouldn't hurt to keep the room for longer than they needed.

"I have only one left."

It would have to do.

He handed her the coins, and she led him up a wide stairwell sitting at the far left of the entranceway. The wooden steps squeaked as they climbed. At the landing they stepped onto a dark red carpet, probably hiding several stains. A hallway extended in front of them with doors on either side. She opened the third door on the left and ushered him in. The room was small but comfortable enough. Two narrow beds jutted out from the wall, a low table wedged between them. A stack of blankets and pillows was nestled into an armchair near the door.

She handed him a key and told him the dining hall would be open late.

With a nod of thanks, Kalen dropped his bag on the floor as she ambled down the stairs. He took a moment to pause and look out the window and get the lay of the land from this angle. Their view was of the sprawling city beyond. Rays of pink and orange light filtered through the glass structures and reflected off the metal-and-wood fixtures.

He took a deep breath. They'd escaped. They were here, in a foreign city, in search of a banished princess.

For the first time he allowed himself to dwell on the futility of this quest.

A veritable needle in a haystack.

———•———

"WHAT'S THE PLAN?" Cirrus sprawled on one of the beds, his ankles neatly crossed and his hands behind his head.

"We need information," Kalen said. "And I think the best way to do that is to split up." He glanced at Cirrus. "You've been here before. Do you have any sources?"

"Of course I do. Girls tend to run their mouths." He glanced at Luna. "No offense."

"Hmph," Luna said. "I'm assuming you mean you're going to head to the nearest brothel?" She sighed and continued pulling clothing out of her bag. She clutched her cloak in her arms like it was a security blanket.

Kalen turned to her. "Any chance you can return to the docks and keep an eye out for the *Impérial*? We need to find out if they're here asking about us, and if so, what they discover."

She nodded. "Glad to put my skills to use. What are you going to do?"

"I'm going to start off downstairs and see what I can gather from the patrons. Bawdry tales usually are based in truth. Perhaps some of them will involve magicked items or projected emotions."

Cirrus launched out of the bed. "Sounds horribly boring. I think I definitely got the better end of the stick here." He tossed them a rakish grin.

"Please be inconspicuous," Kalen said. "It wouldn't serve to have anyone talking about us."

"The girls know how to keep secrets, and any royals who would recognize me wouldn't be caught anywhere near where I'm headed." He opened the door. "Don't wait up for me."

The door shut, and Luna shook her head. "Doesn't he need sleep?" Luna herself looked like she was fighting a yawn. Kalen imagined that the nausea had kept her awake most of the previous night.

"Cirrus doesn't sleep." He glanced at his bag and debated changing. As much as he preferred his conservative attire, he figured his gloves were enough to set him apart and he should remain in the Antioegen clothing.

"What do you mean he doesn't sleep?"

Kalen played with the key around his neck. Unsure how

many secrets to divulge, he modified his statement. "He doesn't sleep at night. He'll catch a nap at some point during the day."

The truth was Cirrus was terrified of the dark, especially of being in the dark in an enclosed space. He'd been known to sleep in the forest clearing where he could see the moon and stars, but if the prince slept indoors, it was with a vast amount of candles or flickerfly bulbs to keep the shadows at bay.

"Weird."

Kalen's stomach rumbled. "I'm going to head down."

Luna glanced at the basin on the table between the beds. "I'm going to rinse off some of this dirt and change. I'll see you later."

"Stay hidden."

"As if you need to tell me that."

"I know. Still, it makes me feel better to say it."

He stepped into the hall and walked downstairs.

The hall was almost filled to capacity when Kalen entered. The innkeeper was behind the bar, filling cups of ale and keeping up a steady stream of conversation with two men seated in front of her. A serving girl slipped through the crowd, mopping up spilled drinks on tabletops and taking orders from anyone who needed a refill.

Kalen claimed the only remaining chair at the bar and waited for the innkeeper to come over.

"Anythin' to eat or drink?" she asked.

"Whatever your special is tonight. And a hot tea please."

She turned and yelled into the kitchen for a bowl of cassoulet.

"Name's Adelaide," she said as she placed a steaming mug in front of him. He thanked her and took the cup. Her eyes cut to his gloves.

"Frostbite when I was younger," he said.

A softness appeared in her eyes, and she asked after his childhood. Kalen felt strangely at odds, guilt over the lie but also a sense of freedom that she wasn't afraid of him and his abilities. Naturally, he couldn't talk to her of his youth, so he steered the conversation to another topic of more use.

"Are there any upcoming festivals or events that my friends and I should know about?"

"Jus' the tournament tomorrow evening."

"What kind of tournament?" Kalen imagined jousting or some other nonsense sport.

"Cards, of course."

Kalen's eyes widened. A card tournament, now that sounded more his cup of tea. It would allow them to gather information—Luna and Cirrus from the crowd and Kalen from the players.

"How does one enter?"

"You don't enter," the gentleman to his right said with a sneer of his thin lips. "You earn it. That's why we're here tonight. Adelaide is hosting a game, and the winner gets entry."

Kalen looked him up and down, taking in his false-jeweled rings and the fraying hemline of his shirtsleeves. He was someone desperate for a win.

"And how do you join the game on this fair evening?" Kalen asked.

"You jus' tell me," Adelaide said as she took a bowl

from the serving girl and arranged it in front of him on the counter. "Entry's open to anyone."

"Except young boys," the patron said, his sneer growing as he stared at Kalen.

"He's not a boy." Adelaide swatted at him with a damp towel. "Leave 'im alone, Reiland. Anyone with the entry fee can play—you know the rules."

"When does it start?" Kalen dug his spoon into the thick casserole in front of him. Beans and mutton, mixed with onion and a simple broth.

"As soon as I set up," Adelaide said. "If you'd like to join, best eat quickly."

Kalen needed no further encouragement, finishing the bowl and a crusty piece of bread in a few short minutes.

Reiland shook his head. "Starved, are ya?"

Kalen ignored him and slid off his seat to allow the serving girl to clean and rearrange the tables and chairs for the tournament. Kalen sat as far from Reiland as possible. A dealer approached, and Kalen reached into his pocket to dig out the requisite entry fee. He handed over the coins and took inventory of the room. Two tables with nine players each. The dealer explained the rules of the game, nearly identical to the one he played in Mureau. Once each table was down to three players, they would gather at a single table, and play would reset. "And no cheating. That means no magick, either." The dealer looked at the only two women who had joined in, identical twins with thin faces, long noses, sharp slashes of lips, and straight dark hair.

Play began in earnest, and Kalen relaxed into his chair. He quickly guessed the players who would be out of the running first: a sloppy bettor on his left and a nervous player across the table from him. Kalen purposely lost a round, giving the table a false confidence that the kid wouldn't be winning anything that evening.

He folded the next two hands, watching as Sloppy and Nerves went all in and lost to a quiet player sitting to the right of the dealer. He wore dark glasses, and his muted green shirt was buttoned to his neck. Kalen had yet to pick up on his tells but watched him closely as the dealer passed cards around the table. The player lifted each card individually, looked at it, and placed it on the table instead of keeping the cards in his hand. His pinky finger curled inward on the fourth and fifth cards, and Kalen watched to see if he would keep or discard them.

Those were the two he kept.

Kalen had been dealt two pairs. He raised the bet and asked for one more card. He didn't look at it until Pinky Finger looked at his individual three cards. His pinky only curled once, so Kalen figured at best the player was dealing with three of a kind.

With a glance down, Kalen saw that his new card was a three of moons. It didn't help his hand, but the pairs were royal cards and would beat a three of a kind. With a heavy sigh he pushed more coins into the pot. Two other plays matched the bet, and, with nonchalance, Pinky Finger added his coins as well. The dealer had them turn up their cards, and Kalen won.

"Beginner's luck," Kalen said as he clumsily swept the coins to his side of the table.

Less than a dozen hands later and their table had been

whittled to three. Kalen, Pinky Finger, and a large-bellied man with luck on his side. They left their chairs to join the other table, where Reiland and the twins waited.

Some of the patrons had left as the night wore down and the losers nursed wounded egos. Kalen fought a yawn and asked for another cup of tea. Reiland sneered at him again from across the table.

The twins sat stoically upright, their opposite hands resting lightly on the table in front of them. Each had auburn hair pulled into a single braid trailing over their mirrored shoulders. Their heads tilted slightly in toward each another, and they sat in complete silence.

Kalen sipped the tea as the cards were dealt. Reiland was a noisy player, sighing and drumming his fingers, but nothing read as consistent enough to be a tell. He was effective at masking them. The twins were impossible to read. They picked up their cards at the same time, discarded at the same time, and even blinked at the same time.

If magick wasn't at play, Kalen would have licked the bottom of his boot.

Still, he could win.

He had to win.

CHAPTER

11

Within three hands the portly player had lost everything. Pinky Finger was quick to follow, but Kalen couldn't seem to get ahead. Every time he nudged the bet higher, the twins would either fold or bet so high he knew his hand wasn't a winner. There had to be something going on. He felt movement at his back.

"They have a mind link." Luna's words were a mere whisper. "I can hear them speaking. Between their two hands, they can figure out much of the table."

He contemplated Luna's words, wondering if he should bring it up to the dealer or use it to his advantage. The dealer had to figure the twins were in communication.

Kalen only needed to get one of them out. Without the knowledge of a second hand, the other twin would be playing on an even field. Twenty minutes later he had his chance.

He had been dealt four royal clovers and a sword. He bet before the discard, one twin folded, and the other twin stayed in but only discarded one card. He figured she didn't have a great hand or she would have raised the bet, and he would beat her if he got another clover.

The single card was dealt to him, but Kalen didn't even bother to glance at it. He needed to win this hand. He cast his glance toward Reiland, all while counting the amount of coins in the twin's pile. When his time came, he bet just enough coins that she would have to go all in. It left him with little remaining, but not so little as to be put out of the game. Reiland had folded at the first increased bet, leaving Kalen and the twin. She glanced at his card, paused as if in communication with her sister, and gently nudged her stack of coins forward.

He exhaled hard and flipped over the card. Another clover.

The twin expressed no emotion as she turned over her hand. A five-card run.

He had beat her, but the game wasn't over yet.

"Good game," Kalen said in her direction as she stood.

She tipped her head to him and drifted away. Without an advantage, the second twin was easily knocked out. Reiland had a slightly larger stack of chips, but Kalen wasn't concerned. He'd finally worked out the man's tell. It was in the space in his movements. The length of time it took him to discard and pick up his new cards directly correlated to the strength of his hand. Within four more deals, Kalen had won.

Reiland rose from the table and walked out of the inn without a word. Kalen was used to all types of losers. This was honestly the best kind as it didn't result in a physical altercation.

Adelaide appeared and thrust a large coin into his hand. "This is for entry t'morrow. Congrat'lations on your win." Kalen thanked her and nodded his acknowledgment to the remaining patrons.

A shadow slipped out of the room, and Kalen knew it was time to follow. The hour was well after midnight, and his eyelids kept closing of their own volition.

When he reached their room, he noticed Luna was checking for exits, an obsession of hers. She pulled her head out from underneath the bed and sat on the thin mattress. She yanked off her boots and dumped them on the floor.

"Good job."

"Thanks. And thanks for tipping me off," he said. Luna's ability had many uses, like uncovering the deceptions of eerie card-playing twins.

"I figured you all couldn't hear their chatter, especially since it was so blatantly about the game." She rubbed at her tattoos. "They were odd."

Kalen removed his gloves and splashed cold water from the basin on his face. He took off his too-bright shirt and his boots, tucked his gloves beneath the pillow, and then collapsed onto the vacant bed. He rolled onto his side to face Luna. "So what did you learn?"

She settled with her back against the wall.

"I headed to the opposite end of the harbor. There's a lighthouse and lookout post there, and I eavesdropped to see if there was any word about us having landed or news of the *Impérial*."

"Any word of foreigners disembarking?"

She shook her head. "Nothing of the sort."

"And the *Impérial?*"

"It arrived just as Milo predicted. The Antioegens obviously weren't expecting the ship, as they used some sort of light system to send word down to the wharf. I made my way to the harbor, even passed Belrose's office tucked to the side. He and Jasper were settling in."

"Did they see you?"

"No, I stuck to the rooftops." She lifted her hand to cover a yawn.

"You can skip to the good part. We can talk logistics in the morning."

"Only two people came onshore."

"Admiral Richard?"

She shook her head.

He paused. "Anyone you recognized?"

She shook her head again. "They weren't dressed in royal colors. One of them was tall and thin. Huge black pupils. I couldn't see any white in his eyes."

Ryndel's henchmen most likely. Kalen gripped the key around his neck. The question was were they after Belrose, or had Ryndel sent them after Kalen and the prince, too? "What happened when they disembarked?"

"A group of Antioegens met them as soon as they stepped on the pier, and asked them to state their business. I couldn't hear what they said, as they spoke into the wind. They produced a sealed scroll, which the patrol quickly glanced at and returned, and then wished them a pleasant stay."

"Did they come into town?"

"No, they rowed to the *Impérial*, but it's still anchored offshore. I'm sure they've slipped back onto land by now. We need to be extra careful."

Kalen sighed. "Yes. But first sleep." He threw a couple of blankets on the floor near the door in case Cirrus wandered in at some point, but for now he suffered no guilt in taking the bed.

The moonlight still lit the room after Luna turned down the oil lantern sitting on the night table next to her head. She tugged the blanket to her neck. "Good night, Kalen."

"Good night."

————

THE INNKEEPER WAS still in the dining hall when Kalen snuck downstairs early the next morning. Cirrus had tripped in as the sun rose and fallen asleep among the blankets. After an hour of listening to his snoring, Kalen knew he wouldn't fall asleep again and decided to venture to the main floor.

A broom grasped in both hands, Adelaide swept the crumbs and bits of trash dotting the distressed wooden flooring.

She glanced up. "Good morning. What can I get ya?"

"Tea and pastries to take upstairs?"

She bustled off to the kitchen, returning a few moments later carrying a tray laden with ceramic dishes of all sizes—a steaming pitcher, cups and saucers, a container for cream and one for sugar—and several pastries filled with almond paste.

"You did well last evenin'," she said as he traded her with coins from his pocket.

"Tell me more about the tournament," he asked.

"Starts seven o'clock sharp at the royal amphitheater. You'll give 'em your coin, and they will tell you which table. There's fifty of ya playin'."

"And the entire town attends?"

"Most folks who isn't workin'."

Kalen thanked her and maneuvered his way up the stairs. He shoved open the door with his boot to find Luna braiding her hair into an intricate plait. Her cheeks were red from the icy water she must have used to wash her face.

"That one won't wake up." In the time Kalen had been gone, Cirrus had climbed into the bed closest the window and lain on his side, trying to curl into what little sunlight made its way through the dirty glass.

"Rise and shine." Kalen's voice boomed purposefully in the small space.

Cirrus groaned and yanked the quilt over his head. "What time is it?" he mumbled.

"Time for your nap to be over. We have a task to accomplish. Seriously, is this what you do at the castle every day?"

Cirrus lowered the quilt and squinted at him. "You haven't earned the right to question what I do or don't do with my time."

"Enjoy your nap then. I plan on finding your sister."

Cirrus sat up and reached to pull on his boots, only to find them still on his feet. He frowned and then shrugged. Kalen handed him a pastry, and he nodded in thanks. He took a huge bite, and crumbs drifted to the floor.

"Chew with your mouth closed." Luna looked nauseous. "Didn't anyone teach you manners?"

"I thought we were going incognito here?"

"Speaking of going . . ." Kalen leaned against the door. "I'm curious about your ventures last night. But first . . ." He shared the information he'd obtained about the tournament and how he'd won an entry. Luna revealed everything she'd learned about the *Impérial*.

"And you?" Luna asked Cirrus. "What do you have to contribute to this journey?"

The prince took another bite, making sure to chew and talk at the same time. "The girls really didn't have much to say."

"Oh, were their mouths too busy?" Luna sprang to her feet. "Let's get out of here."

"No, their mouths weren't too busy." Cirrus held up his hand. "They told me that the fortune-teller at the edge of the marketplace could fill us in on all kinds of information. She's a token reader."

"Lead the way."

THEY STEPPED OUTSIDE into an overcast morning. The city looked duller as it reflected the gray of the sea and clouded sky.

They reached the shoreline and made their way through the stalls. Luna drew a good amount of attention, even with her hair wrapped in the Antioegen scarf again. Kalen kept watch for the black-eyed man from the *Impérial* but instead locked eyes with one of the eerie twins from the card game. She was purchasing herbs from a merchant, but her gaze followed them as Kalen urged the trio quickly past.

Farther down the lane, a merchant crooned to Luna. "Polished stones for the silvered jewel?" Kalen paused to glance at the rocks, wondering if anything would have been used for magick or a pendant, but they were mostly opaque, tumbled stones. The merchant followed him for several yards, trying to convince him to buy some for the lady.

A cluster of silk-clad women swept down the aisle, taking up nearly the entire width of the street. Their array of patterns and colors could have been the jewels on a crown, a bit ostentatious for daylight hours. One woman knocked into Luna as she brushed past.

Luna blinked twice and watched as the girls continued along the walkway to stop in front of a booth selling perfumed oils and cosmetics.

Kalen asked if she was okay, but Luna's attention had already moved to a miniature yellow rabbit hopping around on a table just ahead. The lifelike animal was no bigger than a coin. Kalen suspected magick, until the merchant flipped it over and showed them a windup device located beneath its tail. From under the table, he lifted a basket with a variety of animals. Luna picked out a small songbird and gave the merchant some coins.

"I'm surprised you didn't just steal one," Kalen muttered. "You don't have a lot of coin to waste."

"It's a gift for Amya. And don't worry. It wasn't my coin." Luna raised an eyebrow and turned to look in the direction of the woman who had jostled her. A glimpse of fabric appeared at the bottom of Luna's sleeve and then snaked back up her arm. She'd relieved one of the peacock women of her purse.

Cirrus urged them onward. "This way." He wound through the crowd, growing in numbers as the morning began edging toward noonday. At the main walkway he turned right and then made another right down the next path. They finally stopped a few stalls away, and Kalen stared at the woman out front. She was dressed in fluttering silks, her hair braided with colorful ribbons. She called to the crowd, "Embrace your future. Renounce the past. Uncover the answers to even the smallest of questions."

Cirrus waved them toward the token reader's tent. He ducked inside, and Kalen followed through the slitted fabric.

Luna stood inside the curtain, her eyes flitting around the room from one odd object to the next. Finally, she plopped down on a brightly embroidered silk pillow resting near the exit.

"My name is Genevieve." The woman looked at each of them in turn. "Do you have an object you'd like me to examine, or would you rather I read your cards?"

"Actually, we had a couple of questions to ask you," Kalen started. "About magicked items."

"First, I read cards." She handed a deck to Cirrus, asking him to make several cuts before nudging them together in a single pile. Genevieve spread the cards on the low table sitting between her and Cirrus. She reached out her hand and seemed to debate between two cards lying side by side. Finally, she chose one and turned it faceup. She selected another two and turned them up as well. After a moment of brief evaluation, she gathered the remaining cards and piled them at her side.

"The queen of suns." She pointed to the first card, which

showed a queen resting on a chaise longue, her hand lifted high as her palm cupped a sun. "In this first position, this card speaks to your history. The queen is offering you clarity in the form of energy and heat. You have recently discovered something new, but, like the sunrise each day, it's always been there, hovering off the horizon."

That certainly sounded familiar. Kalen wondered what exactly the *sorcier* could see.

"The three of daggers." Genevieve pointed at the second card. It showed three men in a circle, with daggers thrust upward to meet in the middle. "In this second position, the card speaks to where you are today, at this moment. The daggers are a volatile suit, but the three is one that speaks to harmony and a unity of opposites. A compromise of sorts."

That was vague enough. Kalen tuned her out and turned his attention to the objects in the room. A painting sat propped against the tent wall, its gilded-frame corners causing dents in the fabric. A lidded vase rested on a small shelf stretching across the back wall. And next to it was a small chest.

An ornate chest.

A small, ornate chest that looked distinctly like the one they'd seen on the island.

CHAPTER

 12

"The last card is your path forward. The eight of roses," Genevieve continued.

"Thank y—" Cirrus started to say, but Kalen was done with the cards.

"Excuse me. Where did you get that?" Kalen pointed to the chest.

"It was given in payment for a favor," Genevieve said as she lifted the three cards and placed them on top of the deck. She separated the deck into two piles and then shuffled the cards together.

"Can you tell us more about it?" Kalen asked. "Where did it come from?"

"I'm afraid that will require additional coin."

Cirrus handed over several more.

"Let me see where it has been." She held the chest in her open palms and appeared lost in thought. "I'm seeing a mountain range and a cliff-top city. Servaille, I believe. Hot springs. A monastery. A vast library and catacombs. A crystal held in a monk's hands. Sadness. Fear. Loss of control. Travel. Given away quickly."

"To whom?" Kalen asked.

"That I can't tell you."

"Do you know when the crystal was removed?" Kalen asked.

She shook her head. "I've told you the story the chest has to tell."

"Have you heard of any magicked items in Antioege?"

"There have been stories of objects, but I have yet to see any in action or in person."

Luna leaned in. "What about the monk? Where did he disappear to?"

Genevieve's shoulders lifted in a nonresponse.

"She's not as helpful as was promised," Luna muttered to Cirrus and stood. "I'll figure it out another way then."

Cirrus joined her. "Thank you for your time and the reading." He nudged the other two toward the exit. They stepped out of the tent into the glaring noon of the city as light reflected off all the glass buildings. The prince and Luna joined Kalen on either side, and they walked away from the tent toward the city center.

"Servaille, huh?" Luna said. "Is that our next stop?"

"I have the tournament tonight. Let's see what we can figure out before then, or while we're there. I'd like more information before trekking into the mountains." Kalen didn't mind the cold, but the route would take days, even on horseback.

"I'll see if I can get more information on the monk. I'm sure he's the one who gave Genevieve the chest. Perhaps he's still in the city." Luna raised her hood against the sunlight. "I'll meet you back at the inn shortly."

Kalen knew when he saw her again she'd have answers.

Back at the inn, Cirrus was hungry yet again, so they stopped in the mostly empty dining hall. Cirrus ordered the fish of the day, and Kalen asked for tea. Kalen leaned back in his chair to get a better line of sight to the door, in case the black-eyed man appeared.

"Been having nightmares?" Kalen cracked his knuckles through his gloves.

"What? No. Do you mean why I stayed out last night? I just didn't feel like encroaching on you two and your alone time."

Kalen snorted. "You know there's nothing between Luna and me."

Cirrus smirked over the rim of his cup as he took a sip. "You want me to believe you were never interested?"

"Believe me, we make a much better team when we're not distracted by any romantic misgivings." They had kissed only once. Kalen still remembered how awkward it had been. Luna had pushed him up against the outer wall of the Milked Goat and grabbed his shoulders. On tiptoe, she smashed her mouth into his. It was a chaotic meeting of teeth and tongue and frantic hands that resulted in . . . well, nothing. They'd both agreed to forget it had ever happened.

"So, she's free then?"

Kalen almost fell out of his chair. "Free? Yes. Good luck with that, though!"

Cirrus's food arrived, and he speared a bite of the flaky fish. He exaggerated his ability to keep his mouth closed as he chewed. "You don't think I could win her over?"

"She hates you."

"No, she hates the *idea* of me. I'm royalty, but I'll get her to like me—just you watch."

Kalen shook his head.

"I'll even make a wager." Cirrus leaned over.

"For what?"

Cirrus held out a hand. "Your flickerfly ring."

Now *that* was a dagger to the throat. One of his most valuable possessions, even though he never wore it. The ring was a constant source of light in the darkness. He could see why Cirrus would want it.

"Your jeweled short sword." Kalen didn't want it, but he knew Cirrus would have difficulty parting with the ostentatious piece.

"Deal."

Before Kalen returned to the topic of Cirrus's sleep habits, a voice spoke behind him.

"What are you two betting on?" Out of seemingly nowhere, Luna appeared, this time with a boy at her side. He looked about ten years old with black hair cut close to his scalp. Dark brown eyes contrasted with his pale skin. He appeared to be a stranger to the sunlight.

"He's a little young to be a monk," Cirrus was quick to point out.

"This is Robert." Luna put a hand on the boy's shoulder.

Kalen wasn't sure if it was meant to reassure the kid or to keep him from bolting. "He's a ward of the local clergy."

Kalen took in his plain brown clothes and gaunt frame and guessed him to be an orphan. The boy scooted into the chair next to Cirrus and waved his hand for Luna and Robert to take the open seats. "Sit and eat." He called Adelaide over and asked for bread and fruit.

As soon as the tray appeared, Robert dunked a chunk of bread in oil and herbs and stuck it in his mouth. He didn't even swallow before grabbing another piece.

"He had some interesting things to say about one of the monks who came down from Servaille," Luna said. "Robert, why don't you tell my friends what happened?"

Robert's wide eyes flitted from one of them to the next. "It was maybe six months ago. He came into town seeking refuge. The clerics allowed him in, but soon regretted it."

"Why?" Cirrus asked.

"He acted crazy. Hair half-yanked out of his head on one side, like he'd been grabbing fistfuls on his entire journey. Said he heard a girl singing in the catacombs, and she made him fall in love with her."

Kalen and Cirrus glanced at one another. Cirrus took a last bite of vegetables and pushed his plate to the side. The boy eyed the remaining fish, and Cirrus nodded for him to eat it.

"Thank you," Robert said over a mouthful as he took a massive bite.

"You look like you need it." Cirrus leaned back and crossed his arms. "About the girl . . ."

"He called her an angel or a devil, depending on his mood

as he described her. This went on for weeks. The clerics tried to give him herbs to calm him, but he wouldn't take them. They finally requested that he leave—he was too disruptive."

"What is his name?" Kalen asked.

"Brother Gabriel." Robert paused and swallowed. "Now just Gabriel."

"Is he still in town?"

Robert nodded. "He barricades himself in his house. Boards up all the windows. Deliveries are given through a series of doors so nobody can get near him. He only comes out to play cards as a way to pay his bills. Once every three weeks, except he's making an exception to play in the tournament tonight."

"Tournament?" Kalen lifted his eyebrows at Luna. "What does this monk look like?"

"Patchy blond hair. Not very tall. Still dresses in his robes."

"Perfect. Thank you for all your help." It was nice for once to have a responsive subject to interrogate. He tossed Robert several coins and stood. "If you're ever in trouble, find Captain Belrose and tell him it's a favor for the Questioner."

Robert stared at them wide-eyed.

"And feel free to finish the food."

The boy gripped his fork tight and shoveled several bites in his mouth, as if expecting Kalen to rescind his offer.

THE WATER GLINTED gold in the late afternoon sun, and the air felt heavy on the back of Kalen's neck. They stood on a walkway across from town hall, staring at the royal amphitheater. Massive and made entirely of glass, but for the occasional support beam keeping it upright. Even the floor was glass. The tiles were inlaid with flickerflies, so the large room was lit from below. The frantic movement of the insects kept the pale blue glow steady.

They assessed the building from afar, looking for exits and trying to determine how the seating would be arranged. Kalen laid out the plan. "Cirrus, I need you to get in there and find a way to get ex-brother Gabriel and me at the same table. I will try to keep him in the game until we move to the head table, but if he is losing, I'll make sure to lose, too, so we can exit at the same time. Luna, you need to scope out the building. Find any possible exits. Also, keep an eye on the stands. Be on the lookout for any other magicked items and notice any agitation or changes in mood in the crowd." He paused and brushed the key at his neck. "We need answers tonight."

The duo made their way to the center pier, jostled their way through the ever-growing crowd, and split apart. Kalen approached the front door, strolled to the main table, and tossed them his coin. There were forty players spread over five tables, and once each table was down to two play-ers, those would advance to a final table to determine the champion.

The woman directed Kalen to the last table where it sat on the far edge of the main floor. He walked past the tables, eyeing the other players. There he was. Patchy blond hair tied at the nape of his neck. He wore a drab gray robe and pants, loose fitting, as if he couldn't quite give up his role at the monastery.

And he sat right across the table from Kalen, watery eyes staring at the hands he twisted. Cirrus had done his part—whether it had cost him coins or a few minutes of flirting, Kalen didn't know.

The best player at the table was no doubt the troll-like male sitting directly opposite him. He had an expressionless face that would offer no tells. The player at Kalen's right would be out first but most likely would stick around to watch the play, especially since he reveled in talking. Gabriel kept twisting his hands and continually looked around the room, seemingly in a heightened state of anxiety.

The dealer passed out the first hand, and the table quieted. Kalen watched the other players examine their cards, noting any facial movements, tics, and gestures. Play passed to Kalen, and he barely deigned to glance at his cards before tossing four onto the table. Without anyone increasing the bet, it didn't much matter if he won or lost, just as long as he kept close to Gabriel's stack. He needed to lose at the same time so they could leave together or stay winning with him to the end.

Play continued over several hands. Two of the players dropped out, and Kalen held back from attempting to win further hands as Gabriel came precariously close to losing the last of his chips. Sweat beaded on the man's forehead, and his pale cheeks turned red as he contemplated his latest hand. He laid his cards down and cracked each finger on his right hand and then his left.

"It's your turn, sir," the dealer said.

"Fine." He piled his remaining coins in the middle of the

table and nearly collapsed onto it. His elbows caught the edge, and his hands supported his chin.

Kalen readied himself to leave the table if Gabriel lost. He waited with bated breath for the cards to turn over.

Suddenly a voice carried through the crowd.

"Grab that man!"

CHAPTER

13

Shouts echoed off the glass walls.

"He's a wanted criminal!"

Bounty hunters.

Kalen was up and around the table before Gabriel even attempted to stand. He grabbed Gabriel's wrists and pulled him backward. Gabriel kicked out at him, but Kalen side-stepped and remained upright.

Cirrus was at his side within seconds to help him restrain the ex-monk.

"Over here."

Kalen heard Luna's voice from his right, and he and Cirrus dragged Gabriel in that direction. Gabriel managed to hook his foot behind a chair and swung it so it caught Kalen in the side. He grunted but didn't let go.

The crowd surged around them. Cirrus led the way, pushing through while Kalen shoved Gabriel ahead, sandwiching the man between them.

Luna led them toward the glass wall, which overlooked an expanse of water beyond. Kalen's jaw tightened. What was her plan?

They reached the wall, and Luna motioned for them to stay behind her. "There's a lock there, at the bottom. It's a hatch that drops to the water."

Kalen bent over to examine the lock while Cirrus held on to Gabriel. The man continued to thrash around and kicked out, his foot connecting with Luna's shin. She growled deep in her throat and lunged at him. Her hands were on his neck, and suddenly his eyes rolled back and he dropped to the floor.

"Night lily?" Kalen asked as he dug out the lockpicks.

"No, a move Jasper taught me."

Kalen spun the circular bronze cover to the side to expose the lock. He slipped in the pick rakes and twisted.

Shouts continued to echo around them.

"There he is!"

"Grab him!"

"There's a reward!"

The crowd surged forward. Cirrus began to shove at those who got close, yelling at them to stay away.

Kalen finally heard the lock release and grasped the hook to lift the cover open on its hinges. He dared a glance over his shoulder, and what he saw made the key around his neck turn to ice. A figure stood off to the side of the room, tall and thin, his eyes black as midnight. The man from the

Impérial, just as Luna had described him. Even more startling, the eerie silent twins stood on either side of him, their heads tilted toward his, their eyes now equally as black. His mouth moved as if he were directing the other two. Suddenly people close to them began to panic.

"I can't see!"

Within seconds Kalen's vision faded to black. He rubbed at his eyes, frantically trying to see again, but it was like he'd gone completely blind.

Beside him Cirrus spoke in a frantic voice. "What happened? Did someone turn out the lights?"

Sounds of panic and chaos resounded as people fell and elbowed one another in their hurry to get out. Something drove into Kalen's shoulder, and he braced himself with his hands.

A low, soothing voice swept over the crowd. "Please remain quiet and still. I will move around you. If you do as I ask, you will not be harmed."

Silence fell.

Luna spoke quietly. "They're headed this way."

"We need to go. Now," Kalen muttered. "Luna, help Cirrus through the hole."

"Do not move." The voice again. Kalen heard more in the tone now. It was as if the lack of sight had enhanced his hearing. The words echoed inside his mind.

"Get me out of here." Cirrus crashed past Kalen, his elbow digging into Kalen's side. A gust of air and a splash seconds later.

"I said don't move." The voice was closer.

"Hurry," Kalen said.

Luna gripped his arm and whispered in his ear. "Scoot forward. Your feet are right there."

His hands groped around him as he reached to pull his picks out of the lock. He dropped them into his vest pocket, gripped the edge of the hole, and plummeted into the water below.

Kalen spit water out of his mouth as he sputtered to the surface. His eyes peeled open, and he heaved a sigh of relief that he could see again. His cloak billowed around him, keeping him buoyed. He swam out of the way and waited for Luna to push Gabriel through the hatch. Moments later the body splashed, and Kalen swam over. Gabriel floated facedown on the surface, and Kalen wrestled with his gray tunic to flip him onto his back. He tugged him away, and moments later Luna herself plunged into the water.

Lightning fish darted around them as Kalen tried to keep Gabriel from sinking. He worked his arms underneath the man's armpits, leaned back, and kicked himself backward in the water. He tilted his head to motion the other two past him.

"Find us an empty dock," Kalen told Luna. "I need to access his memories before he awakes, and I don't want to do it while treading water."

Luna swam around the massive supports in search of somewhere they could climb out. Cirrus seemed paralyzed by the inky water. His eyes darted from their surroundings to the water's surface as soon as a lightning fish came within view, and his breaths came short and fast.

"Cirrus." Kalen waited until the prince made eye contact. "You're fine. Be glad you can see again. Let's swim slowly toward the shore." They needed to get away from there quickly, before someone followed them into the depths of the water.

They had only swum a dozen yards before Luna reappeared and led them to the right. They swam under one pier, and Cirrus's breath became shallow again. As soon as the sky appeared above, he relaxed, but only slightly. A lightning fish was intent to be their friend, swimming off to Kalen's side.

They reached a dock that sloped into the water. It was small, meant for only one boat. Kalen dug his back against the wood and pushed Gabriel onto the surface before climbing up after him.

"I'm not sure how long he'll be out," Luna said. "But I'll be here and ready if he starts to awaken."

Kalen stripped off his gloves. "Cirrus, you go ahead and find horses. You'll be better at finding ones capable of our journey." They had no choice but to leave now that the bounty hunter had set the entire city against them. "We will meet you at the inn."

Cirrus nodded and walked up to the pier above before turning the corner and disappearing from sight.

Kalen laid his palm flat on Gabriel's bare forearm. He closed his eyes and entered the mind of the ex-monk. A wave slapped the dock, and he registered the disorientation of his body as it swayed, but his mind was locked elsewhere.

He found himself in a library. Each book resting on the shelf held a different memory, but only a few were locked within chains and padlocks. Either Gabriel hadn't done much in his life that warranted secrets, or he didn't care to lock them away.

The shelves were labeled in looping script. Kalen found

one categorized as *The Catacombs* and selected a book. He opened the cover, and the pages fanned to envelop him in memories, pulling him into a dark hall that ended in an open doorway. The utter darkness of the room pulsed, and shadows slipped down the wall and into the hallway to pool at his feet. They writhed up the other side and filled the length of the space. Gabriel stood, frozen. Listening. A song poured through the open doorway, wrapped in colors Kalen had never seen. Yellows with hints of purple and gray. Green with a touch of red and orange. Melancholy laced with poison. A child's lullaby sung by an ageless, soft soprano. The voice was off-key, but the words were clear, the melody discernible.

> *Darling girl, I love you still.*
> *Rain will fall and Reign you will.*
> *Darling girl, don't be afraid.*
> *Reign you will and rain will fade.*

She was sadness, this angel of the catacombs.

Kalen closed that book and opened another. The same room, only this time Gabriel had stepped farther into its depths. In the center of the cavern, light streamed in from above, a narrow, dust-swirled beam of sun. It seemed to come from miles away, its heat long since having dissipated by the time it reached the cold damp of the catacombs.

The singing began again, the colors the same, only darker, more tangible, and more sinister. The tune haunted Gabriel as the words echoed loosely off columns and coffins and the ridges in the dark outskirts of the room.

Ribbons of emotion wrapped around Gabriel, winding up his arms and legs to bind his chest. He wanted to run away and flee this insanity, but his curiosity dragged him forward. His toe caught an uneven lip in the floor, and he stumbled. He caught himself against the wall, wincing in pain.

The singing stopped.

Whisper-soft movements. Gabriel stayed perfectly still. A swirl of dust off to his left. The faint outline of a person, draped in pale panels of fabric. Even paler skin, a face dotted with freckles. Light eyes, blue gray in color, framed by long lashes. Auburn hair, some of it knotted and much of it tangled, fell to her waist. She gripped a desiccated flower in the hand hanging loose at her side. The dried petals dusted a trail of pale pink to line the floor, a narrow path that traced her route through the room.

She almost walked right past Gabriel but then stopped, her bare feet close enough to touch his boots. She turned toward him, and her eyes scanned his face. Her free hand reached up slowly as if lifted by a delicate string, and her index finger traced the skin from his temple down past his cheekbone to his chin.

"Hello." Her speaking voice was liquid over sand, gravelly yet feminine, and lower than when she'd been singing. Her hand fell to her side and was quickly lost in the fabrics draping over her waist and legs. "My name is Reign. Can you please help me?"

Gabriel swallowed. He wanted to help her, but the binds tightened. His lungs felt ready to collapse, and each breath was a struggle. Even as she reached out for him, her expression full of longing and despair, he pushed against the bindings, turned, and ran.

"No . . ." The wail chased him through the darkened tunnels.

Kalen readied himself to leave Gabriel's mind when the memory shifted, the scene brightening as the monk raced out an opening into the dim light of dusk. A man stood there, absurdly thin and tall, with light hair and eyes. He looked like he'd been expecting Gabriel.

"I have to get out of here!" Gabriel practically shouted the words. "I can't stay any longer." He grasped at the man's hands, but the man pulled away. "Can you help? I have no money to travel."

The man tipped his head forward and withdrew a small chest from beneath the folds of his cloak. The chest looked identical to the one Kalen had seen in Genevieve's tent earlier that day.

"Take this to Antioege. You will be met there by someone who will retrieve the amulet. Do what you want with the chest."

The monk began to shake. "I can't be around the amulet's powers, though."

The man shrugged in nonchalance. "The chest will give you some respite; however, if it's too much, I can find someone else to make the journey. You asked for assistance in leaving. I will provide coin and a horse, so the travel will be easier. Be glad it's not winter."

Gabriel twisted his hands together. "Fine. I'll do it."

Shadows curled in at the edges of Kalen's vision, and the memory ended.

So that was how the crystal had been brought to Antioege, and ultimately Mureau.

And the girl. *Reign*. She had to be the princess.

Kalen closed the book and replaced it on the shelf. Then he took a deep breath, knowing there would be pain on the other side, and yanked himself from Gabriel's mind.

His hand slipped off the monk's arm, and he tried to stand, but the needles in his head doubled him over.

"We need to go," Luna said softly. She helped him shakily rise to his feet, and he pushed his hands into his gloves. Luna nudged Gabriel closer to the wall so he wouldn't flail upon awaking and roll into the water.

With tentative steps, Kalen followed Luna up the incline to the pier, where they found themselves in a narrow alley between two buildings. Kalen's arms brushed the exterior walls as he made his way through and then onto the open extension of walkway beyond. They took a moment to get their bearings before heading toward the series of pier and bridge crossings that would lead them to the outer reaches of the shore.

A wind whipped up from the sea, and Kalen began to shiver. The Antioegen clothing was thin and silky and stuck to him, chafing and frigid. His gloved fingers were the only things that remained warm.

It took them a while to make their way across the piers, but they finally reached the shore and slipped off the paved walkway onto the cobblestone streets leading farther into the hills.

In the alley behind the inn, Cirrus waited with three horses.

"Were they difficult to procure?" Kalen asked.

"You'd be surprised at how easy it was."

Kalen looked at him quizzically.

"We had a little bit of a follower. Robert met me as soon as I made it to the upper piers and asked if he could help. I'm not surprised. My charisma is known to bring all types of unsolicited assistance."

"I'm sure the food helped," Luna muttered.

"Anyway, I told him we needed horses, and he said there were several at the monastery."

"Did you pay him?" Kalen asked.

"Of course I did." Cirrus looked pained. "However, I'm not sure if the boy will actually hand off the money. He doesn't seem too thrilled with his current custodians." He reached over to a grab a low-hanging small red fruit from a tree. Before Kalen could stop him, he'd taken a huge bite. His mouth puckered, and he spit it out. He tossed the rest of the fruit down the street. "I wouldn't even give that to the horse."

"Plaeria," Kalen told him in way of explanation. "They use them in some of the sour breads."

Cirrus swallowed and wiped at his mouth. Then he glanced toward the inn. "I was going to suggest we stay the night and leave at sunrise . . ."

Kalen stared at him.

"Teasing. I know we need to get on the road, but I do want to grab our bags."

Luna held up a hand. "We might want to try a different route. I can hear the twins inside the front door."

They stared at her slack-jawed.

"Were you going to tell us?" Kalen asked.

"Once you stopped discussing the local fruit offerings, I was going to tell you."

"What are they talking about? Is the bounty hunter with them?"

"No mention of him, but they don't seem very happy with how the tournament ended." She tightened her hood around her face. "They are pretty chatty for not actually speaking aloud."

Kalen rubbed at his key. They needed their clothing and coins for travel.

"Is there an issue here?" Cirrus asked. "I can take on two girls."

Luna smirked. "I'm sure you could bore them to death with your tales of travel, but it's probably better that we get away without them knowing. I can get to the second story from outside the building."

"Be careful. The other one might be in wait upstairs." One of the horses sidestepped, and Kalen stroked its forehead to keep it calm. "Leave some coins on the nightstand for the innkeeper's trouble. And hurry."

Luna snuck off into the shadows.

Kalen stripped out of his wet outer jacket and draped it over the horse. He looked forward to dry clothes. His own clothes.

"Were you able to get anything from the monk's mind?"

"There was someone in the catacombs. A young woman."

A young woman who had nearly identical features to Cirrus and was named Reign. But Kalen didn't want to get the prince's hopes up. He leaned in and bumped shoulders with Cirrus. "We'll find out soon enough."

The seconds inched by as Kalen paced back and forth beneath the flickerfly lamp. Cirrus dragged his hand through his hair, and they kept glancing up at every little sound, expecting Luna to appear.

They were both ready to charge into the inn when she appeared, a flash of silver with bags in hand. She had already donned her hood and threw them both their cloaks and travel sacks.

"Easy as pie," she said. "Which I actually got!"

CHAPTER

 14

They traveled on horseback through the night and next morning. As they rode, they shared the pie, eating it fingerful by delicious fingerful.

As soon as it was gone, Kalen dug into the extra bag Luna had packed. She'd thrown in food, a pot, a spoon, and some spices. He removed two pieces of fruit and a chunk of dried meat. He unsheathed his dagger and used it to hack off a slice of the fruit, which he handed to Cirrus. The prince eyed it warily. "That's not another sour surprise, is it?"

Kalen shook his head. "Crisp and crunchy. Nothing alike. I would have thought your palate would be much more refined, what with all the royal dinners."

They stopped around noon to rest the horses, and Luna slept for an hour, and then they were on their way again. They reached the foothills and climbed until sunset, when they decided to stop for the night under an overhang of trees.

Luna dismounted, unsteadily rubbed down her horse, and walked a few feet away to a patch of grass beneath the trees. She sprawled on the ground and covered her head with her hood. "I. Hate. Those. Animals."

While she rested, Kalen built a fire and put a pot of water on to boil. He added dry grains and folded in a little spice and roasted nuts Luna had snagged. Nearby, Cirrus brushed the horses, whistling as he worked. He appeared unaffected by the journey, but then he'd spent significantly more time than them on horseback.

Prince training and all that.

"What's for supper?" Cirrus asked as he approached Kalen and dragged his fingers through his hair, which looked like it could use a washing, quite honestly.

They ate, staring at the flames, each lost in their own thoughts. The fire did little to keep them warm, and Kalen sat with his shoulders hunched over his knees. Luna scooted up next to him, her teeth chattering. "The ground is freezing."

Cirrus glanced at them both and shook his head. Kalen figured it was frustration that Luna wasn't seeking heat from him, but then the prince paced behind them and began to gather pine boughs and branches. He spread them out near Luna and then gathered another bundle. After a couple more loads, he layered them and motioned her over. "Nature's mattress. Not the most comfortable, but it should be warmer than sleeping on the ground."

Luna's eyes opened in surprise. She sprawled on the

branches and covered her face with her cloak. "Thank you," she said, the sound muffled.

Kalen glared at Cirrus silently, and the prince shrugged his shoulders. "Want me to help you make one, too?" Together they made quick work of another mattress, and Cirrus said he would swap out when they each took watch.

The pine boughs were on their way to brittle, and Kalen shifted his weight repeatedly to find a spot where he was no longer jabbed in the back. He lay on his side, his chest toward the fire, but even with the discomfort, exhaustion quickly overtook him.

It was short-lived, though, as Cirrus woke him after what felt like mere minutes for his watch. He paced around for a bit and then sprawled on a nearby boulder, staring up at the constellations, naming each one to keep awake.

Suddenly Cirrus jumped up with a scream. Kalen startled, his side scraping along the rock, and pushed himself into a stand. Cirrus danced around, smacking at the back of his neck. A log had popped, and the ember seared his skin.

"What's going on?" Luna rubbed at her eyes.

Cirrus glared at Kalen. "Too bad you can't do something useful with your magick . . . like control fire." He rubbed at his neck and winced before lying down again.

"What did I do?" Kalen threw up his hands "It's not my fault you slept so close to the flames."

Cirrus had been nearly on top of the fire, as if it could burn daylight into his eyelids.

By morning the prince had scooted so his body was away from the heat, but the top of his head almost touched the flames. "He's going to burn his hair again," Luna said as she woke Kalen, having taken the third and final watch.

"Perhaps he wants it to turn a brighter shade of red," Kalen said with a yawn. He stood to pace around their small circle. He stretched his neck side to side and cracked his gloved fingers.

"Shall we wake him?" Luna asked.

"I'm going to go look for water first," Kalen said.

"I'll come with." Luna attempted to run her fingers through her hair, and they quickly snagged. Kalen lifted the canteens and led the way farther into the tree line. Within minutes he heard the babble of a running stream. He removed his gloves, cloak, and undershirt and splashed frigid water up over his head, face, and chest. After scrubbing at his hair and skin as quickly as he could, he shook off the water droplets and filled the canteens. Luna squatted near the edge of the water, her head tipped upside down as she scrubbed at her scalp.

"I was thinking about the tournament," Kalen said as she wrung out her hair.

"What about it?" She untangled the knots as best as she could and began to plait it over her shoulder.

"The *sorciers*. They were obviously working together, but I don't understand how. Could you gather anything from listening to the twins?"

"We were all in a hurry to escape, so I didn't pay much attention, but I don't recall hearing anything in particular." She went silent for a moment. "Actually, I don't think they spoke aloud at all."

It was bizarre. Kalen had yet to hear of a *sorcier* who could project their power so far and wide.

They returned to the campsite to find a lightly snoring Cirrus. His mouth had fallen open, and he looked helpless as a babe.

Luna squatted and lightly flicked the prince on the nose. His hand reached up to scratch at the spot. She repeated the action, and he flailed his arm. She jumped out of the way as his eyes opened.

"Are you messing with me?" He sat up.

"Who, me? I was just brushing the insect from your face is all." Luna reached into the bag and removed a piece of fruit. She took a huge bite and swiped at the juice that dripped down her chin.

"Oh." A wide smile stretched his lips. "How very sweet of you."

Luna's nose wrinkled as if she'd realized the plan had backfired.

"Bloody crow, it's cold out." Cirrus rubbed at his arms and hunched his shoulders within his overcoat. Eyes flitting back and forth, he grabbed at two sticks and tossed one to Luna. "Let's do a round of Hakunan to warm up."

Kalen packed up their mostly dwindled supplies and loaded the horses while Cirrus and Luna moved through the exercises, and then they started for the mountains. The wind whipped through the trees to chill every bit of exposed skin, and by midmorning it began to snow. They'd seen patches of ice and still-frozen snow along the journey, but this was the first time the clouds had decided to grace them with precipitation. They were less than thrilled.

Kalen tightened his cloak around his head and shivered as an errant flake whipped right down the front of his shirt.

The horses made their way methodically forward, even as the snow built into an inch thick. They turned a corner, and the view beyond took Kalen's breath away. He could see all the way to the sea, the world stretching in miniature scale like a game board he could manipulate or knock to pieces with the sweep of an arm.

The road switched back to the interior of the mountain, and they spent much of the afternoon under tree cover. It protected them from some of the snowfall, but the sun failed to warm them through the tangled branches above.

By the time the sun started to set on the other side of the peaks, they were ready to stop for the night and build a fire to combat the chill embedded in their skin. "We should reach Servaille before noon tomorrow," Kalen said as they found an area mostly sheltered by the trees above and clear of snow on the ground below.

Cirrus made quick work of building a fire, and Luna emptied the remaining food. "Looks like this will be the last meal."

They dined on a hodgepodge selection of dried meats, stale bread, and a jar of pickled vegetables that nobody wanted to eat before but now seemed attractive.

Luna took the first watch, followed by Cirrus, who woke Kalen far too quickly for the Questioner's liking. He silently groaned as he sat up. Muscles and tendons, even his breath, were frozen with the cold. Kalen stood and paced, trying to warm up his body. Cracks echoed as he stretched his neck side to side.

The night sky was heavy, dark black between the tree branches. The occasional prick of starlight could be seen, but the moon had already set beyond the mountain peak. He counted what stars he could see, trying to keep his eyes from closing and succumbing to the heat of the fire on his face.

Eventually the stars faded out as the eastern sky turned pale on the fringes. He hoped with sunrise would come warmth.

His mind drifted, visions of catacombs and an ethereal beauty singing as she meandered around tombs. He had thought about Reign often in the silence of this mountain climb, wondering how distorted Gabriel's visions were, and if she had changed since.

Suddenly one of the horses' heads whipped up, followed by the other two. Ears pricked back, and they began to snort and rear from where they were each tethered to the tree.

Kalen looked beyond the horses into the darkness but couldn't see anything in the forest. The snap of a branch cut through the air, and his attention was now needle focused. Glowing eyes appeared, low to the ground.

"Cirrus. Luna." The words were a hiss as Kalen kicked at the prince's foot. Cirrus startled awake.

"What?"

Kalen lifted his index finger to his lips and pointed out of their little alcove.

The animal was coming at the horses from the other side of the fire, unintimidated by the humans resting nearby.

The horses bumped into one another in their haste to distance themselves from the predator. One of them snorted again, and his head reared back.

Cirrus slowly rose and crept toward the horses, his short sword suddenly free from its scabbard and in his hands.

"What are you doing?" Kalen hissed as he nudged closer

to Luna to awaken her. They needed to be able to run—or climb a tree or something.

With light steps, Cirrus slipped up to the horses and crouched between them. The animal wound languidly between the trees as it inched closer. In the lightening sky Kalen could now make out that it was a mountain cat from its pale gray fur and the fierce yellow eyes intent on one thing and one thing only.

Their horses.

They couldn't afford to lose their animals. They'd lose a day getting up to Servaille, having to travel by foot.

Kalen placed his gloved hand close to Luna's mouth and nudged her shoulder gently with the other. She pushed at his hand and glared at him, but he tilted his head toward the cat, and her eyes widened. He waved her to the safety of the trees behind them, but she shook her head.

"What's he doing?" She looked at Cirrus, who had shifted around one of the other horses so he was now at the side farthest from the slinking animal. "He'll get himself killed," she whispered loudly.

Cirrus threw a glance over his shoulder and shook his head as a warning for them to remain quiet.

Suddenly the horse behind which Cirrus had been crouching reared up on his hind legs. His hooves pawed at the air and knocked the prince, who crashed to the ground on his side. Kalen readied to rush to Cirrus's aid, but the prince pushed himself up awkwardly to his feet.

The animal had circled to come up from behind the horses. Cirrus scooted out of the line of view, his sword gripped tight at his side.

The horses kept shuffling, further tangling themselves in their ropes. Luna nudged Kalen. "Let's get the horses out of the way." While the cat and Cirrus faced off, they slipped over and untied the ropes to lead the horses toward the tree line.

The cat crouched low, ready to pounce. Back legs pushed into the hard-packed ground as it prepared to launch. Cirrus jumped forward and stabbed his sword between the cat's ribs. The animal fell, the sword still jutting from its skin as Cirrus lost his grip.

Luna's hands flew to her mouth as she covered a gasp.

Time slowed as the cat gathered its footing and leaped toward Cirrus in a tackle. A trail of red sprayed the ground below. The force of the cat's jump thrust Cirrus off his feet and into the air for a brief moment before he landed with a jarring boom on the ground.

Before Cirrus could scream, the cat sank its teeth into his upper arm.

CHAPTER

15

The prince grunted and shoved at the animal with his free hand. His hand found the sword hilt, and he plunged it farther into the cat. The animal released Cirrus's arm and pitched forward, its chest heaving with whatever few remaining breaths it had left.

Cirrus moaned and rolled to his side. He released the sword to grip his arm, his fingers reaching around his bicep. Beads of sweat gathered on his forehead as Kalen and Luna ran over to help.

Luna gingerly eased off his overcoat, the sleeve now nearly shredded. Blood soaked through the arm of Cirrus's shirt, staining the black material an even darker shade. She glanced at Kalen. "We need to get his shirt off, too."

Cirrus flinched away.

"Knock it off," Luna said as she grabbed at his hand.

"I'm cold is all."

"The cold will feel good. Now let me examine it."

Kalen propped Cirrus into a sitting position, and Luna worked quickly to unbutton the fabric and pull it off the good arm. She slipped it over his shoulders and peeled it slowly down the other arm. Deep, angry punctures stared back at them.

She gripped the shirt and tore it into shreds of fabric before binding them around the arm. Cirrus's jaw tightened, but he remained otherwise still. "Do you have to be so rough?"

"I want to stop the bleeding," said Luna "I'm sorry it hurts." She dug in her pockets and pulled out a vial of bright-yellow liquid. "Take a swig of this, it will help with the pain until we get to town and have someone look at the wound. I would leave the arm exposed, too, as the cold will help with the swelling."

"You are insane."

"Thanks for the compliment, but it's actually proven that cold therapy quickens the healing."

"Healing? Are you sure you don't mean death?"

"I doubt you'll die before we reach Servaille, but whatever you desire."

He shoved his unwounded arm through the sleeve and attempted to drape it over the shoulder of his wounded arm. Unfortunately, he couldn't do it one handed, so his cheeks and ears reddened while Luna bent over to help him.

"Thank goodness you didn't hurt your leg." She rolled her eyes.

Kalen put out the fire and cleaned off Cirrus's sword

before returning it to its scabbard. He soothed each of the horses and gave them water. Luna mounted her horse, and Cirrus stood next to his. "I might need some help here," he said, his jaw clenched in pain.

It took some maneuvering and a couple of grunts from Cirrus, but finally they were ready to depart. The road wound through the forest, offering them occasional glimpses of the pale blue sky above. They finally reached the edge of the mountain, and the path cleared to showcase the valley below and the peaks on the other side. The horses plowed ahead to a switchback and turned the corner.

There in front of them, built into the cliffs, stood the city of Servaille.

With scylee birds circling above and below, it looked like a miniature snow village sold during the winter holiday season at the marketplace. Silver and stone sparkled in the sunlight glinting off the cliff as the sun crested above to begin its descent toward the horizon. The city seemed vertically stacked, building on top of building, precarious because one avalanche could sheer the side and decimate the entire town. When he squinted and looked closer, Kalen made out trails and roads that climbed the side of the mountain, so it wasn't quite as vertical as he'd thought.

But the illusion certainly made for an imposing first glimpse.

Spurred forward by the sight of their destination, they traversed the final mountain pass and neared the outskirts of Servaille.

The path widened again by the time they reached the city's edge, stretching enough to allow a wagon through.

A large archway marked the entrance, connected to a wall extending along the cliff's edge along their right side. The gate was lifted, ready to slide closed and lock when needed, but for now the arch invited all willing to enter. White flags lined the wall, almost invisible against the white sky beyond.

They received some curious glances from the citizens as they approached the first set of buildings cut into the cliff. Fair-skinned and dark-haired, most of the residents were bundled in layers of fur and wool and heavy cloth.

"Shall I board your horses?" A young boy jumped into their path and held out his hands for their reins. "We have a stable right there"—he pointed behind him—"as horses aren't allowed in the city. They've led to too many accidents."

Kalen glanced around and saw that the only animals were small goats pulling carts of sorts. No horses or mules or full-size wagons. He and Luna dismounted, and Cirrus slipped off his animal. Kalen took the prince's pack and added it to his own.

"Do you have any suggestions for lodging?" Kalen asked as the boy gathered the reins.

"There are a few places along this road, or uptown." He glanced up the mountain cliff. "Some people stay at the monastery. They've opened a section to lodging, and it's the cheapest option by far."

Kalen nodded. That was exactly where they would go. "Where is it?"

"Unfortunately, it's on the other side of town. You'll have to wind your way up and along the path."

"Splendid." Cirrus frowned and tightened his cloak. His

teeth had started to chatter, despite the continued beading of sweat on his forehead.

"Where might an apothecary be?" Luna asked.

"Uptown as well."

Luna snaked an arm around Cirrus's lower back and urged him forward. "Come on. The sooner we get you something for the pain, the better your disposition will become."

"I doubt that," Kalen said as he set off at a brisk pace down the path. They reached a break in the road that branched off to the left. Steep steps were cut into the cliff to lead up to the next level.

"Excuse me." Luna flagged a young woman, dressed in furs, who walked along the street. "Is that the only way up to those shops?"

"If you don't want to navigate the steps, you can follow this street to the end where it curves around. It's a little more gradual."

Luna thanked the woman and turned to the boys. "Which way?"

"Stairs," Kalen said at the same time Cirrus replied, "Street."

She took Cirrus's good arm and turned to walk down the street.

"Wait. Why does he win?" Kalen asked.

"Because he's injured."

Kalen eyed the stairs again. "I'll go that way and try to find the apothecary. No sense wasting time." He had bounded up ten steps to a landing before they had walked even a yard along the street.

Kalen's breaths came heavy and fogged the air by the time

he reached the top of the steps and turned slowly around to look at just how many stories he had climbed. It felt as if he could topple over and spear himself on one of the weather vanes sticking out of a rooftop below. A sense of vertigo sent his body swaying, and he backed away from the edge. He took in the length of the street, spotting the apothecary shop sign a few doors away.

A tinkle of bells and a blast of warm air greeted him when he opened the door. A fire popped in a hearth in the corner, and a woman stood behind a marble counter. She wore a long dress and a white fur cape draped around her shoulders. Dark hair was piled high and heavy on her head, with loose strands tumbling haphazardly down her back.

"Welcome, how may I help you?" Her voice was low but soft.

"My friend is on his way. He was bitten by a mountain cat, and I was hoping to get something to ease his discomfort." Kalen glanced at the wall of jars opposite the window. They were filled with powders and liquids—bright blue and dull gray, powdered yellow and glowing green—and loose tea and bits of what could have been bone or bark or stones.

"A mountain cat?" Her eyebrows knit in concern.

"Yes, we were attacked a few hours outside of town. Our horses were the intended victims. My friend chose to intervene."

"I'm glad you escaped mostly unscathed, and of course I can help. I will put together something for infection and pain, but I'll definitely want to examine the wound."

She introduced herself as Jules as she placed a small metal stand on the countertop and filled it with empty vials. Deft fingers opened jars, and she carefully measured powders into a mortar. She used a pestle to grind the coarse powder into something finer before using a dropper to add a pale liquid. A pitcher on the counter held water, which she poured in until the concoction bubbled and turned a burnt amber color. She filled three of the vials and stoppered them.

The door flew open, and Cirrus and Luna stepped inside. Luna stomped the snow off her feet and threw back her hood at the warmth in the room. The apothecary's eyes widened as she took in Luna's hair and eyes before she turned to Cirrus, who stood silent near the door, gripping his arm. She beckoned him over and had him sit on a stool at the counter. He breathed hard through his nose, and his skin paled as he slipped off the cloak and Jules undressed the wound. A hiss escaped him as she slowly removed the fabric from his skin.

"They'll need stitches. At least these two"—Jules pointed where the top teeth had sunk into Cirrus's bicep—"where the punctures are deepest."

Cirrus's face whitened even further. "I'm not really a fan of needles."

"Seriously?" Luna stared at him. "Don't you go into combat and stab people? You're afraid of a needle?"

Cirrus tossed a glare over his shoulder at her.

Jules walked behind the counter. "I've got something to help." She crouched, her dark curls hardly visible over the top of the marble slab. When she stood again, Kalen inhaled sharply.

Nestled in her arms was a small chest, swirls tracing its sides.

"Put that away," Kalen said. He stepped in front of Cirrus to protect him.

Jules frowned as she placed it on the counter, her fingers pushing at the clasp. "Just wait a moment—"

Kalen was reaching out to grab the box when it popped open. His concern didn't seem quite as pressing as it had before. His shoulders fell, and the warmth of the room eased all the tension from them.

Jules lifted a pendant, and the world seemed right again.

Similar in style to the cracked one buried in the chest on the island, this pendant had a silver base, and the crystal was a clear blue. She reached over and draped the pendant around Cirrus's neck.

"What is going on here?" Luna looked at everyone like they'd gone insane.

"It's a calming stone." Jules motioned for Kalen to step behind Cirrus. "Would you mind helping me to keep him still?"

"Where did you get it?" Kalen moved over and gripped his shoulders.

"Someone made it for me, a local artisan in town."

"We need to meet her," Luna said.

"Him." Jules arranged a needle and thin thread on the counter.

Kalen's mind churned, despite the soothing calm of the crystal. Him. Not a her. Not the princess.

Luna leaned in. "We need to meet this person."

"May I ask why?" Jules glanced at Luna as she threaded the needle. "He doesn't create these for just anyone." She positioned Kalen's hands such that he gripped Cirrus's shoulder firmly in one hand and held the prince's wrist with the other.

"We can provide money," Kalen assured her.

"I definitely need one of these," Cirrus said. "I could probably sleep through the night."

"I'll see about making an introduction." Jules held the needle above Cirrus's arm. "Take a deep breath and exhale. This will hurt."

He winced but otherwise remained still as she deftly stitched up the puncture wounds. She knotted the string and bandaged Cirrus's arm before removing the pendant from his neck.

His good hand lifted as if he wanted to grab it, but Kalen kicked at his foot where it rested near the stool.

After Jules locked the magicked jewel away, the room felt suddenly colder, life suddenly less serene. Kalen tensed as the urgency of their mission returned. The sooner they were on their way to finding Reign, the better.

Jules turned to them. "I will send a message to see if he's available this evening, after I've closed the shop. Return here in a few hours?"

Kalen nodded. "We will see you then."

CHAPTER

16

The monastery loomed in front of them, a massive stone structure that seemed like it had erupted from the mountain itself. The portico was tall columns and shadowed stripes as they approached, the sun ready to sink behind the mountain at their backs.

The heavy doors stood open, and Kalen was the first to step through the entranceway and into a small room with arched doorways on either side. Through an opening at the back of the building, he caught a view of the thin columns and darkened lawn of the cloister beyond. Cirrus scooted closer to Luna as they entered the dimly lit quarters. Sconces flickered along the walls, but a heavy blanket of dreariness and cold settled over the trio.

A lone brother stood near a desk; he lifted his head slowly and peered at them. "May I help you?"

"We were hoping to find lodging here, Brother," Kalen said.

The man blinked and then slowly appraised Luna, as if debating allowing her access. He appeared to have all the time in the world. "Two rooms remain vacant. How many would you need?"

"Two would be perfect," Kalen said.

The brother led them down a narrow hallway to the left. After a sharp turn, they entered the chilled and damp dormitory hall. The sconces here were hardly functional, providing very little light outside the small circle around the flame.

Most of the doors were shut, but two at the end remained open. "Here we are," the brother said. "Meals are in the refectory, and a bath can be brought to you for a charge."

"Yes please!" Luna didn't even wait for a response.

They thanked the brother and entered the rooms. Kalen and Cirrus took the first one. Inside, the furnishings and decor were as barren as one would expect: two small beds, two trunks, one round table, and one shelf holding a bowl and folded gray towels. Luna popped her head into their room a couple of seconds later. "Window glass is loose. You can remove it quickly and climb out in an emergency."

"Thanks," Kalen said. "While you enjoy a bath, I'm going to go search for the catacombs I saw in the monk's memory."

"I'll join you," Cirrus said, but Kalen shook his head. "With your *issues* with the dark, I'd rather you stay here for now. Unless you'd like some assistance in dealing with those fears?"

"You're not going into my head again."

"Not even if it might help? Perhaps there's something else locked away in your memories . . . an event occurred that you refuse to recall. If I could find it and unlock it, we could face this aversion and conquer it."

Cirrus shrugged. "I'm good. You go exploring; I'll take a nap and rest my arm."

"And take a bath," Luna said. "You could really use one."

Kalen bid them warm bathing and walked down the hallway to where he had seen a staircase. The steps were wooden planks that led to a landing. They turned the corner, and the steps became natural stone cuts. Some were wide, some dropped farther than others, but all of them were uneven. His footsteps echoed off the rock walls as he approached the bottom floor, where a locked door cut into a side wall. Kalen hoped it led to the underground cemetery. He palmed the key around his neck with one hand while he dug his picks out of his jacket pocket with the other. The stone was cold against his knees as he knelt and began to work on the lock. It seemed new, made of solid silver, and slid open quickly. He tucked away his tools and rose to a stand. The door was heavy and thicker than a simple wooden door. The inside edge was coated in a thick bronze metal, and etchings bordered the door as he walked through it.

Behind the door was a tunnel lined with flickerfly sconces. He followed it, drawn by something he couldn't quite explain, twisting through the tunnels, not knowing if he dove deeper into the mountain or back toward the town. He passed through the occasional room with crypts opening up on either side, but he kept moving forward, almost tripping in his haste.

Time had stalled and he debated stopping. Only one more archway and he would call it a day. He entered a large space and halted. He took it in, the reality of it in some ways clearer and in other ways dimmer than in Gabriel's memories. The cavernous room was supported with columns at regular intervals, and a skylight let in the early evening rays.

Unlike Gabriel's memory, there was no singing. No sound at all.

He walked past the skylight and into a narrow tunnel that led off to the side. A breeze whipped through the hallway, as if it came in through the cracks in the walls. It tugged at his hair, at the hem of his cloak, and he followed it to see where it led.

The tunnel ended, and he entered another wing with high ceilings and multiple skylights down its length. Archways on either side led to small crypts filled with ornate headstones and stone coffins. He peered into each of the crypts but saw nothing.

He began to wonder if Gabriel had been hallucinating in his memory. There was no evidence at all that Reign had ever been in these catacombs. Perhaps she didn't exist. Perhaps this journey had been for naught.

He reached the last doorway and peered inside. The room was dark, lit with three scattered flickerfly lamps along the floor against the side wall. A lone coffin, stone and tiny, sat in the center of the room. The headstone was broken, but he imagined the date range would have been a short one. He ground his teeth together and looked past the coffin.

Scraps of fabric, in varying faded shades, lay scattered along the floor. A book rested open near the wall, the pages yellowed and brittle-looking. A chipped pitcher of water sat next to what looked like a plate filled with crumbs.

Could these have belonged to Reign? Could she have lived here?

He peered at the book, an old edition of children's tales. The fabric looked like what the girl had worn in Gabriel's memories.

There was no way to tell how long the items had been left here. It could have been days; it could have been years. Most likely somewhere in between. And if Reign had made it out, there was no way she would return.

Which left Jules's artisan contact as his next hope. The amulet's power to project emotions was so very similar to Reign's ability that they had to be related.

———•◦•———

JULES WRAPPED HERSELF in a fur overcoat and locked the door to the apothecary shop behind her. "He agreed to meet at a tavern across town. I'll make the introduction, and then I must be getting home."

The street stretched in front of them, the shops all still open, windows brightly lit but doors shut against the cold. Tall wooden posts lined the edge of the cliff drop-off. Atop each sat a large, bright bulb filled with flickerflies. Smaller bulbs were strung on wire to crisscross over the lane where the darkness seemed to sheer off into an abyss.

Jules directed them into a doorway set away from the street. A sticky warmth immediately settled over Kalen. The room was stifling with body heat and the flame from the hearth. He slid his cloak off and draped it over the back of a chair as they settled in at a table in the far corner to wait. Cirrus ordered ale for him and Luna, and a cup of tea for Kalen. Jules declined his offer.

The drinks were arranged on the table when suddenly a thin, tall, fair-haired man stood behind Jules. Kalen recognized him as the man in Gabriel's vision.

She made introductions.

"Nero, these are the people I spoke of."

"Can we get you a drink?" Cirrus reached for the pitcher with his good hand, but Nero shook his head.

"I'm fine, thank you." His watery eyes were hooded as he took in the seating arrangement.

Kalen scooted his chair to the side to make room. Nero grabbed an empty chair from the table nearby and slid it over. "So Jules said you would like to commission me to make a jewel?"

"We are considering it," Kalen said. "I was wondering if you could tell me more about the process. How quickly could we purchase one?"

Nero leaned back and crossed his arms over his chest.

Cirrus took a sip from his mug. "We have the money."

"It's not about the money. I am not divulging information. It takes a certain type of talent—"

He was cut off when the door burst open and a chest-heaving giant of a man burst in. "Jules? Is Jules here?" His eyes landed on the table. "Kristoph is on the ledge. He's raving."

Jules leaped up and raced after the giant. The entire tavern seemed to swell and move to follow them.

Nero's eyes narrowed, and he rose from the table. "I must attend to something. Let's reconvene tomorrow, shall we?" With that he slipped out through the kitchen.

The trio glanced at one another and at the two different doors.

"I'm on it." Luna rose and followed Nero.

Kalen and Cirrus pushed their way through the crowd to the street. The temperature felt like it had dropped another twenty degrees, and Kalen tightened his cloak. A crowd had gathered near one of the posts.

"Step back!" someone yelled. "Let Jules through."

The group retreated only slightly. Nobody wanted to give up prime viewing of the unfolding drama. Through a slight gap, Kalen made out a figure standing at the edge of the cliff. He had his back turned toward everyone, his head tipped, and he mumbled to himself. Jules approached.

"Get away." He clenched and unclenched his hands. "I don't want to hurt you." He glared at the crowd and yelled it again.

"Who is he?" Kalen asked a young woman standing on the fringes of the crowd.

"Kristoph works at the stables. A horseshoer by trade."

"Any reason you can think of why he'd be acting this way?"

She shook her head. "Usually he's the happiest person in the city. Loves his job. His wife is pregnant. This is unlike him."

"I'd like to take a look at his memories," Kalen muttered to Cirrus. He wanted to know exactly what had happened.

A gust whipped up from the canyon and tugged at the

knit cap Kristoph wore on his head. His arms reached out unsteadily to the sides.

"Kristoph, move toward me." Jules motioned him toward safety.

Kristoph blinked in her direction. He glanced over his shoulder and lurched forward as if he hadn't realized how close to the edge he had backed himself.

She held out a hand, and he grasped it.

"What am I doing here?" he asked.

Jules tucked his hand against her side and made her way through the crowd. "I'm not sure, but you're safe now."

He looked behind him again.

"Can we buy you a drink?" Kalen approached Jules and Kristoph as they walked nearer. "Cider will warm you quickly, I'm sure."

Kristoph took a deep breath and tore his cap off his head. He glanced at Kalen and then Cirrus. "Foreigners, ay?"

They nodded.

"I met them earlier today," Jules said, tilting her head in thanks at Kalen for the distraction.

"Why not? Anywhere but there—" Kristoph's eyes cut to the inn a few doors down. Brightly lit windows showcased patrons dining on food.

Kalen slipped off his glove and reached out to put his arm around the large man as they walked toward the tavern door. He knew the second he touched Kristoph's skin he'd dive into his thoughts, and the recent memories would be readily available, nowhere near enough time to be locked away. He only needed a few seconds, and it was easier to do it with a quick contact than to ask for permission.

Kristoph wouldn't even know what had happened.

Bare fingers brushed the back of Kristoph's neck, and Kalen's mind latched on. Kristoph was seated at a table at the inn, telling his friends his fears of taking care of his family when the baby was born. Suddenly anger blanketed his every thought. *How did this happen? Now I'm stuck in Servaille forever. I will never make enough money to support the family, and it's all her fault.*

Kristoph rose from the chair and walked out, barely glancing at two girls arguing at the counter. One of the girls had her hands fisted at her sides, and her chest shuddered as if she forced deep breaths. Auburn hair plaited into a loose braid, freckles dusting pale skin, a loose wool sweater draping low to show jutting collarbones—

Kalen tumbled out of his thoughts as Kristoph sped ahead to walk single file through the door. Pinpricks needled into Kalen's forehead as the sights and sounds came into focus, but he hardly even felt the pain.

Reign.

She looked drastically different from the vision in the catacombs. Chaos and melancholy versus order and anger. It was absolutely the same girl, though, and she was even more stunning now than in Gabriel's memory. Her face had filled in a little, and she had a healthier glow to her skin. Her hair looked soft, even pulled into the braid.

And she was here.

Kalen turned to Cirrus. "I'll be right back." He was sure he looked panicked, like he was out of his mind, but he had to go. Now. "Buy Kristoph here a drink and keep him company."

And he took off at a sprint toward the inn.

He shoved his hand into his glove as he ran, his only focus on the wooden sign that hung from the awning: SNOWBOUND INN. He shoved at the door that led directly into the dining area, stumbling into a room heavy with the warmth from the hearth and deep conversations as the evening neared its end.

Eyes darting to and fro, Kalen searched for Reign, but she was nowhere to be seen.

He grabbed at a serving girl as she passed by. "Excuse me, I'm looking for someone. Auburn hair, freckles—"

"Reign."

"Yes, Reign."

The girl sneered. "She's gone to cope is my guess. She'll be back for the morning shift, I'm sure. Or maybe not." She shrugged one shoulder. "One can never tell with her sort of crazy."

Shift.

"She works here?"

The girl glared at him. "Yeah, how else would she earn her keep? Nobody stays at the inn for free, you know."

She started to walk toward the kitchen.

"Are you sure she won't return tonight?" Kalen called after her.

A toss of dark hair. "Not when she's had an *episode.*"

The door closed behind her.

"Thanks for your help," Kalen muttered.

He shoved his way back out into the cold. In the few minutes he'd been inside, Servaille had started to clear out. Most of the storefronts darkened, all the footprints dulled as the wind caught the loose drifts of snow and swept it over the street. Strings of flickerfly light bounced off the white—dusted road, snowdrifts, pale buildings, clouded sky—refracting and reflecting until it seemed Kalen walked through a foggy haze of a dream.

Kalen hurried to the tavern, where he found Cirrus, Kristoph, and a red-cheeked Luna enjoying freshly poured mugs of ale. Jules had retired for the evening once she'd ensured Kristoph was no longer a danger to himself or the townspeople. He appeared in a much better mood, but Kalen was ready to return to the monastery. They needed sleep and to return to the inn first thing in the morning.

He tilted his head to the door. Luna threw down a couple of coins, and they excused themselves.

"Where did you go?" Cirrus asked Kalen as they exited.

The wind whipped along the street, and they hurried their steps. Kalen filled them in on what he had seen in Kristoph's mind.

"Reign was angry, and Kristoph felt it. The entire crowd seemed on edge. I went to the inn to look for her, however they said she wouldn't be back until morning."

"We should head there first thing," Cirrus said as he stepped over an errant log. He extended his good hand to help Luna after him.

"Were you able to follow Nero?" Kalen asked her. He trudged ahead, picking up the pace in an attempt to keep warm.

She shook her head. "This town has too many alleyways and vertical climbs. I did find some entrances into what appear to be the catacombs, but I didn't delve too deep, because there was no sign of footprints." She shivered in the cold air. "I did find out where he lives, though." She pointed up and to the left. "Farther up the mountain, on the same elevation of the monastery but on the other side of the woods, there is a cluster of homes."

"And he wasn't there?"

"No."

Nero and Reign both missing. It was too much of a coincidence. They had to be together.

But doing what?

CHAPTER

 17

"We need to find a safer light source today." Kalen yawned and didn't bother to cover his mouth.

Cirrus had been unable to fall asleep the night prior, what with the darkness of the room and the interior walls blocking out most of the moonlight, so he'd gone in search of candles. After collecting a dozen or so, he'd clustered them on the table closest to his head before promptly dozing off. The brightness, and the fear that the room would catch on fire, jolted Kalen awake every hour or so. He wasn't exactly well-rested.

"Either that or I need to get inside your head."

"A light source would be great, thanks." Cirrus, on the other hand, acted downright chipper.

"Seriously. I would only do it once. I'm not going to invade your privacy," Kalen said.

"No way, no how." Cirrus tugged on his cloak, taking care with his injured arm. "Let's get some food."

"Let's get on the road, we can eat at the inn," Kalen said. He donned his gloves and rapped on Luna's door. Before the second knock, she had thrown it open and slid out beside them. Then it was back into the frigid brightness of day. The sun taunted them with a false sense of warmth, but every gust of wind sent tiny pinpricks of ice crystals down Kalen's neck and up his sleeves.

More snow had fallen overnight, making their progress slow as they trudged along the path to the main thoroughfare and into town. They passed the apothecary on their way to the Snowbound Inn, which looked somehow more foreboding in the light of day.

The building was thrust slightly forward and stretched longer than some of the other storefronts, probably owing to the necessary space for rooms. Narrow windows stretched floor to ceiling in reflective stripes that mirrored the trio and the landscape behind them. A series of three wide steps led to heavy double doors. Kalen strode ahead and opened them. They stepped into a lobby that seemed bent on contradictions. Ornate gilded molding lined the ceilings, while a stained chaise rested in the corner, lopsided pillows stacked against the arm. Newer flickerfly bulbs rested in polished brass holders, a sharp contrast to the massive, rugged landscape painting hung in the middle of the wall. The half-naked cherubs, with their bulging eyes and exaggerated features, were almost the size of Luna.

A small bell rested on an empty desk, and Cirrus reached over to give it a shake.

"One moment please," a husky voice answered from one of the hallways leading to either side.

Kalen's chest tightened as he recognized Reign's timbre and realized he would finally see her, in person. A curtained doorway parted, and out stepped the princess. Her hair was loosely piled on the top of her head, and her freckles stood out against her pale skin. Soft lips were parted, and she breathed heavily like she'd just completed a chore. Heavy skirts enveloped her hands as she wiped them off and stepped forward.

"Will you be needing a room?"

Luna stared openmouthed at the girl before turning to Cirrus. "She looks just like you."

He inhaled a sharp breath. "She looks just like my mother."

Reign edged closer and tilted her chin to look up at Cirrus, who stood almost a head taller. "Who are you?"

"I'm Cirrus." He ran his hand through his hair. "I think I'm your brother."

"I don't have a brother. I don't have any family." She stared past Cirrus at Luna, like she couldn't even be bothered with this discussion.

Cirrus stepped sideways and blocked her view. "Yes, you do. You have to have a family."

"My family abandoned me." Reign reached out with one hand and pushed him to the side, dismissing him.

Kalen couldn't stop staring at the scars that circled her wrists, wondering what had happened to her, if she had been shackled. The heavy weight of sadness settled over him, and he tried to shrug it off, tried to tell his mind that it was only his reaction to Reign and her magick. When he finally tore his gaze away, he realized silence had descended and they were all staring at him expectantly.

"Did I miss something?" He rubbed at his neck with his gloved hand and tried to look anywhere but Reign's wide eyes.

"She told us to leave," Luna said, her voice a mixture of disbelief and frustration.

"No!" The word was nearly a shout. Kalen exhaled slowly. "We need to talk to you. It's imperative that we talk to you."

Reign closed her eyes and took a deep breath. Her hands were clutched in her skirts. "You are strangers and know nothing about me, and you also don't know the consequences of pushing me to do something I don't want to do."

Kalen shuddered as a wave of anxiety crested over him. Cirrus took a full step backward as if he'd been punched in the gut, while Luna stood there, a look of disinterest curtaining her features.

His gloved hand extended, Kalen tried to battle Reign's emotions with a calm of his own. "We know more than you think, and we might be able to help. Please. I promise you we mean no harm. Is there a chance we might sit and talk? We'll order tea."

"Breakfast even," Luna said, her expression deadpan.

"Yes please. I'm starving." Cirrus gripped his stomach.

Reign took a deep breath, her eyes closing for more than a second as if she were trying to calm herself. She tipped her head toward one of the doorways. "Follow me."

They arranged themselves around a small round table,

Luna and Reign to either side of Kalen, with Cirrus opposite. There was only one other table occupied in the dining hall. It was located near the front window, and the girl Kalen had spoken to the evening prior was assisting them. As soon as she was done, Reign waved her over. The girl looked at Cirrus appraisingly.

"Who is he?" she asked Reign, not seeming much to care for Luna or Kalen.

"I'm not sure, Sasha. Your guess is as good as mine."

Cirrus grinned at her. "Can we please get some tea?"

"Why sure, I'd absolutely love to get it for you." She sashayed away.

"Pastries, too, if you have them," Cirrus called after her.

Sasha tossed a smile over her shoulder and disappeared.

"So." Reign suddenly sounded tired. "What is it you want to tell me?"

Kalen leaned in, his eyes on her pale ones. "We came to Servaille specifically in search of you."

"Why? So you could study me? Make fun of me?" Her eyes narrowed in a glare at him.

"Not at all." Kalen retreated. "We came to take you home."

"This is my home—"

"How can you even say that?" Cirrus interrupted. "This place is colder than Kalen's parents. And that's saying a bloody lot." He looked at Kalen. "Sorry, but it's true. Your mother was once able turn a room to ice just by opening her mouth."

Kalen shrugged in answer. He wasn't going to take it personally.

"It's cold," Cirrus continued, "and it's not even your country. It's not your home. Mureau is."

Reign's fingers laced into one another, then released and relaced. Sasha burst through the door, a tray held aloft in her hand. With a flourish, she settled a pot of hot water into the middle of the table and arranged cups at each seat. Warm rolls were placed in front of Cirrus, along with a board of nuts and dried fruit. The last dish was a bowl of boiled eggs, which Luna immediately dug into. With deft fingers she peeled the shell and popped the entire egg into her mouth.

Kalen poured himself a cup of tea, and they waited for Sasha to occupy herself elsewhere, out of hearing.

"Home is wherever I want it to be," Reign said.

"Let's cut to the chase," Luna said after she chewed and swallowed. "He"—she waved her hand at Cirrus, who was now licking his fingers after picking through the dried fruit—"shockingly enough, is the prince of Mureau. You"—she pointed at Reign—"are his sister."

"I'm not a princess." Her hands unclenched. "I'm a gutter rat, an orphan, a menace to the village, and a witch." She ticked off each item on her fingers. "Among other things." Her fingers curled into fists again, and her voice rose. "Royalty is not one of them."

Kalen suddenly reeled away as a wave of anger and anguish pulsed over him.

"Enough." Cirrus scraped his chair back, and his teeth ground together. "You're coming with us." His words sounded strangled and his tone foreign.

"You can't just take me. I won't go with you. I don't even know you."

The voices at the other table picked up in volume, and two of the patrons began to argue.

"Please, just leave," Reign said.

Another pulse of anger.

Kalen's own emotions, his interest in Reign, and his excitement at finally finding her were tamped by this frustration. It made him antsy, made him want to run and take out his anger on something.

Reign stood and brushed past him as she headed toward the kitchen. "Sasha." Her voice was strong yet distraught. "Can you please send for Nero? Have him meet me as normal."

The trio rose and followed close behind her.

"Where are you going?" Kalen asked as she wound her way through the small kitchen and out the back door. They spilled into an alleyway that stretched behind the buildings.

Reign didn't answer, only picked up her pace and dashed down the narrow path. "Leave me alone!" She hurled the words behind her, along with another pulse of emotion. Kalen tried to shove it aside, tried to reject the notion of anxiety and flight.

"Reign, wait. We are trying to help. We need your help," Kalen yelled up to her.

She turned and disappeared into the face of the mountain. Kalen reached the corner and was the first to see it, an entrance carved into the stone. Darkness spilled out from the tunnel beyond, and he wondered where it led. He stalled for a brief moment and then charged into the darkness.

"I can't do it. I can't go in there," he heard Cirrus say.

Bulbs lined the tunnel at irregular intervals, not a lot of

illumination but enough to go by. "There's light," Kalen called out behind him, hoping Luna could convince the prince to enter but not stopping to do it himself. It probably wouldn't hurt Cirrus to get a little distance from his sister's emotions anyway.

The tunnel twisted and turned, branching and forking. Kalen kept seeing glimpses of Reign as she flew down one corridor and then another. At one point he paused and had to listen for her footsteps before continuing. There was no way he would make it back out on his own.

Finally, he spilled into a side room of the catacombs. He looked up, where he assumed the monastery must be right above him, before taking in the small space. The room was dominated by a gilded table tomb. The top featured an or-nate sculpture of a couple lying on their sides, facing one another, limbs entangled.

Reign stood on the opposite side of the tomb, in the vaulted opening to the main hall, facing away from him, her body heaving. Her hair, a darker red in the catacomb's shad-ows, had come loose and tumbled over her shoulders.

"Reign?" He spoke softly and stepped closer, not want-ing to scare her or cause her to run again. After he reached her side, he recognized the space and the room beyond as the one she must have slept in. She drifted over as if in a trance and sank into the pile of rags in the corner. Her fingers played with one of the strips of fabric.

"What do you want with me?" She looked up at Kalen, her eyes swollen with unshed tears. "Everyone always wants something. What do you truly want?"

Kalen felt the urge to scoop her into his arms, run his

fingers through her tangled hair, and hold her close to his chest. He squatted down a few feet away. "I want to help."

Her mouth opened in a sort of half laugh. "By taking me away?"

"We would never force you to go, but you belong there. At least give it a chance. Your father is there." Although Kalen wasn't sure how welcoming the king would be. "And your brother needs you. Your people need you. It's your kingdom."

She shook her head. "Nobody needs me. They always send me away. And how can I believe you anyway? How do you know I'm the princess?"

Another smaller pulse of anxiety washed over Kalen, and he felt a heaviness weigh him down.

"You fit the description for starters," Kalen said, trying to figure out a way to make her see. To alleviate her fears. "But I could ascertain the truth by delving into your memories. Cirrus has a particular one that involves his sister. She was an infant at the time, but if you have the same recollection . . ." His voice trailed off, and he figured she could make the obvious inference.

Footsteps and muffled voices erupted from the other side of the hall. A few moments later, Cirrus and Luna appeared in front of the large tomb. Cirrus eyed the skylight in the main hall and mouthed the words *thank the gods*.

They spotted Reign and Kalen and made their way over.

Reign ignored them. "How would you be able to get into my memories? What does that mean? What does that involve?"

He looked at his gloves. "It doesn't hurt. I only touch you and enter your mind."

She sat there in silence, unsure.

"Oh bloody crow," Cirrus said from where he lounged against the wall, taking in the scene. "He's done it to me before. Do you want me to prove to you it doesn't hurt? Fine." He sighed and shoved up his sleeve. "Go on, show her."

Kalen and Luna turned to Cirrus. Before the prince could change his mind, Kalen ripped off a glove, rose, and stepped over to him.

He plunged into the prince's mind, and even though he was out again shortly, his forehead pulsed and threatened to drown him in pain. Kalen sank to the ground and curled his head to his knees. He reached for the tea leaves in his pocket and chewed on a few of them. It eased the agony a fraction.

"What's wrong with him?" Reign's voice soothed the pain's intensity.

"He reacts this way every time," Luna said. "It's an after-effect of his power."

"If it's painful, why do you want to do it again?" Reign asked Kalen.

"It's important to me that I seek the truth. Always. I believe you're a part of this truth, and a path to saving the kingdom." He inhaled a shaky breath. "You'll notice he has no idea what I saw. It's harmless to him."

"Other than knowing you're creeping through my thoughts." Cirrus's words were a mumble.

"There's the animosity I was expecting." Kalen would have laughed if his head wasn't still throbbing.

Reign walked over to sit in front of him.

"Can you do it quickly? And then when you're done, and you discover I'm not the princess, will you all please leave?"

Her sleeves fell to reveal the scars on her wrist, and she grabbed his hand.

He tumbled forward, his mind falling into hers.

He stood in a mirrored foyer. Images reflected back on one another to infinity until he wasn't sure what was real and what was a mere replica. A hallway stretched in front of him, with doors on either side. Most of them were open, and the few that were shut had the simplest of locks.

The mirrored image was the one he couldn't stop staring at. It drowned out nearly everything else. In it, Reign tucked into herself, biting her lip hard enough to draw blood but also to prevent herself from crying out. A man stood over her, features hard to distinguish, all grays and muted tones. One hand lightly gripped the back of her neck. The other held a jewel. It must be Nero. Moments passed, and then Reign seemed to feel relief, her body sagging and her teeth releasing her lip.

The reflections all had minuscle differences. How many times had Nero done this?

Kalen walked farther into the recesses of Reign's memories. Hallways stretched in front of him, with doorways open on either side. A simple turn of the key and he pushed them open. Through each doorway, Kalen caught glimpses of the images. On a rare occasion Reign had a pleasant memory, but they were few and far between. Most of them were depressing. A young girl trudged through the snow, wearing mere rags against the biting wind. A confused toddler stared up at a woman who screamed at her with green and yellow words and then slapped her across the cheek. He wanted to explore further, but he didn't have the time or luxury, and it felt intrusive.

The end of the hallway loomed. He peeked in the second-to-last door and saw an infant crying in a bassinet as it jostled with movement.

He approached the last room. This one was locked, but one twist of the key and the door opened silently on its hinges.

The scene was disjointed, the focus strange in the lack of understanding of a newborn. He saw her mother, the queen, looking down at her. Love, sadness, and something that looked akin to terror filled her eyes. Her lips, feather soft, brushed Reign's cheek, and she began to sing softly. The words were silver threaded with pink, and the tone carried something of a confession, wrapped in longing. A tear dripped from the queen's eyes to tickle Reign's cheek. She winced and turned her head away. The queen straightened, still holding Reign in her arms and singing the exact same lullaby Reign had been singing in the monk's memory.

The tears kept falling, and Reign kept twisting in the queen's grasp. Her mother's agitation grew, and Reign's heart began to race. Her lungs felt near to bursting, but she couldn't cry, couldn't wail, or she would only add to the queen's melancholy.

Something wrenched inside her, an agonizing feeling of burning and pain. Reign didn't know what it was, how to control it, and so she released it. The relief was instant, but only for a brief moment.

The queen tensed. Her hands squeezed at Reign hard, and the infant began to cry. The mother sank onto the bed and curled around Reign. Her eyes were wide, staring off into nothing, her breaths slowing until they no longer came at all.

The baby stopped crying.

A boy walked in.

The king walked in.

The baby started screaming again.

All hell broke loose.

CHAPTER

18

"What's going on here?" The voice was familiar, but Kalen couldn't place it, couldn't do much other than cradle his head.

"What is he doing?" The same voice. Kalen became aware enough of his surroundings to realize it was Nero who spoke. Of course. Reign had asked him to come.

Reign stood, cold air rushing to replace her body heat. "They wanted to speak with me."

"About what?"

"That's private," Luna said, an air of authority coating her words. "What are *you* doing here?"

"She called for me."

"I . . . I think I'm fine now." Reign stalled on the words, and Kalen wasn't sure if she spoke the truth or if she didn't want Nero to help her in front of them.

"Are you sure? They can leave us in privacy."

She shook her head. "Thank you for coming."

Kalen finally looked up and saw Nero standing in the doorway, his gray cloak pulled tight around his thin shoulders. His watery eyes had turned to steel, and his gaze swept back and forth across the room. Kalen was certain they made an unimposing picture, what with him incapacitated on the ground, Luna lounging with her foot against the wall, and Cirrus crouched on the balls of his feet opposite her.

Kalen forced himself to stand. "What have you been doing to Reign?"

Nero turned slowly to face him. "Nothing that she hasn't asked me to do."

Reign touched Kalen's shoulder, the sensation searing into his skin. "He helps me control my emotions, that's all."

"Reign." Nero's word spoke sentences.

Suddenly Kalen felt devoid of motivation or much action at all. He sank to the ground.

"I'm exhausted," Cirrus said, fighting a yawn.

Reign looked quizzically at Nero but didn't say much as she slid down the wall to sit at Kalen's side. Her head fell to his shoulder.

Nero practically vibrated with energy, shifting from foot to foot, his hands trembling at his sides. He glanced at Luna, who was the only one still standing. She kicked Cirrus's knee, and he barely flinched. She stepped toward Nero. "What did you do to them?"

His eyes widened, and he fled the room.

"Wait!" She ran after him, her boots kicking at loose

pebbles that went flying to ping off the walls. The sound seemed to echo in Kalen's brain, and his eyes finally closed.

He didn't know how long they stayed like that. Minutes. Possibly longer.

Luna shook him awake. "I lost him in the corridors."

"Lost who?" Kalen felt as if he spoke around a mouthful of marbles. A tendril of Reign's hair tickled his cheek, but he didn't dare push it away.

"Nero. What did he do to you all?" She kicked Cirrus's knee again, and he opened his eyes.

"He drained our desire to do anything." Reign peeled her head from Kalen's shoulder. "Took our energy." She paused. "But it didn't impact you."

"Nothing does," Cirrus said as he pushed himself into a stand.

"Honestly?" Reign was suddenly much more alert. "Do you . . . You don't . . . Do my emotions affect you?"

Luna shook her head. "Sorry."

"No." Reign launched upright. "Don't be sorry. That's amazing!" She threw her arms around Luna, who stood as still as the sculptures on the tomb across the corridor. When Luna didn't return the gesture, Reign dropped her arms to her side. She glanced in the direction Nero had fled. "Why did he do that?"

"That's an easy one," Cirrus said. "He wanted to get away without pursuit."

"But why?"

Kalen answered this time. "He has something to hide." And Kalen knew exactly what. "Why did you call Nero down here? To take your emotions? Is that what he does?"

Her lips pursed together, and her hand gripped a fist-ful of her skirts. "Yes. I should return to the inn." Reign stepped out of the room and began to cross the catacombs to the opening behind the tomb.

"Where does he put the emotions?" Luna hurried after her.

"He used to absorb it himself, like he did just now in draining us. Obviously the negative emotions take a toll on him. That's when he learned he could transfer them to ob-jects." She ducked into the tunnel, and her pace increased. Kalen practically shoved Cirrus ahead of him so he could hear Reign as she continued to talk. "He tried different items, but learned crystals are not only the best at absorbing the energy of the emotions, they are also easily destroyed."

"Destroyed?" Kalen called out from the back.

"Yes, he fills them and then takes them to the mountain edge to shatter them."

"Are you sure about that?" Kalen's shoulder brushed against the edge of the tunnel as it narrowed.

"Of course I am. Why would he want objects full of neg-ative energy?"

"Reign, he's not destroying them."

She stopped so fast that Luna tripped, and they all stalled in the tunnel. "Yes he is. I trust him; he's been nothing but helpful these past couple of years. You have no idea what it felt like, being trapped down here. It was only when he worked with me for several months that they allowed me to leave, and even then only for short periods of time until we got a process that worked and my ability somewhat under control." She paused. "I'm telling you: I'm not a princess. I'm only a danger to those around me."

Sunlight filtered in as they reached the tunnel's end.

"You're all better off without me."

————•·•————

"I DON'T KNOW if we can take her home." Cirrus smacked Luna's stick. The brothers would not allow the practice of Hakunan inside the cloister, which was fine by Kalen, as their silent, judgmental stares disturbed him.

Cirrus had led them outside the monastery walls to continue the training while they brainstormed options. He and Luna each held a long, thin branch in an outstretched hand as they danced inside a small, invisible space. Cirrus's injured arm hung at his side, and he kept his elbow tucked against his waist.

"She's your sister," Kalen said. They hadn't talked much on the trek to the monastery as Kalen's mind whirled and tried to make sense of everything. "She has the same memory."

"She has no control," Cirrus said. "How do we even deal with her? I can't breathe when she starts to get angry."

Kalen rubbed at his arms. "I'll help her. Perhaps she can better lock up some of her painful memories, or I can search her mind to try to find patterns of when she releases the emotions." He paused and stared at Cirrus. "Speaking of . . ." He waited in silence for Cirrus to stop tapping Luna's stick and turn to him.

"Have you returned to the vaulted memory?"

"I'm not that fond of it."

"No, you're afraid of it. Or rather, you're afraid of getting to it. Do me a favor and go sit with the memory for a bit. I think it will help, and perhaps you can unlock some of the knowledge on your own."

"Could you possibly be more cryptic?" Cirrus asked. Luna smacked Cirrus's good shoulder, and he whirled around to counter her next move.

Kalen waited for them to finish attacking each other.

"When I was in your mind earlier, I went to the vault." Cirrus's lips mashed into a thin line.

Kalen told him what he'd seen.

He'd raced to the memory of the princess and watched again as a young Cirrus approached his baby sister and began to choke. The king threatened to send her away. The prophet spoke. Then another woman swept in and took Reign, wailing red ribbons of cries and waving her baby fists in the air.

Cirrus wanted to run after her, he knew something bad was about to happen, but the king made him stay. A tall man in tight-fitting garments arrived shortly thereafter.

"I can't promise this will work." The man's voice was thin and high, the words pale blue and light as snow. "I'm a crafter, but I can't be sure that a mental room will stay over the years as the boy's mind develops."

"Do your best," the king said, his words threaded with black ribbons of threats.

Kalen tried to observe Cirrus's mind and the vault, while at the same time watching what the *sorcier* did in the memory. The vault didn't exist, and then suddenly it did, which was odd, because Kalen had seen it this entire time.

A confusing paradox to be sure.

The memories were nudged inside, even though they were already there, and then the *sorcier* encouraged Cirrus's mind to lock them before adding locks of his own after.

"Is there a way to discourage him from unlocking the memory himself?" the king asked.

The *sorcier* pondered this briefly. "I could build in an extra layer of protection, making him leery to go near the door at all."

And it was then Kalen saw it. He hadn't before, with his focus on the door itself and opening the locks. He hadn't seen it because it hadn't bothered him, but now that he could, it all made sense.

The exterior of the vault was shrouded in darkness. A thick cloud that seemed to pulse and retract to a beat of its own.

And then, as the *sorcier* retreated from Cirrus's mind, he crouched and faced the boy. "The darkness is absolutely terrifying. Be wary of it, as there are dangers at every turn. Always seek the light."

He rose and faced the king. "Continue to foster this fear if you want the secret to remain hidden."

The king nodded and expressed his thanks.

And then Kalen had removed himself from the prince's mind.

Cirrus leaned on his staff, his focus somewhere in the tree line behind Kalen.

"Reflect on it," Kalen said. "I think you'll find you can rid yourself of your fears." He then turned to Luna. "We need to go get those amulets. It's the only way to prove to Reign that Nero is not destroying them."

"Count me in," Cirrus said.

"No. Absolutely not." Kalen stared at him like he'd gone daft. "You're way too susceptible to the pendants' powers. Can you imagine if we find more?"

"You can't leave me here."

"Of course not. You go into town, ask to meet with Nero so we can make sure he stays away until we are clear. See about your sister, how often she's out of control, and how much she's progressed in controlling her emotions."

"Seems like a rather boring assignment," Cirrus said.

"If you dare say 'it's not fair,' I'm going to punch you." Luna undid her braid and began to replait it, tucking the strands that had loosened during the training now tight against her scalp.

"I think a kiss might make me feel better." He closed his eyes and puckered his lips. Luna dodged and brought her stick up under his neck. His eyes widened in surprise, and then she winked and leaned in to quickly brush his lips with her own.

Kalen didn't know who was more shocked by the move, him or Cirrus. Luna stepped back and released the stick from his neck. Cirrus grinned at him over Luna's head. *I win*, he mouthed.

Kalen rolled his eyes. Of course the prince was still thinking of the silly bet.

He turned to Luna. "I think it's time to visit Nero's."

LUNA AND KALEN stepped out of the monastery and hugged the outer wall behind the grounds. They moved quickly to keep warm in the falling temperature of the late afternoon and stepped through the gap cut into the tree line ahead. The sun shone through the lattice of branches above, casting a pattern on the ground. They skirted bushes and larger rocks that lined the hard-packed ground. When they reached the other side of the forest, they found an entire village of homes. Some were set farther back from the road, while others were cut into the side of the mountain at an angle that wasn't visible from the approach into the city. The residents clearly didn't want to be seen, or visited much, up this way.

Luna led Kalen through the streets and walkways toward the far outer edge of the homes. "It's that one." She pointed.

The house was two levels high and had wings jutting out over a cliff. Supports had been attached to the mountain to hold some of the weight, but the overall result was a precarious-looking structure.

"You unlock the door and stand lookout. I'll go inside to steal the pendants." Luna waited for Kalen to agree, and they inched forward. They clung to as many shadows as possible, but there was a fair amount of open space between the last house and Nero's. They dashed to the front door and stood silent on the front steps.

Kalen cracked his neck and listened for any noises within the house. An eerie silence had descended over the entire mountain. Not even the sound of a scylee bird in the trees or a rustling of the wind through the leaves.

He slid out his picks and crouched to work on the lock. Within seconds the heavy wood door opened on whisper-soft hinges. Luna swept up beside him and slid into the house. Kalen decided it would look less suspect for him to wait inside the home instead of lurking outside it.

He eased the door closed behind him, locked it, and took in the strange room he now stood in. The walls were covered in dark velvet, black or navy, he couldn't tell in the lighting. Pedestals stood in a line along one wall, each supporting a glass orb. The bottom of each sphere glowed a pale blue color, providing the only light in the space.

Curiosity got the best of Kalen, and he scooted closer to the nearest pedestal. Inside the orb a miniature frog rested, squarely in the middle of the base. Kalen assumed it was stuffed, or a toy, because it sat immobile for several seconds. Then it blinked its eyes. He startled away and then peered closer. The container was seamless, not a single hole marring its surface. The next sphere held a large, iridescent moth and the third, a small mouse.

"Kalen," Luna whispered from somewhere ahead, "you'll need to open the chest."

Kalen met her in the next room. She waved him through the space, which contained a mismatch of furniture, and down a couple of steps to a hallway that stretched to either side. She turned left, and they climbed yet more steps before she led him into an expanse of a bedroom chamber.

Kalen felt like he was falling forward.

The bed took up a large portion of the room, but it was what was beyond it that left Kalen off-balance. Two large panes of glass covered almost the entire length and height of two adjoining walls. The view was staggering. The sun had started its descent, casting a contrast on the canyon below, all dark edges and slashes of light and deep shadows. Opposite them, beyond the chasm, another mountain stretched high, its peaks only slightly lower than where they now stood.

"Over here." Luna crouched next to a chest in one of the corners. Ornate in style, it looked similar in design to the one they'd seen on the island, only this one was significantly larger.

Kalen walked past the bed and squatted next to Luna. He recalled the placement of the bits in the lock of the other chest and started there with his picks. It took only a few adjustments before the lock opened, and he stepped back.

Luna lifted the lid. The inside was lined in metal, the same bronze shade as the door in the catacombs. Two pendants lay in a velvet-lined drawer, but the chest could have easily held dozens of stones. She scooped up the jewels, and they disappeared into the folds of her cloak.

An immediate wave of anger washed over Kalen, and his gaze tore to the windows. He felt drawn to shatter them. He could imagine the shards, the piercing glass, and how it could be used as a weapon.

His gloved hands pushed him away from the window. How had he even gotten close enough to touch it?

Luna eyed him warily. "Are you all right?"

"Yes, let's go."

The pendants were clearly affecting him, and he couldn't wait to destroy them. The anger pounded in his brain, blanketing his thoughts with a heavy cloud of frustration and a desire to lash out. He closed his eyes and took a deep breath, trying his best to push away the emotion to uncover his own, more stable thoughts.

He felt in control and opened his eyes, ready to lead Luna to the front of the house. Suddenly she threw out her arm and blocked him. Her finger lifted to her lips to quiet any questions, and then he heard it, too. The sound of a door opening and casual footsteps.

His eyes darted around the room. There was no place to hide, not that he wanted to be trapped here anyway.

"There aren't any exits," Luna said. "I already checked."

They could fight their way out the front door, but Nero's powers could overcome Kalen. He didn't want to leave Luna to the task alone, so he did what any sane person would do.

He grabbed the chest and threw it through the glass window.

CHAPTER

19

Luna kicked out the glass shards jutting up from the floor and quickly flattened herself. She stuck her head over the edge and inched forward until her torso draped through the open space. Seconds later her legs flipped out into the air, and she disappeared from view.

There was no scream nor sounds of bones breaking, so Kalen knew she'd figured out a path of escape. He also knew Nero was seconds away from entering the room, based on the thunder of footsteps running down the hall.

Kalen angled his body out the window. What seemed like dozens of yards of empty space, and then the mountain, sloped beneath him. The rocks were silver blades, their edges thin and sharp and ready to pierce him.

He peered down and to the side to see that Luna had latched her legs around one of the series of long beams supporting the room and was now shimmying toward the point at which it met with the mountainside.

Kalen reached for the beam, his gloved fingers slipping. He wrapped an arm over and then pushed with his toes to shove his lower body out the window. His other arm flung around the beam as gravity took hold and yanked him down toward the maw of rocks below. He pulled his chest against the length of wood and swung his legs to lock around the beam.

Taking a couple of calming breaths, he worked his way along like an inchworm. Luna had reached the edge and released her grip to stand on the narrow ledge jutting out from the mountainside. She assessed the hand- and footholds and began her ascent, leaving the ledge open for Kalen. She was already halfway up when he finally disentangled himself from the support beam and dropped to the ledge with his back to the mountain. The ledge was so narrow that his boot tips edged over it. His back scraped the rough wall as he stepped sideways and turned to find his own path.

The temperature continued to drop, and moisture collected on the rocky surface. He found a handhold and reached out, but his gloves slipped against the frost. He quickly removed them and shoved them into his vest pockets. The frigid air bit at his fingertips, but he preferred the more stable grip.

He focused his gaze on Luna, who had reached the top and now stared down at him. He stretched his arms up, found grooves, and then did the same with his toes. His muscles screamed from the climb by the time he hauled himself up next to Luna and sprawled flat on the ground. Mountain climbing hadn't quite been on his list of recreational activities in Mureau.

"Could you imagine if Cirrus had been with us?" Luna whispered as Kalen caught his breath and pulled his gloves on. His fingers curled into the warmth of the leather as he snorted.

"There's no way he could have climbed with his arm."

"He would've charmed his way out with words."

"Or asked for a kiss?" Kalen noted the faint tinge that dusted Luna's cheeks as she ignored him.

Kalen pushed himself to his feet and paced away from the cliff. He felt the anger creep over him in proximity to the pendants again. His skin itched, and every nerve was on edge. They needed to find Reign, show her the proof, and destroy the stones.

"Nice try."

Kalen heard the words before someone tackled him from behind. The weight pushed him forward, and he barely had time to catch himself with his hands before an arm wrapped around his neck. Kalen immediately rolled, so his weight was on top of his attacker. There was a grunt, and then a knee jammed into his side.

Kalen fought to breathe, but this time he let the anger from the amulet overwhelm him. The arm around his neck held tighter, and he jerked his head backward, wincing as it connected with something hard. A growl in his ear and then release. Kalen thrust forward, launching upright before he turned around and glowered at Nero.

"Return them to me." Nero pushed himself up, brushed his hands on the leg of his pants, and stretched out one hand as if Kalen would kindly hind over the amulets.

Kalen looked to Luna, who stood off to their side. Nero's

eyes narrowed, and he lunged for her. She tried to dodge, but he gripped her shoulders and tore at her cloak. "Where are they?"

Kalen felt his legs and arms begin to weaken and knew it would be only a few moments before Nero absorbed his energy. With a last burst of effort, Kalen rushed behind Nero and grabbed his wrists. He pulled them against the *sorcier*'s lower back, trying to keep him immobile. He wished he had his Hakunan staff for a proper fight, but he would have to make do with his rudimentary wrestling skills. Nero kicked away and connected the heel of his boot with Kalen's shin. Kalen stumbled, teeth grinding together at the bloom of pain that shot through his leg, but he didn't break his grip on Nero's wrists. They fell together onto the ground. Luna was suddenly there. Her fingers gripped Nero's neck, and the *sorcier*'s head slumped forward.

Kalen took a moment to catch his breath and then crawled away from Luna to get control of the anger that had overcome him.

When he felt more himself, he stood and walked over to Nero. With deft fingers, he reached under the man's collar and grabbed the cord that hung around Nero's neck. It snapped, and Kalen removed yet another pendant that he tossed to Luna. She quickly tied the loose ends in a knot and tucked it away with the other two.

"We need to find out how many there are so we can destroy them all."

She nodded, but concern wrinkled her forehead. "Can you do this a third time today?"

"Do I have a choice?" He hesitated only briefly. "If I appear to be under duress, please pull me away. I'm not sure exactly what he—or his magick—is capable of. I don't want to be caught in a mindlock with him."

Luna nodded. "I'll be right here the entire time."

Kalen removed his gloves for the second time in the past hour and plunged into the man's unconscious mind.

He knew he had to make quick work of finding the secrets and unlocking them. Nero surely had hidden away the times he had extracted Reign's magick as well as who had purchased the amulets from him.

Kalen walked along a dimly lit tunnel lined with locked doors. This man had more secrets than a murderer. The doors themselves glowed a pale gray color. Kalen approached one midway along the hall. He gripped the key nestled against his skin and lifted it over his head. Within seconds he had the lock picked and opened the door.

A young boy huddled in the corner of a library of sorts. He sat with his head tucked into his knees, his shoulders shaking with silent sobs. An adolescent Nero paced in front of him. "Did he whip you again?"

The boy nodded.

"Let me take the pain from you. You know he was just angry with me and taking it out on you." The words were a yellow stream that increased in pitch as they left Nero's mouth.

The boy glanced up, and Kalen could see that he resembled Nero. A younger brother or cousin for certain.

"You can't keep doing it. They don't like it. Plus it hurts." The words were jagged whispers.

"I'll find somewhere else to put it. I don't have to

continue to absorb it all." Nero grabbed a book off the shelf and moved to stand beside the boy. Nero's fingers lightly gripped the back of the boy's neck, and he winced. His lips pressed together until they were colorless.

A silver thread appeared, unspooling from the boy's chest. It lengthened and twisted, winding into the pages of the book. Nero's eyes narrowed in concentration, but the thread twined through the pages and out the top, only to snake into the boy's torso again. The boy's lungs expanded, and he gasped for breath, finally wrenching from Nero's grasp and running from the room.

The shadows crept in as Nero stood still, hands in fists at his sides.

Kalen locked the door and opened the next. The lock even easier to pick now that he'd learned the *sorcier*'s wards.

This time it was a girl, and Nero tried to place her emotions in a wooden chest, which also failed to work. The girl fled the room crying.

It finally worked with a jewel, which held a silver strand without release. Nero's excitement at helping the young man, who appeared to be his friend, was short-lived as the memories shuffled and Nero increasingly was called upon to help people.

Kalen moved on, knowing he would soon be out of time. He glanced at secret after secret in the hopes of finding memories that included Reign. Finally, he found her. The princess was slumped in a pile of rags on the floor, begging Nero to help. Pale blue, the words were heavy with sorrow. "Take it away. Take away the sadness, the rage.

The brothers said they will release me only if I get it under control; please tell me you can help. I can't live like this, in these conditions." Her dirty hands reached out in supplication.

And Nero did. The crystals absorbed her emotions, time after time, growing brighter with each visit. It appeared he could use one over multiple sessions until it filled to capacity.

Kalen opened more locks, trying to figure out how many times Nero had extracted Reign's emotions, how many pendants were out there. There were obviously ones that did good, like Jules's pendant in the apothecary shop. But the ones specific to Reign were the only ones Kalen cared about.

Two . . . three . . . four . . . five . . . six.

Kalen shut the door, locked it, and exited Nero's mind.

His forehead creased in agony, and he curled into himself.

"He's starting to come to," Luna said. She tried to keep her voice soft for Kalen, but it still felt as if she were stabbing a sword through his brain. "I ran inside for some rope and bound his hands while you were in his mind, but I was almost ready to pull you out."

And with that Nero began lashing back and forth. His elbow connected with Kalen's skull. The pain exploded, and Kalen nearly passed out. He crawled away from the man and reached into his pocket for tea leaves.

"What have you done to me?" Nero eyed Kalen's uncovered hands and tried to shift to a sitting position.

"Who sanctioned the amulets?" Anger made Kalen's

question short, his patience even shorter. He had to verify it was Ryndel.

Nero's nostrils flared.

"I'll give you one chance to tell me"—Kalen touched his fingers together—"before I figure it out myself."

"Yeah, it seems questioning is *not* your preferred method." Nero glared at him.

Kalen hoped Nero wouldn't call his bluff. There was no way he could dive into the man's thoughts again without being swept under. A part of Kalen was terrified at the thought that he might exit someone's mind one day and the pain would kill him.

"Just stay away from me, and I'll tell you the truth," Nero said. "Your King's Law reached out to me via scylee bird over a year ago, asking after my talents. He wanted to know about the jewels and if there was a way he might commission them. I wondered only briefly what he wanted with the amulets, but it was none of my business. I only cared that I got to be creative and that the money came in on time."

It was a punch in the stomach to hear that Ryndel had been planning this for quite some time.

Kalen kept his face calm and nodded. "As I figured. Thank you for confirming." He rose to his feet.

"Aren't you going to untie me?" Nero wiggled his fingers from where his wrists were knotted behind him.

"I suspect you would tackle us again before we moved three feet."

They turned and trudged down the road that climbed up from the town.

Minutes passed with only the crunch of their boots, and then Luna spoke. "Perhaps we destroy them now?"

"You know we need them as proof to show Reign."

"I only thought I would suggest it, before you wear your teeth to nubby little stones."

It was then Kalen realized he'd been grinding his teeth together. "I can't believe Ryndel turned out to be such a rat. I never trusted him, but he didn't seem capable of anything larger than chasing after girls."

Luna's boot caught a stone that went tumbling away, setting Kalen's jaw to clench again. He wasn't sure if his chaos of thoughts was tied to the amulets or rather his anger that his kingdom might be in jeopardy at the hands of a manipulative rodent.

What kind of game was the King's Law playing?

It was time to find out.

———•———

A WARM GUST of air flushed his cheeks as Kalen held the door open for Luna to walk through. Cirrus lounged in a corner of the small foyer, a mug of most likely ale clasped in his hands and his makeshift Hakunan staff resting against the wall behind him.

"Took you guys long enough," he said as he lifted the drink to his lips.

"We ran into a few complications," Kalen said. "You obviously didn't do your job well."

"It's a sad story." He took a long sip and winced. "I stopped by here to ask if anyone knew where Nero might be this time of day, and then that girl wouldn't stop talking and bringing me drinks."

"What girl?" Luna tapped her foot impatiently.

"The serving girl. Sasha." Cirrus leaned in. "I swear, I tried to escape, but I didn't want to be rude."

"Right." Luna drawled out the word.

"I swear on the royal treasury. She's not my type." He turned to Kalen as if desperate to change the topic. "I'm guessing you ran into him, but successfully got away?"

Luna shook her head in disbelief. "Yeah, we ran into him."

"I'm going to find Reign." Kalen ducked into the lounge to see if the princess was serving anyone. He nearly laughed at the absurdity of the thought. *The princess. Serving food and drinks.*

She wasn't in the crowded room, so he made his way toward the swinging doors, just as Sasha walked through them in his direction.

"You're not allowed in the kitchen." She balanced a tray of food.

"Is Reign back there?"

"Yes, but you can't bother her. She has work to do." Her eyes flashed with disdain and then brightened. "Your friend is adorable by the way. I'm trying to convince him to stay at the inn tonight."

She winked, and her hips gained momentum as she walked toward the foyer.

"Good luck with that," Kalen muttered as he slipped through the doors into the kitchen.

The smell of roasted meats and fresh-baked breads made his stomach growl. He spotted Reign on the other side of open shelves filled with dried beans, baking ingredients, and spices. Her fingers danced along the different seasonings.

"I have proof."

She jumped, her eyes widening in his direction.

"I'm sorry! I didn't mean to startle you." He dragged his hands through his hair. "I thought by speaking I wouldn't scare you. Apparently that was a bad idea." So was his blunt choice of words, he knew.

Reign stepped out from behind the shelves and smoothed her hands on her skirt. "You're here, too?"

"I'm guessing you saw your brother then."

Her nose wrinkled. "Is he really my brother?"

Kalen nodded. "You both have the same memories of the day your mother died." He paused and swallowed. "And when you were banished from the kingdom."

"Banished." Her voice was low, like she hadn't meant to repeat the word aloud. "Banished." Louder this time. "And you expect me to return?"

"I don't expect you to." In fact, Kalen realized he would be surprised if she had any desire to return at all. "However, I hope you do. There was a prophecy that the kingdom would fall if the king went through with his plans to exile you."

"Good. I hope it does fall. I hope he falls, too." Her hands clenched.

He wished he knew the words that would make her want

to return with them and thus save the kingdom—her kingdom, her people. But, even more than that, he wanted to comfort her, to pull her against his chest and run his hands over her hair.

The door flew open.

"Help! He's trying to attack her!" Sasha's chest heaved as she pointed toward the foyer.

CHAPTER

20

K alen raced out ahead of Reign into the lounge. His pulse thundered in his ears, but then he heard it above his heartbeat.

Scuffles and a yelp.

"Cirrus, don't!" The words echoed down the short hallway from the foyer.

Luna.

Kalen burst into the foyer to see Luna half-hidden behind the desk, her arms extended in front of her. The amulets dripped from her fingers. Her eyes shot to Kalen, and she nodded at the jewels. "Take them and run."

He shifted forward, but before he could reach her, Cirrus lunged and yanked at her hair. He spun her around, her back to his chest and his good hand gripping the makeshift staff tight against her throat.

"Cirrus, let her go!" Kalen shouted.

Luna dropped the amulets to the carpeted floor and clawed at his arm with her fingernails. Her eyes bulged with panic. Cirrus's lips squeezed together, and he tightened his grip around her neck.

"Cirrus!" Kalen reached them and grabbed at the wound on Cirrus's arm. The prince didn't even react.

One of Luna's arms dropped, and she dug into her cloak.

"She was talking behind my back." His eyes locked on Kalen. They had turned from pale to a dark, searing midnight.

Luna thrashed again, her leg kicking into the desk.

"She can't be trusted." Cirrus scooted away from Kalen, dragging Luna with him. "We need to leave. Now. We need to go home before the prophecy comes true."

Reign gasped from behind Kalen, and Cirrus's focus turned to her. With his attention diverted, Kalen took action. Instead of lunging for Cirrus's arm again, he shot his hand out toward Luna. Her fingers released the vial he'd seen clasped in her hand. It fell, small and cool, into his palm. He uncapped it and brought it up to Cirrus's nose in one swift motion. Cirrus whipped his head to the side in an effort not to inhale the vapor, but he wasn't fast enough. The prince collapsed to the ground, taking Luna with him. Luckily, his chest broke her fall, and his arm collapsed, pulling the staff from her neck.

She scrambled away on hands and knees. Once she'd gained some distance, her hands flew to her neck, fingers spread to cover and soothe the red marks now staining her skin. She stared at Cirrus for several long seconds. With a jagged breath she reached out for the vial. Kalen corked it and dropped it in her hand. Without even looking at it, she tucked it into her cloak.

"That was my last use," she said.

"Good thing we didn't waste it on Nero," Kalen said.

Reign stepped closer. "What happened to him?"

Luna reached over to grab the amulets from where they lay scattered on the floor, a mess of leather cords and sparkling jewels, reflecting the sunlight flooding at an angle through the front window. She gathered them and held them up.

Reign's hands fluttered to her mouth. "Those are my crystals."

"Yes, and you can see what they do to people." Kalen felt the agitation settling over him like an acidic mist. "They turn your brother into a murderous lunatic. They turn everyone angry. This is what we have been trying to tell you."

Reign extended her arm toward Luna, who handed them to her. She cupped them in open palms and peered closer. "I don't understand. He was supposed to destroy them. He promised he would destroy them." Her voice tripped on the last of her words.

Luna buried her hands in her cloak. "He didn't." The words were quiet, no trace of her characteristic biting tone.

"What is he doing with them?" Reign's fingers curled over the amulets protectively.

Kalen braced himself against the pulses of anger flowing from the crystals. "He's been selling them to our kingdom to use as weapons. Ryndel, the King's Law, has been turning our people—your people—against one another. He's inciting unrest, but I worry that there's a bigger plan at work."

"Where are they? How many are there?"

Kalen paused. "I believe Ryndel has two of yours. We already destroyed one, and there are the three here."

"You have to take them from Ryndel." She paused and took a breath. "We have to take them." She swallowed hard and spoke louder again. Her fingers released the amulets and then clenched tighter as she seemed to reach a level of panic. "We have to get them. And then I'm going into hiding. This can't happen again."

Kalen's stomach twisted with nausea as he fought against the combined despair flooding from her and the magicked anger coming from the crystals. "Reign, if you're able to calm down, without Nero's help, please try." He spoke through gritted teeth. "We absolutely plan to do as you ask, and we want you to join us. However, first things first." He paused and looked to Luna. "We have to destroy those."

"I'll do it," Reign said. She clutched the jewels to her chest.

"No," Kalen said, the word loud and harsh in his ears.

"They are mine. I want to be the one to do this." She stepped backward as if expecting Kalen to take the crystals from her.

"Reign." He inhaled a shaky breath and tried to conjure positive thoughts to negate the magick. Unfortunately, there wasn't much positivity in his life. His parents abandoning him, his delving constantly into the minds of criminals, his increasing headaches. But one glance at Reign and he realized how similar they were. They both had had rough childhoods, but they had moved beyond them, they were still standing, stronger, about to do something that mattered.

Something like saving a kingdom. "You can't be the one to destroy them."

"Why?" Her lips turned down.

Luna swept in and plucked the amulets out of Reign's hands. Reign lunged to grab them, but Luna danced away. "Because we've done it before. There's some strange vapor that releases from them that may be the emotions trapped inside. The last thing we want is for them to absorb into you."

Kalen nodded, thankful for her explanation.

"Then who is going to do it?" Reign's empty hands fell to her sides. She glanced at Kalen. "Not you."

"Not me." He agreed with her.

"I'm going to do it, just as I did the other one." Luna grabbed Cirrus's staff from the floor and headed toward the front door. Kalen followed close behind.

"Where are you going?" Reign asked, reaching for Kalen's arm. He felt the heat from her touch travel up his arm and into the center of his chest.

"She's my friend. I need to be there to help if necessary."

Reign's hand fell, and with it the heat.

"You need to stay here and watch your brother," Kalen said as Luna opened the door and stepped through. "He will awaken soon."

Reign's eyes flicked to where Cirrus still lay sprawled on the floor.

"Just don't get too close to him. He reacts to you, too," Luna called as she bounded into the street.

Kalen let the door shut behind him, leaving the prince and princess ensconced in the lounge area.

Knowing they needed privacy so the emotions wouldn't latch on to anyone, they paced toward the end of the road, where it curved sharply in on itself and to the upper elevations. Instead of turning to follow the path, they walked toward the cliff's edge. The flat surface gave way to jagged rocks right before the ledge stopped in a sheer wall to the valley below. Kalen let Luna walk ahead, hoping the distance would be enough that the emotions wouldn't seep in his direction once they were released.

Luna faced away from Kalen toward the abyss in front of her. She removed the hood of her cloak, allowing her silver hair to tangle and twist down her back. The wind tugged at the strands as they shone near-white in the horizontal rays of the sun behind them. She reached into her cloak and pulled out the cords. The faceted edges of the jewels blinded him as they reflected the sunlight. She dropped them to the ground. Booted toes nudged the amulets next to one another. She took a deep breath, and then, with a hefty swing, she bent over and slammed the staff head onto the surface of the first jewel.

Wisps of airy black tendrils pushed through the crack and twisted into the air. Kalen poised, ready to rush forward if they turned toward Luna, but they continued upward, thinning further and separating until they were no longer visible at all.

She smashed the second one, and before the black trail fully disappeared, she lifted the staff to swing again.

"No!" The shout erupted from seemingly nowhere, yet somehow Kalen had been expecting it, tense with anticipation. Nero would not let such masterful work be destroyed so easily. "Those took years to create. They're my life's fortune. Stop!"

Nero came running at Luna from the switchback above. Kalen sprinted forward in an attempt to stop him.

It was a collision of arms and legs, heads and staff.

An unfortunate collision.

The staff struck the jewel just as Kalen and Nero reached Luna. The black thread wound its way upward but then twisted, latching onto the object closest to it.

Nero.

His eyes bulged. His chest heaved. His rage built.

And he shoved Kalen. Hard.

Kalen flew through the air like he'd been kicked by a massive beast, the force of Nero's hands lifting him off the ground. Kalen's arms whirled as he tried to regain his balance, but he kept moving away, shifting, scuffling.

His feet fought for purchase.

And then there was nothing.

He plummeted as if the weight of the world clung to his ankles. His gloved hands grabbed for something, anything, to keep him from falling off the edge of the cliff. His boots dug at the wall, searching for holes as he continued to slip and fall. Gloves grasped at anything, the errant stone or wisp of a root. He slid farther, until he stopped suddenly. Hands gripped his own, and his head jerked upward.

"I've got you."

Luna, little Luna, lay on her stomach, her arms stretched down the mountainside so her hands held his own. He knew she couldn't hold him for long. He frantically tried to find a groove wide enough to support his weight. He slipped, one leg swinging wide, and his toes finally caught a small ledge. A gasp escaped his lungs as he fought to hold himself steady.

Suddenly his gloves slipped, and Luna's eyes widened.

"Hold tight." She adjusted her grip.

The arms of his cloak slid down, allowing the barest gap of skin. The leather of his gloves continued to slip from her hands.

"Help!" she screamed, the sound wrenched from her mouth. "Is anyone around? Please, can anyone help me?"

His hands slipped farther, and his pulse thundered in his ears. He looked down at the gaping jaws of the mountain beneath him and then up at Luna.

A shadow cast her in darkness. Nero loomed over her, ready to thrust her into the abyss, and Kalen along with her.

CHAPTER

21

Nero's eyes were darker than a starless sky. His palms lifted to propel Luna forward.

Suddenly he jolted sideways. A glimpse of red hair and then Reign started beating on the *sorcier*'s chest.

"How dare you?" she shrieked. "How dare you use me as a weapon?" She shoved him back a step. He blinked repeatedly at her, as if she spoke a foreign language.

Luna adjusted one hand so she gripped Kalen's wrist. It allowed for a little more stability as he looked around for another foothold. A pulse of anger enveloped him, but he isolated it and continued to concentrate on staying alive.

"You used me. You told me you were helping me, and you used me." Reign's voice wavered between anger and hurt. She shoved him again, and he shuffled, unbalanced. "I trusted you, and you destroyed it. You destroyed me, everything I've built and tried to accomplish. You made it all worthless. Even worse, you turned it against innocent people." Another shove. Nero tilted off-balance, as if his legs couldn't support his own weight.

"Reign, stop!" Luna shouted. Her grip on Kalen tightened as she twisted her head to watch the duo.

"You."

A shove.

"Destroyed."

Another shove.

"Me."

"Reign, no!" Cirrus's voice rang over the edge of the cliff.

Nero collapsed like a marionette whose master had dropped the crossbar, allowing the arms and legs and body to fold in on itself. He listed to the side and, helpless to stop the momentum, tumbled over the edge of the cliff. He didn't utter a sound as he fell through open space. Kalen closed his eyes, not wanting to watch what would happen when Nero's body connected with the chasm floor below.

A stronger grip replaced Luna's. Cirrus appeared in Kalen's view and his good arm now locked around Kalen's.

"Hold on."

Kalen dug his feet in and scrambled up as Cirrus lifted him from above. Luna had led Reign farther up the road, still on the switchback but away from the boys, as if to prevent Reign's emotions from overwhelming them and causing further harm.

Once his feet were on solid ground, Kalen bent over, chest heaving. "Thank you," he managed.

"Thanks for not killing me when I"—Cirrus swallowed hard—"tried to hurt Luna."

"Yeah, I think I'm going to be holding on to that flicker-fly ring for a while longer," Kalen said.

Cirrus traced a circle in the dirt with his boot. Kalen straightened, and they looked over to where Luna spoke to Reign. "What do we do now?"

Kalen squatted and gathered up the cracked amulets. Even ruined, they blinded him with their brilliance.

"Four down. Two to go," he said. "We need to get home."

They walked over to Luna and Reign.

"Everything okay?" Cirrus asked as the girls' conversation stalled.

Reign gave a shaky laugh and backed up several yards. "Everything is far from okay. I just killed a man—"

"You lost control," Kalen said. He took a step closer, but she held out her hand so he would maintain his distance. He wondered if it was a gesture of protection for herself or to keep him farther away from her emotions. "It wasn't intentional, and we can work on that."

"You saved Kalen's life," Luna said. "And mine. If you hadn't arrived when you did, Nero would have surely pushed us both over the edge. He was like a man possessed when he absorbed the crystal's negativity."

"But"—her hands rose to her mouth, as if she could prevent a wail from escaping—"he's dead. And I am a part of that."

Cirrus ran his fingers through his hair. "He's dead. I'm not dismissing that, but we need to keep moving. We have the ability to save others from these amulets, if only we can return in time."

"Spoken like a true prince there." Kalen nudged Cirrus's shoulder with his own.

"Hey." Cirrus winced and rubbed at his still-healing wound.

Reign shook her head. "I don't know if I should go. I don't know if—" But her words were interrupted by several voices shouting from the direction of the shops.

"What happened?"

"Is it an eclipse?"

"I can't see!"

"Don't move. Everyone stay back from the edge."

The foursome glanced at one another and came to an unspoken agreement. They had to figure out what was going on. They ran toward the center of town but stopped short. Townspeople rubbed at their eyes or held their hands out in front of them so as not to run into something. Several lay on the ground where they had tripped in their haste to flee. And there, facing them, cloaked in black, stood the *sorcier* bounty hunter from the tournament. His black hair was tied in a low ponytail, and his pale skin seemed to glow.

Kalen threw out his arms to protect the girls, and it was only then that he realized that Luna had disappeared.

"Bloody crow," Cirrus muttered under his breath. "Here comes the darkness."

"Fancy running into you here," the *sorcier* called to them across the crowd, his voice soothing.

Kalen felt a foreign presence pushing at his mind. A pressure nudging his senses. The hairs on his arms stood upright, and he mentally rebelled against it.

"Who is that?" Reign asked in Kalen's ear.

"He followed us from Mureau. He's a bounty hunter with an ability."

"Leave the citizens alone," Cirrus called out. "They wish you no harm."

"Ah yes, it's unfortunate that they are in the way. Perhaps you can make it easy on them and come with me now? I'd be happy to release them. You see, your ransom is my ticket home." The *sorcier* stepped forward, closing the gap to bring them within range of his power.

Kalen felt Reign begin to tense at his side.

Cirrus turned to Kalen. "Let's split up and meet by the stable." He took off at a sprint toward two storefronts directly to their right. Kalen reached for Reign's hand, but the scene suddenly turned black.

"I guess you'd rather make it difficult," the bounty hunter said. "For you, anyway."

The sudden blindness was all-encompassing, throwing Kalen off-balance. His gloved fingers grazed Reign's, and then there was nothing.

"Kalen!" The panic was clear in her voice. He felt movement and then his hand touched her arm. He quickly curled his fingers around her bicep to keep her close.

"Stay calm," he spoke softly to her. "Keep your emotions under control." He didn't think he could handle another wave of her ability. He shuffled her toward the direction Cirrus had headed.

So much for splitting up.

But Kalen wanted to get away from the *sorcier* as quickly as possible.

Reign stumbled, and his grip tightened on her. They kept

moving, and Kalen threw out his other hand in the hopes of finding the edge of a building. Finally, it scraped against a rough brick surface. Kalen scooted along the wall, away from the *sorcier*, his hand grappling for some sort of handle or door to push through.

"You can't hide." The *sorcier*'s voice came from all angles, disconcerting in the blindness. Kalen sensed the movement of something sweeping past him from behind. He tensed, wondering if it was the bounty hunter, Luna, or something else altogether.

His hand finally found a lip, a door frame, and his fingers scrambled for the handle. He pushed down, but the door was locked. A curse escaped his mouth.

Reign's breaths came in frantic gasps. "You can control this." He squeezed her hand as he continued to scoot them away from the *sorcier* in search of another door.

Somewhere in the direction of the cliff, the noise of breaking glass erupted. "Bloody crow," Cirrus yelped. Kalen tugged Reign toward him.

"Don't worry." The *sorcier*'s voice was right next to them, and they both jumped, startled. "I'm sure he's not that injured."

Reign squeezed her fingers into a fist tight around Kalen's hand. She held her breath, and then her magick unleashed. Kalen yelled to Cirrus to run as the flood of panic burst from Reign. A vise tightened around his chest, and his lungs desperately sought air.

The *sorcier* groaned, and suddenly Kalen could see again. The scene flickered from color to darkness as the *sorcier* tried to retain his grip on his magick. As Kalen's vision returned, he made out the bounty hunter now several feet away up against another building. He was bent over at the waist, his head buried in his hands.

"Over here!" Kalen saw a sweep of silver, and Luna waved them toward her. She was on the other side of the *sorcier*, closer to the stables, standing in the middle of the street. Darkness filled his vision again, but he had a grip on Reign and ran.

"Stop." The *sorcier*'s voice sounded strangled and unfocused. Kalen could see again.

"Contain that man." Cirrus had joined them and yelled at the townspeople, who now blinked their eyes and looked around in confusion. "Take him to be questioned."

"No!" the bounty hunter yelled. "Grab *them*! They are wanted criminals from Mureau."

The citizens of Servaille hesitated as the trio reached Luna and continued to run toward the stable. Jules stepped away from a crowd that had gathered outside the Snowbound Inn.

"What is going on?" she asked Cirrus.

"That man is a criminal sent from Mureau. As the prince of that kingdom," he ignored her intake of breath, "I give you permission to arrest and hold him until we send for him for trial. But be careful. He's a *sorcier* with the ability to blind everyone in a short radius."

Jules quickly dispatched two men in the direction of the bounty hunter before she turned to Reign. "Do you need me to get Nero?"

"No." Reign shook her head side to side, the motion frantic. "No."

Kalen urged Cirrus forward to get him out of the way if Reign lost control again. "Have them ready the horses."

Cirrus ran ahead while Jules continued to try to comfort Reign. "He can help; he's always been able to help."

Reign squared her shoulders. "No. He hasn't. He used me. He sold the amulets."

"I don't believe that."

"He did. And he . . . he's . . ."

"He fell over the edge," Luna said, pointing off to the switchback on the road. "It was an accident."

"We need to go." Kalen spoke softly in Reign's ear.

"I'm sorry," Reign said to Jules.

"Wait. You have to explain." Jules tried to step in front of them. "You can't just leave."

"Unfortunately, we must," Kalen said. "Now. Please do as Cirrus suggested and hold that man captive. We will send reinforcements and coin for any damages."

He tugged Reign's hand, urging her to follow so they could leave the city.

"I'm sorry," Reign said again over her shoulder to Jules. "The town will be better off without me. Thank you for everything."

By the time the trio reached the stable, Cirrus stood in the street with the horses. Luna and Cirrus each mounted their steed as the stable boy thrust the reins of Kalen's horse into his hands, as well as a pile of thin blankets. Single file, they made their way through the arch and out of the city walls.

CHAPTER

22

Reign rode in silence for the first half hour. She rubbed at her arms, and Kalen tried to rearrange one of the blankets around them as night continued to fall. "I'm sorry," she finally said. "I thought I had control, but I don't. I don't think I should stay with you. You're better off leaving me at the next town."

"Reign, you saved us."

Cirrus voiced his agreement. "This time your unleashed powers worked to our advantage."

"Do you ever try to control it?" Kalen asked. "I mean, on your own without the jewels."

She released the grip she had on her arms. "I did in the beginning. But then I couldn't stop it anymore. What if it happens again? I can't risk killing someone else."

"You saved us," Kalen repeated. "If it happens again,

please feel free to use your magick to protect us." He waited for the words to sink in. "That's exactly what you did. You saved us from being captured. You released us from the *sorcier*'s control. Your magick isn't all bad. It isn't negative or positive on its own. It's how you choose to use your magick that determines the outcome. If you can control it and harness it, you could be more powerful than anyone I know."

She sat in silence as if considering his words, and while she didn't seem happy about the idea, she didn't protest. After a minute, she took a deep, yet unsteady breath and nodded. "Okay."

"I might be able to help further," Kalen said.

"How?"

"If I were to go into your memories, I could look for triggers or see if there are common occurrences. There has to be a way for you to gain control."

There was silence and then: "I don't know."

"We have several days' travel ahead of us."

"You should let him help," Luna urged her.

"I'll think about it," Reign acquiesced.

The temperature continued to fall as the sun completed its descent. The sky darkened quickly and with it, Cirrus's mood. They agreed to stop, only because they feared the animals would slip on the frost-covered ground.

They stopped in a clearing, and Cirrus made quick work building a fire. As the flame took hold, he kept throwing glances behind him, into the thicket of trees.

"Enough," Luna said. "You're going to make us all crazy, and this time you can't blame it on your sister." She reached into her cloak and removed a glass sphere, the size perfectly matching her palm. She tapped the glass, and the orb lit up against the night sky.

"Where did you get a flickerfly orb?" Cirrus asked.

"Nero had a lot of oddities in his house. I figured this one could be of use. Good thing for us I never had time to drop it off at the monastery. Although I wish we could have had two seconds to gather our things. I am going to miss my change of clothes."

"Forget clothing. I wish we'd had time to pack food," Cirrus said, his stomach grumbling as if to further agree. "But I am thankful for the light." He glanced down at Luna and then quickly kissed the top of her head. "This is probably the best gift I've ever received."

Kalen glanced at Cirrus and then Reign and then Cirrus again. "You know, it might help you further if we talk about your memory."

"No way. Luna just got me the perfect gift, and you want to diminish that? I see where you're going with this."

Kalen grimaced in Cirrus's direction. He tilted his head toward Reign in an effort to make the prince understand. If Cirrus allowed Kalen to help, Reign might allow it as well.

"However . . . ," the prince drawled as he grasped Kalen's intention, "perhaps it might make sense to have you help in case the orb stops working or it breaks."

Kalen swept his hand to the log nearest them. Cirrus reached out to pull Luna down with him. She moved to scoot away, but he patted the seat.

"Stay."

She opened her mouth as if to berate the command.

"Please."

Luna's mouth closed and she sat. Kalen settled on the other side of Cirrus and took a deep breath. "I'm only going to look at the memory again so I can help you understand it. I don't want to be in your mind long. You can't see what I'm doing, so that is not even helpful. I only want to assist you in finding it."

Because that was the problem. Cirrus could see it. The memory remained unlocked. But it was so clouded in darkness that Cirrus wouldn't revisit it again.

Kalen quickly removed a glove and grasped Cirrus's wrist before the prince could back out.

He rushed to the recesses of Cirrus's mind and witnessed again the *sorcier*'s ability. His crafting of the vault and the shrouding darkness placed over it. He saw again the man crouching in front of Cirrus and telling him to always seek the light. Watched as he looked at the king and told him to foster the fear.

Kalen nudged the darkness with his hand, watching as it pulsed and retreated, a swill of dark gray smoke. It seemed malleable; Cirrus only needed to push through.

Kalen broke the connection.

The headache wasn't nearly as crushing this time, considering he had only dived in for a minute or so.

Kalen donned his glove, this time more to protect his hand from the frigid temperatures than to protect him from seeing someone's thoughts. He pushed himself upright and walked around the fire so he sat next to Reign, his eyes locking on the prince.

"You've seen the memory. I left it open the night the king

had me enter your mind and you pulled away. So you know where it is."

Cirrus nodded.

"I think you can push past it. Try using your body." He paused. "Or even better, imagine taking the orb or casting sunlight on it. Search and push past your fears of darkness to see the truth for what it is."

Cirrus nodded and closed his eyes. Over the flames, Kalen saw that he clenched Luna's hand tighter, but she made no effort to wiggle free of his grasp.

"Come," Kalen muttered to Reign. "Let's clear a space for everyone to sleep."

They worked in a synchronized silence to move rocks away from the area around the fire and gather some dried branches to lie on.

Cirrus opened his eyes.

He stood and paced toward the tree line and back several times before he spoke.

"All these years, my father knew of my irrational fear of the dark." His tone was laced with bitterness. "And do you know what he did?" Cirrus didn't even wait for a response. "He perpetuated it. Embellished my nightmares, made me go outside at night by myself—" He stopped abruptly, and his head tipped toward the sky. "Gods, I think he even had me locked in the treasury one night."

Reign flinched. "Maybe I was lucky to be free of him."

Kalen walked over to the prince, his childhood friend, and placed a hand on his shoulder. "I'm sorry. We know his motivation, but it doesn't make it right. Hopefully, you'll begin to work through your fears, knowing that there is nothing behind them but magick and deception."

"I hope so, but it will probably take time to get over this. All of it." He reached for the orb and held it tight against his chest. "In the meantime, I have something else that will help."

Cirrus looked around the circle at the three of them. "I'll take first watch. I have some things to ponder."

Kalen wasn't about to fight him on it, although he did make the prince promise to wake them at their fair turn. He didn't want Cirrus tired and susceptible to his sister's emotions the next day as they continued their journey to Antioege.

———

THE FIRST STRANDS of light colored the horizon as Kalen lay on his back several yards from the fire. The last to keep watch, he had scooted away in hopes the cold would help him stay awake. He'd stared at the darkened sky with its endless stars and the moon hanging off center and couldn't help but think of Luna's story, of the girl who was afraid of the dark and the boy who brought her light and became her moon. It was odd, really. If he were to flip the characters, he would have Cirrus and Luna herself. The boy afraid of the dark and the girl who brought him light in the form of a flickerfly orb.

Kalen stretched and walked toward the tree line, where he thought he'd heard the gurgling of water. A small stream flowed over rocks, and he bent to splash the frigid water on his face. He spotted berries growing on vines, and he gathered them to take to the group. He then set about waking the others so they could get on the road and stay—hopefully—one step ahead of the bounty hunter.

Reign rode with Kalen again, and he was thankful for the warmth as the sun would take a while to provide any semblance of heat. They sat in a comfortable silence for a while before she spoke.

"I will let you help."

He waited as she seemed to struggle with what to say next.

"I know you've gone into my mind before, but what exactly do you see? Everything?" She tensed, the movement causing the horse to shift beneath them.

He was quick to answer. "I don't see everything. I have to search and sift through memories. They are not all exposed and available, so I will be respectful not to view anything that looks too personal. I will look for specific memories where you lose control over your emotions and see if I can identify any commonalities. There has to be a way for you to gain control of this."

"Do you want to do it now?" Her voice was barely a whisper.

"No, I need to be on solid ground. We'll do it when we stop for a break."

Reign sighed and leaned back against him. His breath hitched before he allowed himself to relax as well, just breathing in the scent of her hair and feeling the tickle of it against his cheek.

———•—•———

REIGN AND KALEN sat, facing each other, on a patch of grass while Luna and Cirrus went off in search of something to eat. Reign slowly removed Kalen's glove. The leather slid over his skin as her fingers plucked at the fingertips, causing goose pimples to erupt on his arm.

She gripped his hand in hers, and he was swept under.

Kalen took in the surroundings again, noticing that her thoughts were contained in a space much like the catacombs. In the main cavern were the painful ones, the fractured images that reflected off one another. On either end, the hallways stretched, and he knew other memories were held in rooms there.

Kalen went in search of those memories that might be indicative of Reign's inability to control the strength of her power. He peered into the openings quickly, trying, as promised, not to completely invade her privacy.

His heart felt heavy in his chest as he observed scene after scene of her loneliness. In one memory she was with a group of children in what appeared to be an orphanage on the outskirts of Servaille. Even there she seemed isolated, sitting off by herself in a corner. Finally, a little girl came over and held out her hand. Reign tentatively grasped the girl's fingers and let herself be led to the middle of the room. There was no burst of emotion, only a sense of calm.

Another room showcased a trio of boys standing over Reign. They were a couple of years older than her, perhaps in their teens to her ten years old. They threw pebbles at her bare arms. "You're a witch. Horrible little witch." They taunted her with green ribbons of words. "Go back to where you came from and leave us alone." Tears coursed down her cheeks, but she said nothing. Kalen saw the moment her power erupted, like her emotions had hit a tipping point, and the boys began to choke on despair. They wailed and ran off as if chased by a pack of wolves. He watched her body for tells, as he would the players at a card table. Her hands curled into fists tight at her sides and released, like he'd seen her do with her skirts at the inn.

He moved on. A slightly younger Reign sat on the top step of the monastery entrance. Thin legs poked out of a dress, and her red hair was snarled at the back of her head. "Please don't leave me here." Tears streamed as she watched a woman walk away down the path. "Please!" she screamed before her voice dropped to a whisper. "I didn't mean to. I didn't mean to." She sobbed into her arms until the door opened behind her. A monk stood with his arms crossed in front of him. "Clean your face and come inside. We have just the place for you to stay."

And thus it went.

Reign in control.

Reign alone, without family, without friends.

Reign out of control, her fingers folding into fists and waves of emotion rolling away from her.

He extracted himself from her mind.

The pain hit him so fast and hard that he fell forward. She caught his shoulder with one hand and reached for his hand with her other. He was immediately swept into her mind again.

Her most recent thoughts were vivid in front of him.

Vivid *of* him.

Of his hand gripping hers and his eyes closed in concentration. His forehead furrowed and his eyelids twitching.

He felt Reign's concern, and she whispered aloud.

"The slower you can come out of these episodes, the less pain you will feel."

She was talking to him, through her memories of talking to herself.

"Relax. Close your eyes. Try to acclimate yourself to your surroundings out here. Imagine the log you're sitting on, cold and hard beneath your legs. Picture the sun and the cool breeze. Place yourself here, and then release my hand when you're ready."

His eyes closed, but his fingers gripped hers tighter. He didn't want to let go; he didn't want her to let go. The pain had disappeared, and he didn't want it to return. He pictured the clearing, using all his senses, and severed the connection.

She waited, expectantly, her gaze traveling over his face to look for signs of pain.

"Thank you," he said as he put on his glove. "I've never . . . I've never had someone do that for me."

"You're doing the same, trying to help."

He nodded and told her what he'd seen in her memories and how her fists clenched before her emotions erupted. "It's not a trigger, necessarily, but it's a sign we can look for. If you could find another way to release that tension, instead of sending out a wave of emotion, you might be able to better control the magick."

Cirrus shouted in their direction. "Come on, you two. We need to get on the road."

Reign frowned but Kalen stood and held out a hand to assist her up. "Best be listening to your brother. He'll be king someday."

"My brother." The words were a whisper that bled into silence. "I assumed I was an orphan all these years. Now I have this person in my life, this whole other history of who I am, and I don't know what to do with it." She paused. "I don't know if I want it."

"Come to Mureau, help us destroy the crystals, and then you can decide. Learn about the town, meet the people. You have an entire continent to explore if you find you don't want to stay."

Her gaze focused on the grass at their feet. "A continent to destroy."

"No. You'll get control of this. I promise."

By MIDDAY, with only berries in their stomachs, they were ravenous. Cirrus attempted to distract them.

"Maybe some more Hakunan training?" he asked Luna.

She rolled her eyes. "On horseback?"

"It's not all physical, Little Pebble. And don't knock it. Are you feeling prepared for that sea travel home?"

"Little Pebble?"

"Yeah. The moon is only a rock that orbits our planet. A small rock comparatively."

"That's the only nickname you could come up with? How about Oh Stunning Beauty of the World?" Luna attempted a bow from her horse.

Cirrus shook his head. "No. No way."

"What are they talking about?" Reign asked Kalen.

"Hakunan," Cirrus said, while at the same time Luna replied, "Exhaustion disguised as meditation."

"Did it help you on the ship or not?" Cirrus asked.

She sighed. "It helped."

Kalen agreed. "I do it often after a draining questioning to clear my mind of all the negativity I've seen."

"It must be hard, seeing what all these people have done in their lives." Reign looked over her shoulder at him.

"It is. It's why I have to unlock the secrets. They aren't locking them from me; they are locking them from themselves. Their deepest darkest secrets are hidden away so they don't have to remember, don't have to reflect on or examine the consequences of their actions on others. I see their flaws and lies in full, vibrant reality."

A loose tendril of Reign's hair brushed against his cheek as the wind picked up. They neared another switchback that would cut across the mountain face.

"Try it. Close your eyes," Cirrus instructed Reign. "Not you," he said in Luna's direction. "You can try it later, when you're not guiding an animal ten times your size."

"Thanks for pointing out the obvious," she said.

He continued. "Locate your center of gravity and then focus on each of the directions. This will bring you to the present and allow for more control of your emotions. Concentrate on your body's movement and reactions to each of your senses."

"It's similar to what you said to try to help me exit people's minds," Kalen whispered in Reign's ear.

Single file, the horses wound their way down the trail, and Kalen waited in silence for Reign to work through the meditation. Her breathing fell into a rhythm of deep inhalation and exhalation that he could feel against his chest.

"It tastes like a storm." Her voice was hoarse when she finally spoke.

Kalen nodded, his chin grazing the top of her hair. He'd been watching the gathering of clouds and darkening of the sky in the distance. "I'm hoping it moves slow enough that we're under the cover of the trees when it hits."

The last thing they needed was to be caught on the open trail and unable to see.

CHAPTER

23

Cirrus, at the head of the line, increased their speed as much as was safe for the horses' footing on the path. The wind picked up and the clouds swelled as they hurried along the switchbacks in hopes of finding a road that would lead away from the cliff's edge. Sleet began to slice from the sky, hitting their faces and slipping into the gaps of their clothing.

"Hurry," Cirrus shouted, the word ripped from him to scatter in all directions.

They reached another bend as the storm continued to worsen. Snow flurried, and the horses grouped together in the whiteout. Cirrus slowed their pace. One misstep and any of the horses could tumble off the edge. Kalen refused to imagine the journey ending here and now, on the cliff of a mountain they were so close to reaching the base of.

Kalen noticed Reign's hands begin to fist in her lap. Panic built, palpable, around her, begging for release. He resisted the urge to tighten his hold on the reins and instead leaned in so his mouth was next to her ear. "Close your eyes. Focus on your breath. Inhale as you count to five. Exhale as you count from five. I've got you."

He began to count as she forced a shaky inhale. He stopped at five. "Hold it for a second—now exhale." And he counted backward.

A gust of wind tore at his cloak, and his horse sidestepped toward the steep rock wall on their right-hand side. Kalen's elbow grazed the rough stone. Reign's breath hitched, and he quickly resumed the meditation.

"There's a sharp turn up here. Go slow." Cirrus's voice carried over the screeching of the storm. The flurry had lifted enough to give Kalen a glimpse of Luna in front of him. He wondered if they should have climbed off the horses to lead them along the path but had to trust Cirrus in this. The prince had traveled with the Mureaun military far more frequently than Kalen had ever left the town's walls.

Reign's hand fisted against his thigh, and he quickly started counting again.

The horse slowed, hesitant as it twisted around the sharp bend. The wind battered them now from the other side, buffeting them toward the chasm below.

"It opens up from here," Cirrus called over his shoulder.

Kalen nudged the horse to go a little faster.

It was a mistake.

The animal sped up, only slightly, but enough so that when its hooves hit the patch of ice, it slid. Its head swung toward the wall and its back toward the cliff. Kalen yanked on the reins, desperately trying to keep the animal, along with him and Reign, from tumbling into the abyss.

"Five," he said as her fist balled again. "Four."

The horse scrambled, obtained its balance, and took a shaky step forward.

"Three."

He felt her curve against his chest as she continued her exhalation.

"Two."

The trail started to widen ahead of them, and the wind softened its assault. Kalen found his breaths came easier with each step away from the cliff's edge.

"One."

They entered the darkness of the tree line and could finally see. Cirrus urged the horses onward, toward a cluster of trees with branches reaching high, knotting together to form a canopy that kept the ground dry below. Kalen focused on Reign's fingers, watching as—bit by bit—they uncurled.

She had done it. The meditation had helped her control her emotions. He only hoped it would work when they encountered other people and a situation that escalated quickly.

THE STORM SET them back several hours, but it had probably kept the bounty hunter at bay, too. After another cold night with nothing to eat other than the berries, they finally reached the foothills and left the last patch of snow behind.

Kalen urged his horse to a stop, figuring it was as good a time as any to stretch his legs. Reign slid awkwardly off Luna's horse, which she had ridden that morning. She shifted from side to side, testing her legs to see if they would buckle. "I don't care if I never see a horse again for the rest of my life," she said.

"Oh come now, they're not all that bad," Kalen said, patting his horse's forehead.

"Tell that to my bruised tailbone and aching groin muscles." She tried to take a step and pitched forward. Before Kalen reached her, she had steadied herself again. She muttered obscenities as she paced along the edge of the road, finally sitting, with her legs outstretched and ankles crossed, on a large flat rock.

Cirrus began to sing a bawdry tune and threw an arm around Luna's neck. He pulled her close, her silver hair a stark contrast to his reddish mop. She settled for a minute and then pushed away with a roll of her eyes. Kalen had a feeling he'd be giving up his flickerfly ring sometime in the near future, much to his continued surprise.

Reign lay flat on the rock, her eyes closed against the harsh sunlight that broke through the clouds. Kalen wanted to shake off the stiffness in his body, so he took a quick walk toward the stream they'd been riding next to for the last hour. He bent over to dip in his hands. He cupped his fingers, splashed cold water on his face, and scrubbed at his hair.

"How do you think she'll fare in Mureau?" Cirrus startled him as he burst through the bushes.

"I was able to walk her through some meditation during

the storm and when our horse lost its footing. We'll have to continue working on it, but I think she's strong enough to manage it."

Cirrus sighed.

Kalen shook the water from his hair. "We started this quest to find your sister and stop the prophecy. If we make it back in time, it looks like we will. Her abilities were being used to create weapons for Ryndel. That right there was enough to destroy the kingdom. Had she never been sent away, he couldn't have had her magick siphoned."

"She still has the power to destroy us, though." Cirrus toed the ground with his boot.

"Everyone has the power to destroy something," Kalen responded. "I could pick up a sword today and run you through with it."

Cirrus nodded. "I guess time will tell. I only hope that we're preventing the destruction the prophet saw, not causing it."

Kalen hoped the same.

———•———

THEY FINALLY APPROACHED the outskirts of Antioege, and Cirrus led them down side streets to a long, low building. The bounty hunter had known about the inn, so they needed a new place to rest. A brick wall extended the length of the yard, and they passed through a narrow gate into an enclosed courtyard. A path, lined with flat stepping stones, wound up to the front door, which was brightly lit in preparation for evening.

Luna sighed as they stared at the entranceway to the

brothel. "Why am I not surprised this is the place you chose?"

"I know it's not ideal." Cirrus had the decency to look chagrined at having brought them there. "But it is safe. They know me, and they're discreet. Plus, it's a roof over our heads for a night if Belrose needs time to prepare for our departure."

Reign's eyes flitted everywhere as they entered the lobby. Two girls lounged against a bar top in the corner while another draped herself across the lap of the only patron. A tall brunette wearing a silk robe tied at her waist—and little else—approached Cirrus.

He leaned in close to her. "We need two rooms. No company necessary."

She hooked a finger and led them through a door at the far end of the room. They climbed a flight of stairs and walked down a hall until she pointed at two rooms on opposite sides. "Yours for the rest of the night. You'll have to double up or sleep on the floor. We don't exactly cater to guests who need multiple beds."

Cirrus thanked her, handed her several coins, and then watched the sway of her hips as she walked away. Luna smacked him on the chest. "Let's get word to Belrose and eat."

"Can we switch that order?" He held his hands together and begged.

"How about Luna and I do the former, and you two do the latter?" Kalen glanced at the siblings. Reign's hand clenched a little, but then she nodded. She slowly reached out to grip Kalen's biceps and pull him close.

"Be safe and come back quickly." Her voice was low and hoarse.

He could only imagine the discomfort of being in a strange city and feeling a fear of abandonment yet again. The majority of her memories were filled with people leaving her for one reason or another. Why wouldn't she fear Kalen's leaving, too?

"We'll return shortly."

It was all he could offer her before he and Luna headed out of the building and down the slope toward the city. The entire landscape was a display of lit-up glass, backed by twilight. They walked in a meandering route to the harbor, weaving their way through the outer edge of the web of piers.

"Do you think it's okay that we left the royals to fend for themselves?" Luna asked as they ducked behind a pillar and looked to see if anyone was ahead.

"It seemed the best option," Kalen whispered. A pause, and then: "You seem to be developing a fondness for the prince, though."

Luna snorted and led them forward. "Please."

"You're a much better liar than that," Kalen said as he made his way through a row of barrels smelling of salt water and rotting fish.

"I'm not lying. What good could come of it? The crown prince and the bastard daughter of the town madam. Sounds like a lovely tale to be sung by bards across the kingdom."

"Is that self-pity I hear? Because that's not the Luna I know. The Luna I know doesn't let anything get in her way. If something blocks her path, she climbs the nearest building and jumps over it. Since when do you care about titles and social status? Next thing you're going to say is that you don't feel comfortable borrowing coins from the upper class."

"True."

"And hey, you would have access to the royal treasury if you married the prince."

Luna smacked his shoulder. "Enough. He hates me."

"He far from hates you."

Luna finally nodded at a building, the glass walls frosted so they were opaque, lending it a sense of age and secrecy. Pale light glowed from within, making it its own light source.

Kalen stepped forward and knocked on the door.

It swung open, and Jasper stood there, clean and clean-shaven. Kalen almost didn't recognize him.

"Oh, it's you two." He spit a stream of tobacco out into the street, and Luna jumped to the side, narrowly avoiding having the juice splatter her boots. "How may I be of service?"

"Is your captain around?" Kalen asked.

"He's out on the ship with the rest of the crew." He chewed quietly for a moment. "It's almost as if he knew you'd be coming here."

Kalen wondered if the tracker, Milo, had been following their journey.

"How soon could we set sail?" Kalen asked.

"I don't know that he intends to take you at all. I can't see how the captain would be eager to sail to enemy territory." Jasper spit again.

And yet Belrose had tracked them and was at that moment preparing his ship to sail. Kalen sighed, knowing this was most likely about coin. He reached into his pockets and began to pull out what remaining funds they had. Jasper stared blankly at the growing pile, like it meant nothing.

Kalen was down to the few remaining coins he needed to procure supplies, but Jasper only stared at him. "Really? That's all you got?"

"There's more in Mureau if needed," Kalen said. "Take it to the captain, and remind him that he owes me his life. Now our lives are at risk. We have a bounty hunter on our trail. Belrose can consider all debts repaid."

"Fine. Let me row out there. Assuming he's ready to sail by morning, where can we find you?"

Kalen told him where they were staying, and Jasper's eyebrow lifted. "Interesting choice."

"Yet not somewhere you would think of, correct?" Kalen asked.

"This is true." He glanced around. "It's best you're not spotted."

He went to shut the door, and Kalen stuck his foot in the opening. "Let the captain know there's an additional passenger."

"Fabulous," Jasper muttered, and slammed the door shut.

They turned away toward the glass buildings of the inner city, sparkling with the backlight of the sun. Kalen began a path that led right through the heart of the piers. There weren't many stands left open, but they needed to procure a change of clothes, and he had a gift to purchase. His promise to Luna's sister was that he would return with a book.

Kalen never went back on a promise.

CHAPTER

24

They were up with the sun, waiting in the front hall, restless and anxious to return to Mureau and get away from the bounty hunter.

Cirrus was the only one able to eat a full meal. Luna was already pale at the thought of getting on the water again, and Kalen and Reign had shared a pastry.

They had paced a web of circles and lines into the floor by the time the door flew open and Belrose walked in.

"Fancy finding you all here."

Kalen was surprised to see the captain, figuring Jasper or another sailor would have been sent to fetch them. Then again, they were no ordinary passengers. And Belrose had yet to discover that he would be carrying not one, but two members of royalty.

Cirrus and Kalen clasped hands with the captain, and

they introduced him to Reign, who smiled quietly. They grabbed their bags of clean clothing, having washed them the night before and let them dry near the hearth all night, and followed Belrose out the door into a morning heavy with a brewing storm. The wind whistled a miserable tune, and dark gray clouds collected on the horizon.

He led them down and across the streets until they finally hit the jagged line where the land met sand and the pier lifted up and away to the glittering glass walls of the inner city. Instead of encouraging them onto the wooden platform, Belrose pointed to the left, and they followed the lip of grass that butted up against the beach.

"Where are we going?" Kalen had assumed the shortest path would have been straight to the harbor.

"You'll see."

The land began to incline, jutting upward from the sand, which narrowed and then disappeared at a rocky wall just in front of them. They finally reached the beginning of the wall, the land now level with the stone. The expanse of sea spread beyond, a blanket of blue except for the flash of whitecaps reflecting the sunlight. The wall widened and extended to their right as it wrapped around the bay to protect the city from the crash of the incoming tide, a narrow edge that sliced apart two worlds—a troubled sea and an awakening city. The outside was built as a battlement with alternating crenellations and merlons, and the wall walk followed to what looked like a building at the end. As they drew closer, Kalen could make out the shape of the lighthouse.

The group finally reached the building's base. The walk had widened, and the structure was narrow enough to slip around to the opposite side. Kalen was the last to make his way along the rough lighthouse wall. He reached the opposite end and stopped short as he spotted Belrose's ship anchored a few dozen yards from the wall's edge.

The captain directed them to a ladder cut into the wall, where they made their careful way down the stones to a dinghy. Belrose and Kalen rowed the small boat to the ship, and within minutes they had boarded.

It was midafternoon by the time the anchor was weighed and the sails raised. The wind caught the canvas, and the vessel began its journey to Mureau. The foursome headed to Belrose's quarters to ask what had happened in their absence.

"The *Impérial* left the day after you did," Belrose said.

"But you don't know where it went?" Kalen asked, looking at Milo.

He shook his head. "I stopped tracking it."

It made more sense to start tracking us, Kalen thought. Aloud he said, "I assumed as much."

"There was no reason," Belrose said. "They most likely traveled to the island or returned to your country. In either case, they didn't get what they wanted."

Kalen stared out the window at the horizon. He wouldn't be surprised if the *Impérial*'s crew had finally discovered the location of the island and gone there. Perhaps he and Luna should have removed the chest or buried it somewhere else, but there wasn't anything they could do about it now. They could only focus on their impending arrival.

Jasper banged in through the door with a gust of wind at his back. "Sir, the storm is closing in. We need to begin preparations."

Outside the window the dark gray skies blended with the sea as if to form a barrier with no means of escape.

Milo and Jasper walked out, with Belrose at their heels. He turned at the last second and rubbed at his temples. "I'm going to have to ask that you all go belowdecks. The crew is worried, and I need them focused on the ship." He glanced at Reign.

"Of course." Kalen asked after the enclosed room that had held the chest. "It may make sense if we stay there."

"You can stay wherever you need. The crew won't be sleeping much."

Kalen led the way to the galley to gather food in case they were hungry for the supper hour. He grabbed two lamps, handed one to Cirrus, and kept one for himself. "Reign and I will take the closet space; you two take the cabin where we stayed before."

He and Reign entered the windowless room. It had appeared smaller in Belrose's memory. The corners had seemed to close in on his vision, but the compartment itself more than accommodated the two of them. A pile of blankets rested on top of a shelf that stored books and a stack of rolled maps. He hung the lamp on a hook on the wall, grabbed the blankets, and spread the top one on the floor. He laid down the food in the middle, slid off his cloak, and sank beside it. Reign settled next to him.

"So, they don't like me?" she said.

"Fondness isn't the issue, although I imagine the crew isn't thrilled any of us are on board." He braced his hands against the floor as the boat rocked violently. Reign reached in to grab biscuits and pickled meat out of the basket Kalen had hastily put together. They ate in silence, and Kalen's thoughts began to race, thinking of Reign and her past and her fight to control her emotions. It all stemmed from the king banishing her.

"Do you hate him?" Kalen glanced at her in the flickering light.

"The captain?"

"No, sorry," Kalen said. "I was thinking of the king."

"I can't hate him; I don't know him. I have empathy for what he did. He mourned his wife and blamed me. I understand that, but in some ways I think it would have been more merciful to kill me then." Her voice had fallen so low he barely heard her.

A crash of thunder rumbled the walls, and Kalen could only imagine the lightning that must have slashed the sky a mere second before. Belrose shouted orders and footsteps echoed, but after that it was mostly silent except for the perpetual sound of howling wind.

Reign's fingers clenched, relaxed, and clenched again. Kalen scooted closer and wrapped an arm around her. Her head fell to his shoulder, and his cheek rested against her hair.

"I know you had a hard journey to get to this point," he said, finding it easier to talk without her pale eyes searching his, "but I'm glad you're here."

She didn't answer. They sat in silence, the boat swaying beneath them, the thunder rolling outside the walls, and their breath falling into unison. Eventually they sprawled, side by side, on the blanket. Their fingers laced together; they stared at the dark ceiling above as footsteps pounded along the deck.

"Should you offer to help?" Reign asked. "They might appreciate another body."

Kalen shook his head, his scalp rubbing against the hard floor. "If they need me, they will come down and ask. Belrose won't hesitate. Until then, I'll stay here with you."

"My brother is the one who is afraid of the dark."

"I know," Kalen said, but he didn't want her anxiety building here if the storm continued to worsen.

Or at least that was the reason he told himself he stayed.

———

THE STORM LASTED through the next day. Reign and Kalen spent most of the daylight hours in the cabin with Luna and Cirrus, where they talked about Ryndel and made plans. Reign interrupted with questions about the city, the politics, and how one person might have obtained so much control without anyone noticing.

At that, Cirrus stormed upstairs.

Reign's concerned eyes followed him, but Kalen assured her he was probably asking himself the same question she had voiced aloud.

They returned to the closet for another night. The storm began to ease, and Kalen and Reign lay in the confines of the damp room.

"You've seen into my head," she said, rolling onto her side to face him. "Why not give me a glimpse into yours? What's your worst memory?"

He lay in silence, eyes staring at a spot on the ceiling.

"The day my brother was kidnapped."

"What happened?" A breeze of compassion drifted over him.

He had never talked about it with anyone. Never. But Reign was right, he had seen much of her dark past, and he felt obligated in a way to tell her.

"My mother had taken him to the marketplace to shop for whatever it is that she shopped for. Mathew was timid, tentative, so I'm not even sure how he strayed away, but he must have, because suddenly he was missing."

Reign laced her fingers through his gloved ones and squeezed them.

"She came home, frantic, and dismissed my tutor so I could go find my father. Everyone went searching for Mathew. I thought . . . I thought he was dead." He swallowed. "I was the one who found him. On the edge of the woods on the opposite side of town from the marketplace. He stood there, his eyes blankly staring ahead. Nothing was amiss. Not his clothing, not his hair. But he wouldn't speak. Hours passed. My mother bathed him and tried to feed him, but he wouldn't do anything.

"My mother hated . . . hates most likely still . . . my ability, but she asked me to go inside Mathew's mind to see what had happened."

"He hadn't wandered off. He had been taken by zealots who were intent on eradicating magick. They took him because of me, to see if he had any abilities. Pushed him, prodded him, threatened him, but he could only sit there and cry. They released him ten hours later. I struggled to tell my mother this, as I knew she would only blame me further.

I can still see the hatred in her eyes as she bundled Mathew close to her."

"And then?" Reign asked, her hand still in his.

"They left. My mother, my father, and my brother. In the middle of the night, just gone. A note sat on my brother's bed, explaining they couldn't risk living with me anymore and that the king would take me in."

"So you were abandoned, too." Her voice was barely a whisper.

He nodded.

"Have you ever heard from them?"

"Not a word."

"I'm so sorry," she said.

He turned toward her, their faces merely inches apart. Her lips were slightly parted, and he was suddenly distracted with the desire to kiss her. He wondered if it was her own longing that pulled him in, or if the desire was his. Based on the way his skin hummed in her vicinity, he felt confident that his feelings were not the result of magick, but he still found himself pausing.

They stared at each other, basking in the comfort of similar backgrounds, shared pains. Finally, the ship settled as the storm relented. Their eyes closed, and they fell asleep, fingers twined.

THE AIR WAS dense with fog and salt, heavy on Kalen's face as he and Reign climbed the stairs the next afternoon. Above deck, the clouds had thinned enough to let weak rays of afternoon sunlight pass through. The water had calmed, and for that they were thankful. Kalen and Reign had gotten little sleep with the constant listing of the boat, but the crew looked even worse for wear, bleary-eyed and yawning as they lounged wherever they could find a somewhat dry surface.

Luna rubbed at her eyes, her face pale, most likely from a night filled with nauseous swaying, while Cirrus leaned nonchalantly against the rail, his perfect hair somehow motionless in the gusts of wind.

Mureau was a speck on the horizon, and they watched in silence as the city grew larger in front of them. The sun kissed the water's edge by the time Belrose lowered the sails and directed Jasper to row the foursome to shore. He then turned to face the group. "Be safe and I wish you the best of luck."

They shook the captain's hand solemnly and thanked him before boarding the tender with Jasper. They navigated slowly and silently toward the coastline. The sun shone down, but the wind continued to lash around them, whipping up sprays of water that might as well have been rainfall. It gathered in Kalen's hair and on the back of his neck, with the occasional drops coursing down his spine beneath his shirt.

"Here's to hoping you don't need our services any time soon," Jasper said as they spilled out of the small boat onto the rough wooden dock. He dipped his oars into the shallow water to row silently away.

They turned away from the sea and braced for their homecoming.

CHAPTER

25

They swept up the docks only to slow as they heard shouting ahead.

"Hoods up," Kalen said. His gloved hand found the hilt of his dagger, and he edged along the street, keeping as close to the warehouse walls as possible.

Around the corner, a throng of sailors clustered in the middle of the street. They scuffled with one another, fists flailing and swords drawn. Shouts and accusations echoed down the main street as more men shuffled along, having stumbled out of the taverns.

Tension wafted off them, more sour and tangible than the sweat dripping down their backs as they fought. There was no evidence of magick, but if Belrose's earlier assessment was correct, the King's Law had been inciting further unrest while they had been gone from the city. Many of the same sentiments as at the riot Kalen and Luna had stumbled on the night they left Mureau were being thrown around, only this time stronger and more definitive.

"It's time. We need to act soon."

"We need to expand our borders. Down with the confinement."

"Down with the king!"

Kalen glanced at Cirrus, whose lips pressed together.

Suddenly he felt compelled forward. An invisible thread, leading him toward the eastern end of town, in the direction of the castle. The din had quieted, and the crowd had all turned to face the same way as Kalen. The pull released, but several of the men began to move almost blindly away from the harbor in that direction.

Cirrus's eyes widened as he looked at Kalen. "Did you feel that?"

He nodded.

"I did, too," Reign said with a shudder. "What was it?"

"I don't know," Kalen said, "but something is definitely going on. We need to find Ryndel."

"Shall we check with the harbormaster first?" Luna asked.

Ryndel was known to spend time there, inquiring after civilian trade and naval movements. With the prince and the Questioner having disappeared, Kalen imagined the Law asked for information there even more frequently. It seemed worth exploring before they moved inland.

"If we get separated, let's meet at the castle walls," Kalen said as they made their way across the docks.

Reign's gaze shifted to every part of the port, seeming

to soak up all the details. Kalen encouraged her to pull her cloak tighter around her face, and they ducked their heads as they made their way toward the stout building that housed the harbormaster.

Muted lamplight shone from within the room, but there didn't seem to be any movement. Luna slipped closer to listen at the door and then waved them all away.

From the port they wove through alleys and into the streets beyond. Kalen turned to Luna. "What's the fastest way to the Sea Serpent?" That was the tavern where Kalen and Luna had last seen Ryndel. He might be there further working the crowd.

"Fast but safe," Kalen told Luna.

"I'm guessing rooftops aren't an option?"

"No, let's stick to the roads."

She tilted her head to the right, down another alleyway. The buildings closed in, and the space was narrow. Kalen led the group as he sprinted through puddles and around a pile of what looked like fabric scraps but smelled like rotting compost.

Reign threw her arm up to her face and covered a cough.

"Don't worry," Luna said. "The rest of the town is much better kept."

Kalen and Cirrus exchanged a glance. Mureau could definitely use some cleaning up.

The street was surprisingly empty when they reached the tavern. The same barkeep glanced up as they slipped inside single file. His eyes narrowed, only to widen again when Cirrus stepped through the doorframe. "Your Highness."

"I wasn't here," Cirrus said.

"Of course." He bobbed his head like a marionette. "What can I get you? On the house of course."

Cirrus looked tempted for a moment but then shook his head as if to clear his thoughts. "We only wondered if the King's Law had been here recently?"

"No," the barkeep said. "I can't imagine he'd have interest in my establishment."

"Has there been much unrest this past fortnight?" Kalen asked.

"Yes. Foreigners coming and going. Although nobody much cares to be here tonight."

Kalen felt that sudden tug again. Like they were one, they leaned in the direction of the kitchen. Everyone but Luna, who drummed her fingers on the sticky bar top. "Anything else you can tell us?" she asked.

"No, I'm sorry."

The pull released, and Reign shuddered again. "What kind of magick *is* that?"

"Is it magick?" the barkeep asked. "It's been happening all day. It's uncomfortable if nothing else."

"We're going to find out," Cirrus said as they moved to the exit.

"I'm glad to see you safe," he called to Cirrus. "Be careful, though. Everyone's looking for you." His eyes cut to Kalen. "And you as well. You might want to be extra careful."

Great, Kalen thought. He gripped the key at his chest as they regrouped outside.

"Shall we try Ryndel's residence?" Luna rubbed her hands together. There was nothing that girl liked more than breaking into a noble's home.

Kalen led the way into an alley and made a couple of sharp turns. He stepped onto the cobblestone of the next cross street, only to nearly be impaled as a guardsman yanked a sword from his scabbard and pointed it at a group of men standing opposite. "In the name of the king, tell me your intentions."

Kalen held his arm out to keep everyone behind him, but Cirrus crashed into him and, as if they'd become a tumbleweed, they all spilled into the street. They now found themselves between the guardsman and his apparent foes. Kalen took a closer look and realized the group of men were all dressed in the lightweight fabrics normally found in Pantes, a city at the southern tip of Sandrasia.

The barkeep had been right.

"The King's Law hired us," one of the men said as the guardsman shoved past Kalen to get closer to them. "Step aside and let us do as we've been asked."

The guardsman frowned, and then his eyes widened as he spotted Cirrus at Kalen's side. "What are *you* doing—"

"Run!" Kalen grabbed Reign's hand and urged her away from the men.

Luna and Cirrus raced off in the opposite direction. If Kalen had to guess, Luna would route them past Ryndel's residence before meeting them at the wall.

The guardsman paused only a moment before yelling after Cirrus and following their path. The foreigners decided to chase after Kalen and Reign. It appeared nobody cared about sides; they just wanted confrontation.

Kalen nudged Reign's shoulder to the right, and she instinctively turned down another side street. Their feet pounded the cobblestone lane, past closed storefronts and several open taverns. Music spilled forth, but little laughter. The entire city was anxious for a quarrel.

Two of the foreigners kept pace and chased Kalen and Reign as they turned down an alley and then onto a side street, this one leading toward the edge of the town where it butted up against the forest.

Several men walked slowly but methodically down the center of the street, in the direction of the castle. The two pursuers had fallen slightly behind, but they still followed. Kalen wasn't sure if they saw him when he moved off the street and ducked into a nondescript building coated in ivy with a small painted sign hanging outside.

Kalen and Reign stepped through the door and into an opium haze. The mood was less intense than outside, and nobody seemed inclined to grab a sword and race toward the castle. Kalen wondered if it was the opium that counteracted the magick at play.

"Another brothel?" Reign asked under her breath.

Another brothel, but not just any brothel.

"Kalen!" Luna's mother swept in, her loose skirts swirling around delicate ankles. She was almost as tiny as Luna, only without the silver coloring. She enveloped Kalen in a hug and kissed him on both cheeks. "Where's my daughter?"

"She's safe and will be home shortly." Kalen urged Madam into the far hallway and nodded for Reign to follow.

"And who is this lovely young girl you brought with you?"

Kalen thought Reign blushed at the comment, but it

could have been the rose tint of the lighting in the hallway they had stepped into.

"Reign, this is Madam, Luna's mother. And this is Reign; she's visiting from Servaille." He quickly introduced them.

"There's something about you that looks familiar." Madam cocked her head to examine Reign.

"I'll explain more later." Kalen urged Reign forward. The last thing they needed was Madam realizing Reign was royalty.

"We are going to slip out the back. Two men might follow me here. I actually hope that they do." He glanced around. "If they ask, you haven't seen us. Have Jezebel entice them." The curly-haired brunette would certainly keep the men ogling for the precious few minutes Kalen needed to lose them.

"Of course," Madam said.

"Have the girls heard anything that might be of use since we left?"

"Business has been good, although we've had more trouble with customers than we normally do."

"I imagine. Anything else?"

"The other *sorciers* . . ." Her voice trailed off.

Kalen halted midstep. "What of them?"

"The Law had them rounded up the day after you disappeared. Nobody has seen them since."

Kalen's mind churned this detail. Would Ryndel have decided to punish them all for Kalen's desertion?

"When will Luna return?" Madam asked.

"I'll send her as soon as we're done. It could very well be later this evening." He reached into his jacket to pull out the book he'd purchased their last day in Antioege and pressed it into Madam's hands. "Please give this to Amya." He gave her a quick hug before leading Reign farther toward the exit.

A door flew open, and Jezebel stepped out. "Kalen!" Her fingers trailed along his arm as he passed, and he threw her a lopsided grin.

Several of the girls peeked out of their doors, and each one called him by name, blowing a kiss or reaching out to run a hand over his check or back or arm. He'd spent enough time there over the years, first when he'd lived there for a few months after his parents abandoned him, and then later, gathering secrets and spending time with Luna. All the girls knew him. They also knew he wouldn't touch them.

Reign didn't know that—couldn't know that—but she kept her gaze at her feet as they passed.

Kalen grabbed the handle just as he heard Madam's sultry voice from the doorway at the opposite end of the hall. "Hello, gentlemen. What might I be able to do for you this evening?"

Kalen slipped out and eased the door quietly shut behind Reign. Then they were down the darkened alley and headed toward the castle.

They followed a street that curved along the tree line and would eventually land at the castle wall. Reign tugged her cloak tighter against the cold air of night and the drizzling rain that had started as soon as they left the brothel. It seemed the storm had followed them from the sea.

Suddenly she stopped and tugged on Kalen's sleeve. "What's that?" She pointed deeper into the woods.

Kalen squinted into the twisting trunks and tangled

branches, his gaze settling on the flickering lights in the distance. At first he thought they were flickerflies playing tag, but the lights were brighter, and then he heard the murmur of voices.

It could only be more men, waiting in hiding. But for what? And how had Ryndel been able to rally such a vast amount of people?

Wind whipped through the branches above, coaxing the few remaining leaves to fall to a peaceful demise. Up ahead, the castle walls spread from the trees toward the sea. Kalen increased his pace. They reached the wall and headed for the side entrance. He checked that Reign still had her hood pulled over her head. Based on Madam's reaction, he didn't want people wondering who she might be.

He paused outside the gates to see if any guards would stop them. Silence greeted them, and he led Reign through, only to find two of the guardsmen lying incapacitated and Luna and Cirrus waiting casually beside them.

"Took you long enough," Luna said.

"We had to ditch the foreigners," Kalen said, his voice low. "I take it there was no sign of Ryndel?"

Luna shook her head. "He has to be here."

They stuck to the shadows of the inside of the wall, following it along for several paces. Above them the clouds continued to gather. Shouts and stamping echoed from outside the main castle gate. The mob was growing as people continued to feel pulled in this direction.

Kalen tensed as he felt it again. His chest turned toward the right, almost on its own volition. The familiar buildings stretched before him—the kitchens, the barracks and training field, and the dungeon beyond.

He glanced at Cirrus and Reign, who had turned in the same direction. Reign's eyes were wide, and her fingers began to fist. She saw him watching, and her hand opened slowly as she took a deep breath.

"What does it feel like?" Luna asked.

"It's like a hook," Reign said. "I'm urged forward, attracted to something."

That was it. One of the female *sorciers* could attract things to her, but never something this significant in scale. She attracted small objects and animals, maybe a single person if she concentrated on it, but certainly not crowds of people from as far away as the harbor. He didn't understand how it was possible.

The tug severed again.

Cirrus took a deep breath, then his eyes narrowed. Kalen felt it, too, a sudden blanket of anger and rage. On the heels of the other magick, it felt even stronger, as if they'd been disarmed by the pull.

Cirrus spun toward Kalen. "What are you looking at?"

Kalen's hand gripped the handle of his sword. Shouts erupted and footsteps sounded on the other side of the wall. The mob was closing in.

Luna stepped between them. "Knock it off, you two. Let's go find the king."

Kalen mentally pushed against the anger, but it suddenly cleared just as quickly as the attraction had. Whatever Ryndel was doing, it came in pulses.

Cirrus yanked at his hair, pulling it further on end. "Bloody crow. We need to stop this madness."

Lightning flashed, illuminating the stretch of exterior courtyard between the wall and the side of the great hall. Thunder crashed above them, and they made a run for it, hoping the darkness and noise would cover their approach and they wouldn't be spotted. Time was not on their side, and they couldn't afford the delay of a conversation with the guardsmen.

They followed the arched stone corridor that lined the front of the great hall. A high ceiling jutted above them, held aloft by columns evenly spaced along the length of the building. To their left the courtyard stretched down in wide, stepped tiers to the castle wall, where lanterns hung at regular intervals, showing the guardsmen stationed outside. Clouds darkened the horizon, and more lightning danced in the heavy clouds still hanging above the sea. The rain began to fall harder, echoing off the roof and dancing in puddles in the courtyard. The shouting continued to erupt from outside the wall.

"How easily can the mob get in?" Reign asked as she tried to peer past the wall and gate that held them out.

"It's been decades since we've been attacked," Cirrus said. "I really have no idea. I would hope that we are safe here."

Finally, they reached the midway point of the corridor. To their right stood a marble slab of flooring and two massive double doors, ornate with jeweled carvings. Reign's mouth dropped open as she took it in. A two-headed dragon stared out at them, the eyes inlaid with sapphires and the talons encrusted with rubies. Flickerflies, dusted with diamonds, dotted the background. The dragon's tail wrapped around and split to form the handles.

"You ready?" Cirrus looked at Kalen, who nodded.

They each grabbed a handle and pushed inward. The doors parted enough for them to slip in, Luna and Reign just after. They lined up side by side, a united front, as the heavy doors closed behind them.

A cross the length of the massive room, at the far end
where the throne sat at the apex of a rounded dais,
the court council, minus Ryndel, all turned their
heads.

Terrack thrust his chair behind him, rose to his full
height, and lifted his sword.

Cirrus stormed forward. He tipped his chin up and
threw his shoulders back. Gone was the charismatic jokester
from their journey and in his place was the stern and serious
prince. "Put your weapon away."

"Terrack, stand down." The king stood, his robe settling
around him as he took a step in their direction. "Cirrus, my
son. Where have you been?"

"Nice try." Cirrus waved him back toward the throne.

Kalen and the girls caught up to Cirrus as he continued across the floor.

The king's eyes narrowed, and he remained standing. "Be careful how you tread, son. I don't suggest you anger me further. You disappeared without warning—the same day a prisoner was set free. I imagine your friends had something to do with that." He paused to glare at Kalen. "However I still maintain it was mere coincidence that you left the same exact evening and are only now returning."

"The captain was wrongly accused," Kalen said to the king before his gaze turned to Terrack. "I told you to set him free."

"The Law disagreed with your conclusion," Terrack said.

"Speaking of . . . where is our old pal, Ryndel?" Cirrus asked. "We have a few things we need to clear up. Things you all might want to know about, considering the mob outside your door."

"We are waiting on him so we can address the very problem of which you speak," the king said.

"He *is* the problem," Kalen interjected. "You're not likely to have him join you unless it's to put a sword tip to your throat."

The council members began to mutter among themselves.

The king dismissed the comment with a wave. "I don't know that I can believe you any longer, Kalen. My son departs after you've gone into his mind, a prisoner is freed from my dungeon, and now you return with two harlots at your sides."

"Harlot?" Luna jumped forward.

Cirrus held her back as Reign stepped toward the king and let her hood fall.

"You might want to reconsider your choice of description . . . Father."

All conversation halted, and two of the council members rose, dark cloaks folding around them as they stared in confusion.

Cirrus burst into laughter. Inappropriate, but he seemed unable to help it or even to care. He chuckled and bent over, clutching his side. "The look on your face," he said to the king before he took a deep breath and straightened. "Did you think with Kalen's abilities we wouldn't figure out the truth eventually? Let me introduce you to your daughter. My younger sister."

As one, the king's council shifted their gaze from Cirrus to Reign and back again. Anyone could see that they were siblings. The same hair color and freckles. Even the way they both glared at their father. It was a bit uncanny. And then the council all turned to face the king. His face drained of color while his fingers fisted at his sides. "Why did you bring her here? She's destined to bring on the destruction of the kingdom." His voice climbed as he repeated himself. "Why did you bring her here?"

Reign continued to stare at her father even as the council began firing questions at the king.

"What are you speaking of?"

"Destruction of the kingdom?"

"Who is this girl?"

Reign stepped forward. "My name is Reign," she said. "Although I have no idea if that's my birth name or not."

"It is," the king said, his voice dropping to a loud whisper. "Your mother used to sing you a lullaby."

Kalen remembered the song from her and Cirrus's memories.

"So, she's a princess?" another member asked.

The king looked her up and down. "Assuming she's who she says she is, yes."

"I can vouch that she's the princess," Kalen said. "I've been inside her memories, and they match Cirrus's."

"Plus, just look at the two of them," Luna chimed in. "You can't all be that dense."

"You've been hiding this from us?" the only female council member spoke directly to the king.

"Of course he has. He hid it from everyone." Cirrus practically spit the words, and then he turned to the king. "To answer your question from before, we brought her here because she *belongs* here. The bigger question is why did you send her away? The prophet *told* you her banishment would bring destruction upon the kingdom. You only need to look outside your castle gates to see the truth of that."

The council members again began to speak over one another, expressing confusion over the prophecy and banishment.

"Silence!" The king shouted over them and then spoke to Cirrus. "What does the unrest have to do with"—he paused as if struggling to come up with a word to describe Reign—"her?"

"Quite a bit, unfortunately. That's why we need Ryndel. We have a few questions for him."

And a few amulets to destroy, Kalen thought.

"If you could only point us in the direction we might find him," Cirrus continued, "we'll be happy to leave you to whatever mundane matters you were discussing before our arrival."

"I doubt the conversation will be so mundane now," Luna muttered with a snort.

Terrack leaned forward. "The kingdom is under attack. I think we can all agree that is the most important matter at hand. What exactly does the Law have to do with the men advancing on the city?"

"He's using magick to influence the subjects, even ones from other cities," Kalen said. "I saw residents of Pantes outside earlier."

"He's been scheming for a while now, from what we can tell. Possibly years," Cirrus added, his eyes never leaving his father's.

"Enough of this." The female council member waved her hand like she was bored with the conversation already. "Throw these four in the dungeon and deal with them later. It's obvious they are part of this revolt."

Before anyone could respond, the door behind the throne swung open, and a young page rushed in. "They're through the gates, sire. The mob is headed this way."

The council erupted in panic. This type of unrest or attack was unprecedented.

Cirrus and Kalen looked at each other. They needed to be out there, protecting the kingdom, not indoors explaining matters to a council incapable of action. Kalen turned to

Reign. "Stay here with the king. This is the safest building on the entire grounds."

"No." She grabbed his arm. "I'm coming with you. I can't stand by idly while the fighting happens outside. So much of their anger is because of me."

"It's not because of you. You can't take any of the blame." Kalen wanted her safe, not out where she could be impaled on a weapon.

"Their anger *is* mine." She swallowed hard. "Ryndel is projecting my emotions on the citizens. Please, Kalen. I have to help. I have to find a way to stop it."

Kalen nodded. He didn't like it, but he understood.

Luna stepped to Reign's other side. "Don't think for a second I'm staying behind to babysit these fools."

"We will go fight your fight, Father." Cirrus freed his sword from its scabbard.

"No." The king's voice rose. "We are not yet done talking. You must stay here."

"Talking will solve nothing. We are going to go stop the attack, find Ryndel, and destroy his magicked weapons. Then we can talk."

The king walked down the steps and toward them. "Cirrus, you must see reason."

"Father, I was trained to be a soldier. I'm not letting others fight and die while we hide."

The king dared a glance at Reign, but she spun around and walked toward the doors.

"Terrack, please keep an eye on them." The king's eyes narrowed. "As much as I would like to believe they are fighting *with* us, they did free one of my prisoners. I'm not quite sure I trust them yet."

The head guardsman jogged over, and they all moved toward the heavy double doors.

"Godspeed to you all," the king called. And then, in a lowered voice: "Someone barricade the doors behind them."

———•◦•———

TERRACK LED THEM to the bailey. Subjects and guardsmen alike streamed in through the gate, eyes glazed over, swords drawn and ready to fight. It was going to be a bloodbath. There weren't enough people within the castle walls to defend the king.

They stormed forward, the ragtag group of five, a bizarre sight to behold, from the tiny, silver-specked Luna to the giant-framed Terrack. Rain pelted from above, cold yet searing as it dripped down Kalen's back, and lightning raced through the heavy clouds.

Terrack tossed Luna one of his two short swords and turned to Reign. "What will you use for a weapon?"

"I'm not fighting." She turned to Kalen. "Get me to the wall."

His gloved hand reached for her bare hand, and they raced forward.

Anger surged through his thoughts, and he seethed. Was Ryndel nearby? Did he have an amulet? Kalen would cut him down. He dropped Reign's hand and pulled his sword from its scabbard. He lifted his weapon high, ready to plunge it into the Law's throat, but Ryndel was nowhere to be seen.

Off to his right, Cirrus let out a war cry and raced into the mercenaries. Luna called after him, ready to have his back, but he outpaced her. She turned to help Terrack as he fought off a group of attackers.

Two men split apart from the pack and came at Kalen. He swung his sword down and to the side. The man on the right jumped out of the way, but the force of Kalen's swing sliced at the mail on the other mercenary. Kalen wasn't sure if the blade cut through, but the man groaned and fell.

He took a deep breath and made sure Reign was still just behind him. She pushed damp tendrils of hair from her eyes and pointed at the stairs leading up to the parapet. "We need to get higher."

Kalen pressed through the crowd, his sword swinging side to side to ward off attack, until they reached the steps. They sprinted up to the parapet and stopped short. Beyond the castle walls, the mob seemed to stretch to the harbor. People funneled up the streets, pushing and shoving, anxious to join the fight. Reign's eyes widened as lightning flashed and further illuminated their crazed looks and tense bodies.

"Somewhere inside, I would wager most of these men don't want to be here," Reign murmured. "Perhaps they're trying to resist the amulet's projections, perhaps not, but if I can give them a mental shove in another direction, they may retreat, or at least come to their senses."

If Ryndel could use the amulets to increase the citizens' anger and anxiety, surely Reign could project her emotions to counteract him, but would it be enough? How was he controlling such a large number of people?

"I'll help," Kalen said. "Try to intensify your magick through me."

He feared that's what Ryndel was doing now, using the other *sorciers* to project the magick—of one another and the amulets. It would explain how the *sorcier*'s attraction drew so many people toward the castle grounds.

Reign's eyebrows lifted, and she looked at him with uncertainty.

"How would I push it through you?"

"I don't know, but I've seen it before. We ran into the bounty hunter in Antioege on our journey to Servaille. He projected his magick through two other *sorciers*." He paused. "I think he may have tried to do the same in Servaille as we were fleeing the city." He had felt a foreign presence and pressure in his mind seconds before his vision had turned black.

"I felt something then, too," she said. "But I don't know how to replicate it."

Someone screamed below. Kalen couldn't tell if it was a war cry or the shriek of a mortal wound, but he knew they had to act fast.

"Perhaps we try it a different way. I can go into your mind and see your memories as they happen only a second delayed from real time. As you project your emotions, I will try to do the same, and together maybe the magick will be magnified."

Reign wiped the rain from her brow and glanced out over the land stretching away from her. Kalen could only imagine the thoughts going through her mind. She had been cast out from this castle, from the king she was now trying to save. A part of her probably wanted to let him die a slow death and watch his kingdom fall. But she had come to right any wrongdoings enabled by her emotions and the magick Nero had siphoned from her.

She turned to Kalen. "Let's do it."

He lowered his sword to the ground, and she tugged at his glove with her fingers, removing it slowly from his hand. Reign's eyes closed, her fingers threaded through his, and his mind plunged into hers.

Kalen easily found her in her most recent memory. She stood in the same spot on the walkway, in the same position, with her eyes closed. The scene was more exaggerated, as it always was in someone's mind. They stood in a more precarious position, on a much higher wall. The mob came at them from an even farther distance, shouting and thrusting their weapons as they ran at a full sprint.

In this continuing evolvement of her thoughts, Reign reached out for him and tugged him closer. Her eyes fluttered open, and her fingers reached up to trace his cheekbone. Her lips searched his, soft at first, and tentative. She pulled back briefly, and then her hands dug into his hair, and her mouth found his again, yearning, full of longing and hope and destruction.

Their tongues and breaths entwined. She tasted of loss and sorrow, and he wanted to take it all away from her. Her teeth tugged at his bottom lip, and he groaned somewhere deep in his throat. His hands tangled in her hair. He couldn't get enough of her, her taste, her lips, her tongue.

He forced himself to pull away. "You need to focus."

"I am." The words were a ribbon of yellow, brighter than any sun could have been. "This is the emotion I need."

She grabbed his hand and placed it against her chest. Her skin radiated warm through her shirt, and her heart beat a fast rhythm. The beats grew more intense, until he felt them permeate his own body, his heart pulsing in time with hers.

Time froze. She reined in the pulse and then threw it forth. Kalen felt it immediately, an overwhelming sense of peace and calm. His mind cleared, and he let her magick flood his senses. All his anxiety lifted. He willed the feeling farther, away from him, away from Reign, trying to push their thoughts together to the outer edges of the city and beyond.

She released his hand, and his mind released hers. Her lips sought his again, this time soft and hesitant and salty in the rain. He rested his forehead against hers, and they breathed in each other.

Then she collapsed to the ground, nearly bringing Kalen with her.

CHAPTER

27

"They're stopping." Terrack had joined them on the wall. Shocked, they watched as the men put down their weapons and looked around in confusion. Kalen held Reign in his arms as her eyelids fluttered and she came to.

"What happened?" she asked.

"You did it." Kalen hugged her close.

"For now." She straightened and stepped back. "Ryndel still has the amulets and he could start it again."

"I saw flashes of light and movement in the top floor of the dungeon," Terrack said. It made sense that the coward would lock himself away, and that was one of the buildings in the direction Kalen had been drawn to earlier.

"Do you want to stay here?" Kalen asked Reign, but

she had already begun to make her way down the stairs. He grabbed his sword and followed her.

They searched the courtyard for Luna and Cirrus. Subjects, mercenaries, and guardsmen alike appeared stunned by their actions. Moans and whimpers from the wounded competed with the sound of the pouring rain. Those who had been attackers suddenly turned into comrades and began treating injuries and moving men indoors.

Kalen craned his neck, searching the wounded for his friends. He exhaled in relief as he spotted them ambling their way across the courtyard. Luna's braid had come loose, and her hair fell in wet tangles down her back. Cirrus seemed to be babying his injured arm, but they looked unharmed otherwise.

Kalen and Reign ducked under the portico that bordered the great hall and offered a welcome respite from the rain. As they walked its length, Kalen let his hood fall to see better by the occasional flickerfly bulb swaying in the wind. Some had been knocked loose and shattered, leaving broken glass to snap under their boots, but freeing the insects within.

All too soon they were out in the open again, sprinting toward the dungeon tower. Lightning flashed and thunder clapped an echoing sound as Kalen shoved open the door and they raced inside. Kalen headed for the stairs and took them two at a time, hardly stopping at the second floor before taking the next set of stairs to the highest story. He strained to hear any noises.

"I won't do it anymore." A woman spoke, her voice hoarse and trembling. "You're going to get us all killed."

"You'll do what I say," the Law nearly shouted. "Or

your family will pay for your disservice. The fighting has stopped—you can see with your own eyes." The sound of feet shuffling and a muffled sob. "We need to attract them all onto the castle grounds. The kingdom will be mine tonight. This time I want you to project through all of them."

"No," more voices chimed in.

Cirrus elbowed past Kalen into the antechamber. "Enough of this."

Kalen took long strides across the room to the cell where Belrose had been held. He glanced through the bars, and his entire body froze.

Ryndel stood at the far end, staring out the small window cut into the exterior wall. Lightning flashed again, and in the reflection of the glass Kalen could see Ryndel's wide, unfocused eyes and a tilted half smile that made him look crazed. "You think you've stopped me?"

"Yes. Yes we do." Kalen found his voice, but his eyes kept cutting to the other figures in the room. Jenna and the other *sorciers* sat on the floor, their feet bound with a thick metal rope and their arms tied behind their backs. They ranged in age from ten to sixty years old, all of different coloring and backgrounds, and yet in this moment they all looked terrified of the Law. The attractor stood next to Ryndel, a line of dried tears tracing down her cheeks to her jaw. His fingers were locked around her elbow.

"Do it," Ryndel spoke right into her ear.

Her body trembled, and her eyes fluttered closed.

"You don't have to," Kalen said through the bars.

Ryndel shoved her against the window. "Use him, too!"

The other *sorciers* moaned, and then Kalen felt it, that

same foreign pressure he'd felt with the bounty hunter. His hands pressed firm against his forehead, and he mentally fought against it. The presence left as quickly as it had come, almost as if she refused to push him.

Cirrus stood beside Kalen, yanking on the handle. "Enough of this. Come out and face your consequences. Why are you locked in the dungeon, of all places?"

"Nobody can get to us here. I can see and control everyone from this vantage point."

If Kalen could have reached through the bars to throttle the man, he would have. "I can unlock it, you idiot. That's what I do. That's what you taught me to do."

"Good luck, boy." The last word was spoken as a condescending insult, thrown across the room with more force than a dagger.

Kalen removed his pick tools and inserted one into the lock. A twist and turn and the lock opened.

Suddenly Ryndel turned in Kalen's direction. He held an amulet in one uplifted hand, thrust toward Kalen as he maneuvered the *sorcier* so that she stood in front of him as some sort of shield.

"You coward!" Anger flooded Kalen's thoughts as he strode toward Ryndel, ready to attack. Before he was halfway across the cell, he was suddenly thrown to the ground from behind.

"Cirrus, no!" Luna shouted.

A punch landed on the side of Kalen's cheek, and pain bloomed from his cheekbone up to his ear. He rolled to the side to try to escape and stared up into Cirrus's rage-glazed eyes. Kalen's own anger flared as well. He shoved Cirrus away and leaped to his feet. His hand gripped his short sword as he aimed it at his friend.

Something began to scream at him. He couldn't tell if it was within or without, but it was a long wail that told him, *No, don't do this.*

His body wouldn't stop.

Cirrus seized his own sword, and within seconds they were attacking. They parried and lunged and circled around one another. The small cell seemed to close in on them until Kalen saw an opening and plunged into the antechamber. His arm swung up and around to parry Cirrus's step forward. The steel blades crashed and echoed around the room.

Kalen's mind felt splintered, a push and pull, a tug-of-war that wouldn't stop. He fought to keep focused and from being impaled on the end of Cirrus's sword. But even Cirrus seemed unable to concentrate. His thrusts were weak. His feints were easy to spot. Cirrus was one of the most renowned swordfighters, and even Kalen somehow kept up with him.

Circle. Lunge. Riposte. Attack.

"Stop," Reign cried from where she stood at the top of the stairs. "Stop it, you two!" She took a deep breath and then stepped over against the wall, where she closed her eyes.

Kalen lunged, and his sword sliced at Cirrus's side. The cut was shallow, but the prince grimaced as he leaped to the side. Blood seeped through his white shirt, visible where his cloak fell open. He swung his sword up to block Kalen from further attack.

Luna lunged forward and tried to shove Kalen. "Enough, you two!" she shouted at both of them. "Use your training.

Use the Hakunan." She spun and faced Cirrus. "Use every-thing you taught me."

Kalen's mouth gaped at the wound, and it was enough of a distraction that he could focus on something other than anger for just a moment. His senses acclimated to the room. To the sounds of the metal of the swords as they slid off each other. To the smell of the rain as it seeped in from outdoors. To the feel of his lungs gasping for air and the tension in every muscle in his body.

He danced away from Cirrus, refusing to lift his sword toward the prince again. "I'm sorry," he panted.

Cirrus's teeth gritted, and he lunged forward. Kalen eas-ily moved aside.

Without warning, another feeling permeated the anger. Love. Unconditional love. It was filled with apologies and healing and friendship, and both Cirrus and Kalen dropped their weapons to the floor.

Reign.

Even through her anxiety over the fighting, she had been able to harness the emotion and project it over them.

As if they were one, the siblings both collapsed to the ground where they each stood. Reign was exhausted with the continued use of her magick and Cirrus fell to his knees, his hand immediately going to cover the blood spreading to stain his shirt. Luna ran to him.

"I'm sorry," Kalen said again. Self-loathing overwhelmed him, and he thought he might never stop saying those words.

"Don't." Cirrus held up a finger weakly. "Don't do that to yourself. Neither of us is to blame."

"You're right," Kalen said. "Someone else is to blame."

He wanted to run and comfort Reign. He understood all too well what continued use of their abilities could do, but first Ryndel had to be taken care of. Kalen strode into the room where the Law stood again near the window. His arm was now locked around the *sorcier*'s neck, and her expression was a mix of pain and panic. The amulet was held at chest height, directed at the masses outside. The traitor still seemed intent on his original plan.

"Enough, Ryndel. Put the amulet away." Kalen was almost within arm's reach.

Ryndel pushed the girl to the side, crammed the amulet into his coat pocket, and yanked his sword from its scabbard. He stabbed the weapon in Kalen's direction, and Kalen barely danced to the side out of the way. Kalen realized too late that he'd left his sword in the other room. He tried to run out of the cell, but Ryndel had stepped around him and blocked his path. Ryndel swung his sword again, and the sword sliced through Kalen's sleeve. Kalen jumped backward, only to find he was up against the wall, the window behind his head.

He was going to die.

"Use your magick," Kalen shouted at the *sorciers*, where they still stayed bound on the floor. "Whatever you can do."

"We can't," Jenna said, her voice hoarse. "It's the metal rope. He can project through our minds, but the binds remove access to our own abilities."

Ryndel sneered at Kalen. "I've been planning this for years, and I've thought of everything." He advanced again. "I've bested you, Questioner."

His sword sliced through the air. Kalen knew he couldn't

get out of the way fast enough, but suddenly the attractor was at his side. Ryndel's sword swung at an awkward angle, as if she urged the weapon in her direction. It barely missed Kalen's cheek as it swung past.

Ryndel's hand twisted, and the sword slipped from his grasp to clatter on the floor before it slid over to the *sorcier*'s feet. She reached down and grabbed it, holding it in both hands as she aimed it awkwardly at Ryndel.

On even footing, Kalen launched himself at Ryndel, his gloved knuckles connecting with the man's jaw. Ryndel's head snapped back, and he fell to his knees. "You'll pay for this," he said, as his mouth began to swell.

"Free them," Kalen said to the attractor. She lifted the sword and used it to start hacking at the rope.

He bent over Ryndel and reached inside the Law's coat to pull out two amulets.

"Luna." He raced out of the room to find her and Reign leaning over Cirrus. The prince was curled on his side, his face a sheen of sweat.

"He's not doing well," Luna said.

"It's little more than a scratch," Cirrus said.

"I'll bind the wound. You take care of these." Kalen handed Luna the amulets and pointed to the other empty cell where the door stood open. He reached down to grab his sword off the floor and gave it to her before she walked away.

Kalen squatted and helped Cirrus sit to pull his shirt over his head. The cut looked shallow, a slice along his rib cage. Kalen gripped the garment in both hands and began to tear it into strips. One of the wide ones he folded into a square and pressed against the prince's side. Cirrus inhaled sharply.

"Hold that for me," Kalen told Reign. Her hand replaced his to hold the fabric in place.

Kalen knotted two more strips and wrapped them around Cirrus's chest over the first bandage before he tied the ends together.

The sound of an amulet shattering echoed from the cell.

"No," Ryndel moaned. "All my work for nothing. You will all pay for this."

Another sound of crystal breaking.

It was done.

Outside a flash of lightning and then thunder, and then something more.

The sound of footsteps and voices.

———•———

EARLY THE NEXT morning, after everyone had a chance to bathe, eat, and rest, Kalen and his friends gathered in the throne room with the council and the king.

The king sat on his throne, his head buried in his hands. His voice was hardly audible. "Start from the beginning."

So they did. Kalen recounted finding the memory of Reign as an infant in Cirrus's mind, and together they told of the journey to find the princess. Luna filled in some of the gaps, but Reign stayed stoic and silent, as if refusing to grant him any of her story. Not her past, not her present. She only kept her pale blue eyes on the king, waiting and watching for reactions.

When they had told of ending the battle and destroying

the last pendants, the king appeared stunned, his eyes glassy and his mouth slack-jawed.

The foursome stood facing him. He composed himself and rose from the throne. "I appreciate all that you've done for the kingdom. Without you I would probably be dead." He turned to Ryndel, who had kept his mouth closed ever since Terrack had dumped him on the floor, his arms and feet now bound in a stretch of the same metal rope he'd used to tie the *sorciers*. "Do you have anything to say for yourself?"

"The kingdom will still fall." He spat at the floor. "The prophecy will come true. Look at the amount of power the girl holds. You should kill her now."

Luna glared down at him. "You used her same power to your own advantage. Someone should kill *you*."

The king looked at Terrack. "Throw him in one of the lower dungeon cells. With their magicked wards, nobody should be able to free him." He glanced at Luna. "Besides that one, but I'm guessing she won't be inclined to do so. Have your men interview the wounded in the infirmary. I want to know everyone connected to Ryndel. If they joined this movement for personal gain, they will have to answer to me. And if they won't answer, I'll have Kalen go inside *his* head." He tipped his chin toward Ryndel.

Ryndel snarled at the king. Terrack reached down ungently and hauled Ryndel to his feet. The man kicked, flailed, and tried to bite Terrack, but the guard was undeterred. He lifted him by the collar of his jacket so Ryndel stood nearly on tiptoe before he dragged him off to the exit on the side.

The king then approached Reign. He opened his mouth and closed it again, lips pursing together. He cleared his throat and finally spoke. "You look exactly like the queen." The words were whisper soft, and his lip trembled. "I can't presume to know what you've been through, and I don't know what this means for our country. But thank you for everything you've done. For freeing my people—our people—from under Ryndel's control, and for destroying the amulets."

Reign stared at him, the silence growing increasingly uncomfortable.

"I'm sorry about what I did to the queen," she said. Her hands twitched against her sides, but then she reached out and gripped Kalen's hand tight. "However, you had no right to send me away. I was your daughter."

The words hung in the air, heavier than the weight of the humidity.

"You still *are* my daughter."

She stared at him. "I don't know who I am or what I want, but at this moment, you're not going to dictate my life. I have some choices to make, and I'm not sure yet where they will lead."

The king's hand lifted slightly, and he leaned forward as if he wanted to reach out to her, but he refrained. "I'm not sure that I can allow you the freedom to make those choices. You are still a threat to the kingdom, after all." He stared off into the distance. "Your power is stronger than any I've seen. I may need you to stay close at hand."

"No, Father." Cirrus stepped in. "You are done controlling all the *sorciers*. If there's anything we've learned in this, it's that they are not weapons to be used at one's disposal. They are our subjects, not our slaves."

"And she's not a threat." Luna moved closer, her fingers twining with Cirrus's. The king's nostrils flared, and he refused to look at her. "The prophecy was if you sent her away. You did that, and she has returned."

The king stared at Cirrus. "The prophecy is only over when she's dead."

"Then that is your fault," Cirrus said. "You banished her. Everything that comes after is on your head."

The king waved his hand in dismissal. "Let me speak to the council, and we will make a decision. In the meantime, stay close."

Reign nodded and turned for the exit. Kalen was quick to do the same, followed by Cirrus and Luna.

"Cirrus, we need to discuss your upcoming training," the king called after him.

The prince ignored him.

They followed Reign through the double doors and into the courtyard, which had brightened with sunlight as the storm had now completely passed. She picked up her pace, moving out into the bailey and up the stairs to the top of the ramparts, where the wind whipped at her hair. She yanked it free of its braid and stood still, looking out over the town below. Kalen stood beside her, their fingers laced together.

Reign was the first to break the silence. "Is it safe if I stay?"

"If not, we'll go elsewhere," Kalen answered.

"You can't leave," she said.

Kalen didn't want to leave. He would have preferred to stay, support Cirrus, and help strengthen the kingdom. But if Reign left, he knew he would go with her. "My parents abandoned me years ago, and the king took me in only so he could keep me close and use me as a questioner. I certainly can't stay in his employ and continue to delve into people's minds. It's slowly killing me; I can feel it."

"But where would we go?"

"Anywhere. We can board Belrose's ship and travel south if we want."

"Great, more time on the open seas," Luna said from Cirrus's other side.

"It would be fun, Little Pebble," Cirrus said.

"You can't come with us," Kalen said. "You're next in line for the throne."

"Exactly. I can do whatever I want. My father is in good health; I should be traveling and learning about the subjects. Ryndel was able to use the amulets to incite unrest far before the revolt, but perhaps they would have pushed past the anger had they been more aligned with the king."

"I'm in," Luna said.

A smile had crept across Reign's lips while they all talked around her, and Kalen squeezed her fingers tighter. Cirrus threw one arm around Kalen's shoulders and gripped Luna's hand with his other hand. The road hadn't been the easiest to traverse, but they'd found one another, repaired friendships, made new ones, and helped save the kingdom.

They stood there, the four of them, looking out over the city that would one day be theirs. Not yet. But one day.

ACKNOWLEDGMENTS

THE KING'S QUESTIONER is a book that might never have been written if not for a team of people (both personal and professional) who nudged—and sometimes shoved—me forward. Thank goodness they did or it wouldn't now be in your hands! A huge and overwhelming thank-you to the team at Swoon Reads and Macmillan. Editor extraordinaire Holly West helped both to nail down the plot and characters at the beginning when I sold the book, as well as polish the manuscript to the very end. Val Otarod got me through the exhausting and daunting editorial process and made me kill some of my darling scenes to get the pacing as perfect as possible. I'm also so appreciative of everyone who touched, edited, read, critiqued, and produced the novel: Mandy Veloso, Kat Brzozowski, Jean Feiwel, Brian Luster, and Erin Siu. To Liz Dresner, my fabulous cover designer, I love the ambience and magical elements that bring Kalen's story to life.

To my agent Kate Schafer Testerman, thank you for championing this book from the beginning.

To Demetra Brodsky—we did it again, girl! I can't believe we both have books coming out this year. Thank you for talking me off the ledge and pushing my butt into the chair to write and revise. Love you always.

A special note of appreciation to all the authors in the Swoon Squad for your endless support, answers, virtual hugs, and commiserating! Many tears and endless nights were averted because you guys are always there.

San Diego has an amazing community of local authors, and I'm thankful for the continued friendship of Debra Driza, Shannon Messenger, Mary Pearson, and Cindy Pon.

And if it wasn't for my original critique partners, Andrea Ortega and Lisa Cannon, none of my books would have been published!

To my friends who pick up the phone . . . even at 2:00 in the morning Amy, Cathy, Emily, Jayne, Jen, Jim, Kristin, Maria, Robin, and Ryan. Each of you has been instrumental during this particular book's journey and I thank you from the bottom of my heart.

To my kiddos, Katelyn, Kendall, and Lincoln. Thank you again for supporting me during this process. I know it's not easy when I shut the door and type away for hours. I hope I make you proud with each book that I write.

To my mom, Barb, thank you for your unwavering support these last couple of years. I know it hasn't been easy! To my brother, Kenny, I love you always and I know you have my back no matter what. And to Paul and Brandy, thank you for your encouragement and for being part of my extended family.

To Matt, thank you for loving me unconditionally and for your patience . . . even months before we met. Thank you for being the first nonindustry person to read this book, and for catching the grammar errors! I love you forever and can't wait for our fairy-tale ending.

Check out more books
chosen for publication
by readers like you.

DID YOU KNOW...

readers like you
helped to get this
book published?

Join our book-obsessed community and help us
discover awesome new writing talent.

1 Write it.
Share your original YA manuscript.

2 Read it.
Discover bright new bookish talent.

3 Share it.
Discuss, rate, and share your faves.

4 Love it.
Help us publish the books you love.

Share your own manuscript or dive between the pages
at **swoonreads.com** or by downloading the **Swoon Reads app.**